Praise for Vicki Del

"Charming, entertaining, a.._ ...._..
—*Library Journal* (Starred Review)

"Bestselling crime writer Vicki Delany has penned more than forty hair-raising whodunits—and her latest tale follows suit!" —*Woman's World* (Book Club Selection)

"Find a comfy chair, raise a cup of fragrant, freshly brewed tea to your lips, and settle down for murder and mayhem in a mystery novel set in a tearoom for a delightful form of armchair travel." —*TeaTime Magazine*

"Delany's down-to-earth heroine wraps up this investigation with even more than her customary panache."
—*Kirkus Reviews*

"[A] well-crafted series launch from Delany. . . . Fans of culinary cozies will be sure to come back for more."
—*Publishers Weekly*

"Sympathetic characters, a charming setting, the baking frame, and appended recipes distinguish this cozy, which will appeal to fans of Laura Childs's Theodosia Browning tea-shop mysteries and Cleo Coyle's coffeehouse-set series." – *Booklist*

"Delany's latest work can hold its own against anything in the genre being published today." —*Deadly Diversions*

"It's a crime not to read Delany."
—*London Free Press*

Kensington Books by Vicki Delany

The Tea by the Sea mystery series

Tea & Treachery

Murder in a Teacup

Murder Spills the Tea

Steeped in Malice

Murder Spills the Tea

VICKI DELANY

Kensington Publishing Corp.
www.kensingtonbooks.com

For Isla Gail Webb and Mary Gail Cargo

Acknowledgments

My thanks, as always, go to the marvelous Cheryl Freedman, for applying her keen crime-loving insights to an early manuscript of this book, and to Alex Delany, for her love of afternoon tea. I'd also like to thank Kim Lionetti, my marvelous agent at Bookends, and the team at Kensington, including, but not limited to, Elizabeth Trout and Wendy McCurdy.

Chapter 1

I'm a baker, not a TV personality. This wasn't my idea, and my doubts were growing steadily as the day got under way.

"Sit still," the woman growled as she dabbed muck on my face.

"Is this going to take much longer?" I asked.

"It'll take as long as it takes." She took a step backward, tilted her head to one side, furrowed her brow, and narrowed her eyes as she studied me. I tried to smile. It wasn't easy. "You'll do," she begrudgingly admitted. "At least you have camera-friendly hair."

"Thanks," I said. "I think."

I eyed myself in the mirror. I'd never seen so much makeup in my life, never mind worn it. Thick black lines were drawn around my eyes, my lashes were caked with mascara, dark pink blush outlined my cheekbones, and my lips were a slash of crimson. My naturally blond "camera-friendly" hair cascaded around my shoulders in soft waves.

"You do know this isn't at all what I look like at work," I said.

The makeup artist began packing up her pots and brushes.

"That's what they all say. I'll say, as I say to them all, if you want to be on TV, you have to look the part."

"That's the point," I said to my reflection in the mirror. "I don't want to be on TV."

"They all say that, too."

A rap sounded on the trailer door, a voice called, "Knock, knock," and the door flew open before Bernadette Murphy came in without waiting for an answer. She stopped in her tracks when she saw me. "Oh my gosh, Lily Roberts. Is that really you?"

"No," I said.

The makeup artist chuckled.

"Can you do me?" Bernie asked her.

"Not on my schedule. But I'd love nothing more than to get my hands on that hair."

Bernie tossed her head, and her curly red locks bounced.

"Off you go, and"—the woman glared at me—"don't you dare rub your eyes, kiss anyone, or have anything to eat or drink."

I stood up and gave her a salute. "Yes, ma'am. An important part of my job is tasting what I'm making, but I'll do my best. Do you have a name?"

The edges of her mouth turned up just a fraction. "Thank you for asking. I'm Melanie Ferguson." She was in her early sixties, tall and thin, with a heavily lined face and tired eyes that said she'd seen it all.

"How long have you been doing makeup, Melanie?" Bernie asked.

"Longer than you've been alive, honey. Probably longer than your mothers have been alive. Now, get out of here. Because you've been polite and not demanding, I'll give you a tip, Lily. Josh Henshaw's not a bad boss, as directors go, but he expects punctuality above all else, and I've known him to fire crew for showing up five minutes late."

"Thanks," I said. "But I don't work for Mr. Henshaw."
"Far as he's concerned, this week you do." She lowered
her voice. "Josh was a big-time director once. Now he's
doing reality TV. Hard on the ego, and we all know how
some men react when their ego's hurt."

"I've worked in Michelin-starred restaurants," I said. "I
can hold my own against men's inflated egos. Women's too."

"Glad to hear it. Watch out for Reilly, the assistant director, too. He's on his way up the career ladder, and that
lot can be worse than the old guys on the way down. Here's
another tip for nothing. Tomorrow don't wear red."

"I like red."

"Too harsh under the bright lights for that pale complexion. Now, run along and have fun."

"That's not going to happen," I grumbled.

Bernie linked her arm through mine. "Always the opti-
mist."

We left the makeup trailer and stepped into the parking
lot of my restaurant, Tea by the Sea. Although, if I hadn't
been aware of what was going on, I never would have recognized my own place.

Trailers and equipment vans lined the long driveway,
and on the lawn and the patio thick black cables crossed
all over themselves. Shouting men rolled cameras and
sound equipment through the gate. As I watched, one of
them hit his head on a cracked teacup swinging from a
colorful ribbon tied to a branch of the ancient oak in the
center of the tearoom patio. He rubbed his head with a
muffled curse.

The patio was full, more than full, with TV people as
well as guests here to enjoy afternoon tea at ten in the
morning. It was a beautiful Cape Cod summer day, clear
skies overhead, the blue waters of Cape Cod Bay sparkling
in the background, a light breeze ruffling women's hair

and causing the teacups hanging from the single tree in the center of the patio to tinkle cheerfully.

My friends and my grandmother's gardener had gone to a great deal of trouble to spruce up the space, and it looked great. Moss in varying shades of green and tiny blue and white flowers peeked from between cracks in the weathered stone of the half wall surrounding the patio and the flagstones that made up the floor. They'd refreshed the colored ribbons in the old oak, the ones from which hung a variety of teacups, repurposed after being damaged. The flowers in terra-cotta and stone flowerpots edging the patio had been deadheaded and trimmed and replanted if needed.

The people gathered here this morning either eyed the TV people with excitement or pretended not to notice them. Each table had been set with fine china, pressed linens, polished silverware, and a tiny vase of flowers selected personally from our garden by Simon McCracken, the gardener at my grandmother's B & B, Victoria-on-Sea. Everything looked fabulous but at the same time strange, I thought, as not one person had a cup of tea or a plate of my baking in front of them.

My maternal grandmother, Rose Campbell, had taken a seat at a table for four. She saw us coming and lifted her hand in a wave. I grimaced in return. When Rose arrived at the beginning of the day to take her place, the assistant director told her to go home and change. He didn't want extras dressing up for the camera, he'd said.

Rose genuinely didn't know what the man was talking about. Her attire today—flowing black pants with a print of huge yellow sunflowers, purple T-shirt, red scarf, sparkly pink sneakers—was nothing more than her usual informal attire. As was also usual, she'd applied a heavy coat of blue shadow to her eyelids, dark red lipstick to her lips, and two slashes of blush to her cheeks. Her short gray hair stood straight up in a series of spikes. My grandmother is a woman who likes color. I wondered if she and I would look even more alike than usual today, considering I was almost as made up as she. If you didn't know better, you'd think the bride in my grandmother's wedding photo, the one sitting in pride of place on her dressing table, was me dressed in old-fashioned clothes.

"You there! Blondie. Yes, you." A man broke away from a cluster of people and waved at me. "We haven't got all day here. Come on."

"Actually," Bernie muttered, "I think they do have all day. I'll go and join the peasantry. Enjoy your time in the limelight."

I growled at my best friend.

"You know you're loving it," Bernie said as she skipped off.

The man sitting at Rose's table politely got to his feet as she approached. Rose had invited Matt Goodwill, our closest neighbor, to join them. I thought the TV people would be pleased about that. Not many handsome young men go to afternoon tea. Simon, our gardener, had also been invited to participate, and he'd flatly refused.

I was not enjoying my time in the limelight. Not one little bit. I hadn't expected to. But Bernie can be very persuasive when she wants to be; combined with Rose, they're an unstoppable force.

I went to join Josh Henshaw, director. I hadn't met three of the four people with him, but I knew who they were. The older woman was Claudia D'Angelo, legend of the New York City baking world. The man was Tommy Greene, famously temperamental English chef and star of many a TV cooking show. The younger woman was Scarlet McIntosh, who didn't seem to do much in life other than be on TV. I'd met Josh's assistant director, Reilly Miller, several times as the plans for this show came together.

Rain was expected to move in later in the week, so the decision had been made to film on the garden patio today and move inside the restaurant later if necessary.

"Good morning, Lily. Are you excited?" Reilly asked me as I approached the group.

"You could say that," I said.

Reilly introduced me to everyone. I gushed over Claudia D'Angelo and told her, truthfully, she was a hero to me. She smiled and thanked me. Tommy Greene gave me a wink and said, in his working-class English accent, that he was looking forward to what I had to make for him. He was in his early fifties and not a good-looking man by any means, but there was a certain presence about him. He was around my height, five feet eightish, thin to the point of scrawny, with a prominent nose, too-large and too-white teeth, thin lips, and pale blue eyes. His hair was an unnatural shade of yellow, except for the section at the front, whose tips were dyed a solid black and which stood straight up to frame his bony face.

Scarlet smothered a yawn as she limply put her hand in mine and said, "Delighted, I'm sure." I got the feeling she expected me to be the delighted one, not her. She looked exactly as you'd expect a former beauty queen to look: tall and far too thin, except for the augmented breasts, with dyed blond hair tumbling halfway down her back in sleek waves, sharp cheekbones, plump lips, wide brown eyes, and red fingernails resembling talons. In contrast, Claudia, who I knew to be sixty-five, was considerably shorter than me, slim, and elegant. Her thick black hair was heavily streaked with gray and styled in a chic chignon, her makeup was subtle, and the nails on her manicured hands were clipped short and painted a light pink. Her olive skin was good, but the fine lines around her eyes and mouth were showing. She was, I thought, the sort of woman content to age naturally.

Formalities over, Josh turned to face the onlookers. "Okay, everyone. First, thank you for coming today. Filming out of doors can be tricky, what with weather and all, but this garden is a highlight of your place, so we need to feature it on the show."

I glanced at the assembled guests. Edna Hartwell, who helped in the B & B with the breakfasts, was here, accompanied by her husband, Frank, editor in chief of the *North Augusta Times*. I recognized Susan Powers, mayor of North Augusta, sitting with her husband, Gary, and a smattering of town councillors, along with some of our neighbors, B & B guests, and tearoom customers, who'd called to make a reservation for afternoon tea and been told what would be happening today. We hadn't served breakfast at Victoria-on-Sea, because the breakfast chef, aka me, was otherwise occupied, so Rose had offered guests either vouchers for a restaurant in town or a chance to be on TV and enjoy a full afternoon tea, albeit at ten in the morning. To no one's surprise, every one of them had joined us.

My assistants, Cheryl and Marybeth, both of whom had been given a pared-down version of the full makeup and hair experience, fidgeted in the doorway. Cheryl wiped her hands on her apron, looking as though she wanted to flee. As for Marybeth, I hoped she'd be able to control that manic grin. They both wore their regular work clothes of white blouse with lace collar, black knee-length skirt, and a bibbed apron featuring the name Tea by the Sea. Earlier Cheryl had asked me if her earrings were okay: silver with a stream of sparkling red stones. "One of my grandchildren gave these to me for my last birthday.

She said they were good luck earrings, and she'll get a kick out of seeing them on TV." I'd told her the earrings were fine with me.

"All I need from you," Josh continued, speaking to the guests, "is to act naturally. Can you do that?"

No one said anything.

"Can you do that?" Josh yelled.

The guests yelled back, "Yes!"

"Okay then. The servers will bring out your food, and you'll eat it. Servings will be paced so the judges have time to visit each table to ask how you're enjoying it. Remember to be totally honest, and try to avoid grandstanding or lecturing. Say hello and answer their questions. Now let me introduce you to our judges." He then did so. Claudia D'Angelo smiled modestly, and the older women in the crowd clapped with enthusiasm. Tommy Greene gave everyone a wave, and many of the women squealed with excitement. "Now, remember, ladies and gents," he said, "I know you Yanks like to be polite—"

"No we don't," Susan Powers's husband yelled. Big grin in place, he glanced around at the people at his table, checking for their reaction.

"Don't speak until you're spoken to," Reilly said.

"My bad," Gary Powers shouted. His tablemates tittered in embarrassment, and his wife threw him a poisonous glare.

Josh and Reilly exchanged a glance, which I took to mean they'd keep their eyes on Mr. Powers.

"And last but not least," Josh said, "our third judge is none other than the pride of Louisiana herself, Scarlet McIntosh."

Scarlet took a step forward and waved her fingers. Gary Powers whistled. His wife's face tightened still further, but Scarlet gave the man a smile.

"Now, remember," Tommy said, "*America Bakes!* is all about frank and fair criticism, as well as praise when it's warranted." He turned his bright eyes and toothy grin on me. "You can take it, can't you, Lily?"

I nodded.

He gave me a genuine smile before shouting, "We'll see about that." Everyone laughed. Everyone except Bernie, who leaned across the table and whispered something to Rose. I don't know what she said, but Rose threw me a worried glance.

"As filming progresses, you may talk quietly amongst yourselves," Josh said.

"My wife's never spoken quietly in her life," Gary shouted. He laughed, but no one else joined in, and Susan Powers shifted uncomfortably in her seat. I'd met Susan before, but not her husband; however, I'd heard things about their marriage. He'd been called an anchor around her political ambitions. I could see why. It was ten o'clock in the morning. They'd been here since nine. I wondered if he'd been drinking.

"If," Josh said sharply, "I may continue. I want no shouting, and no one's to stand up without raising your hand for permission first. One crew will be out here filming, while the others are in the kitchen with Ms. Roberts. You can assume the camera's on you at all times, so don't be talking with your mouth full, no sneezing into the linen napkins, and for heaven's sake, people, no mugging for the camera. Do you get it?"

Everyone shouted, "Yes." Rose's accent, full of memories of Yorkshire, rose above them all. My grandmother clapped her hands. Gary opened his mouth to grace us with another charming bon mot, but Susan grabbed his arm and hissed at him.

"If the judges stop to talk to you," Josh continued,

"speak clearly and distinctly. Answer their questions and that's all. I don't want to hear about your new grandchild or what you're doing on your summer vacation. Get it?"

"Yes!" nearly everyone chorused.

"Do you get it, sir?" He stared at Gary Powers, who for once only nodded.

"No eating while you're being spoken to." Josh turned to face me. "You're with me. Reilly, you have the show out here. Let's do this."

He stalked into Tea by the Sea. Marybeth and Cheryl scrambled to get out of his way.

Chapter 2

America Bakes! is currently the country's hottest cooking show. One bakery each season has the honor of being crowned America's best. Restaurants and bakeries are judged not only on the quality of the food by the three star judges but on the ambiance of the restaurant, the friendliness and professionalism of the staff, and the opinion of the "average" customer.

When word got out that CookingTV would be bringing the third season of *America Bakes!* to Cape Cod, I wanted nothing to do with it. I'm a baker, and all I want to be is a baker. I'm a culinary school–trained pastry chef, and I hadn't been joking when I said I've worked at Michelin-starred restaurants. I'd moved to the Outer Cape from Manhattan last winter to set up my tearoom on the grounds of my grandmother's B & B, and I'd worked hard renovating the crumbling stone cottage by the road, creating a patio oasis, planning my menus and testing recipes, and getting the word out. We opened in the spring, and I needed to devote all my concentration to getting the restaurant up and running, as well as helping my grandmother with the B & B she'd bought, in the opinion of everyone in the family, on a foolish whim. Obviously, the publicity generated by being on the show would be valuable, but we've been satisfyingly busy all season both in the tearoom and the B & B. I decided the disruption from having several days of filming at my place wouldn't be worth the exposure.

Bernie and Rose, however, had other ideas. They'd applied to the show without telling me, advance scouts had been dispatched to check us out, and before I knew what was happening, Tea by the Sea had been accepted. Imagine my surprise when Rose gave me the "good news."

Six bakeries in Cape Cod had been selected for this year's competition. Two of them were located in the Lower Cape, the Mid and Upper areas of the Cape had one each, and two were in the Outer Cape: Tea by the Sea and the simply named North Augusta Bakery. I'd never been to any of them, but Rose and Bernie had checked out my nearest competition.

"A coffee shop," Rose had sniffed. "Totally common."

"Best donuts I've ever had," Bernie said. "You'd better up your game there, Lily."

"I don't make donuts," I'd said.

I'd be competing with North Augusta Bakery in the first round. The winner would then be matched against the winners of the other two rounds, and one bakery would go on to compete in the Northeastern US division, then the quarterfinals, and, if they were lucky, the grand finale, titled *All-America Bakes!*

I was secretly hoping *not* to continue. If we kept winning, I'd be tied up all summer with TV crews and special guests. I don't think of myself as a competitive person—I leave that to Rose and Bernie—but I have far too much pride to throw the competition. Now that I was in the show, I'd do the best of which I was capable.

I led the way through the restaurant. No one would be

served inside today, as everything was happening on the patio, so the tables weren't set, and our footsteps echoed around the empty rooms. Sunlight streamed through the east-facing windows, but the alcoves were dark. The trays of food to be served outside had already been assembled and waited on a counter near the kitchen, along with china teapots, airpots to heat the water, and a selection of canisters containing a variety of loose teas.

"Eddie." Josh pointed to the cabinet of things we offer for sale. "I want shots of those teacups and stuff. Adds to the atmosphere."

"All the jams and preserves we sell," I said, "are made in Cape Cod with locally grown produce."

"Whatever," he said.

My kitchen's crowded when I'm the only one in it. Today I was not the only one. The cameraman and his camera, the sound guy, the woman who clapped the clapper board, and the director somehow managed to stuff themselves in.

I'd spent almost all of last week baking extra scones and pastries to put in the freezer to serve today, and I'd been up most of last night fixing sandwiches and other things that couldn't be frozen, with the help of Simon and Bernie.

Marybeth and Cheryl had come in early this morning to help me prepare the presentation. Fortunately, everything served at afternoon tea is served at room temperature and brought out at the same time. We normally offer some variety in our menu—traditional afternoon tea, cream tea, light tea, royal tea, and children's tea—but unlike a restaurant where everyone gets their own selection on their own plate, the food is served on platters or stands, from which guests help themselves. That makes it far easier to plan and prepare for an event such as this one than if we had to fill individual orders.

Marybeth and Cheryl would appear to be taking orders,

but the camera wouldn't show them picking up the pre-arranged stands. We simply couldn't function with the three of us working in the kitchen as well as the camera crew.

While all that was going on outside, I'd be happily baking away in here. I'd be filmed rolling and slicing and mixing and stirring and peering anxiously into the ovens, all the while chatting to the camera about what I was doing and why. My plan for today was to do two types of scones, plain and orange, and pistachio and hazelnut macarons. Macarons always look lovely on camera. I normally make a lot more food than that in a day, but Reilly'd warned me things would take a good deal longer under the relentless eye of the camera. The judges wouldn't come into the kitchen today to watch me work and talk to me about it. That was on the schedule for tomorrow.

"Okay," Josh said. "You do whatever you normally do, Lily. Pretend we're not here. Talk about what you're doing, but don't talk too much. And don't try to tell any jokes. People are nowhere near as funny as they think they are. Okay, let's go. I want lots of close-ups of her hands, but she's younger and prettier than most of the old bags we get on this show, so give me plenty of close-ups, too. Tomorrow, honey, wear a tighter sweater, will you?"

"I beg your pardon?"

"Don't get all offended. You look good, so I want you to look even better for our fans. Most of the cooks we get on this show have enjoyed far too much of their own baking, if you know what I mean. A lot of men watch our show, so let's make everyone happy."

"Careful, Josh," the clapper-board woman said.

He waved his hand in the air. The clapper board clapped.

The first thing I always do when I start work is put on my hairnet. I reached for it.

Josh yelled, "Cut, cut. What are you planning to do with that thing?"

"Cover my hair. It's a public health measure."

"I'm not covering up that hair. It's your best feature. Forget it."

"But—"

"No buts. If someone gets hair in their food and complains, we'll cut it out."

I wasn't so sure, but I decided not to argue about it. Not only do I wear a hairnet when I'm cooking, but I tie my long hair back. Melanie, the makeup artist, had insisted on leaving it loose.

Baking is my happy place, and as I got out my ingredients and utensils, I tried to put myself there. It wasn't easy, not with the camera in my face, Josh saying either "Speak up" or "Don't yell," the makeup itching my face, and my hair falling over my eyes and into my mouth.

I thought I was going to be allowed to bake as I normally do. Wasn't that what I was being judged on? Instead, I had to keep stopping and starting. I weighed my butter on the kitchen scale, as I always do, but Josh wanted me to slice it according to the markings on the package, as the home cook does.

"I am not a home cook," I reminded him.

"You're whatever I want you to be," he replied. "Now do it again."

I thought I'd feel silly talking to myself about what I was doing; instead, I started getting annoyed when Josh objected to everything I said. I was, apparently, explaining too much or too little.

"Cut those scones bigger."

"This is the size I always make them."

"I want them bigger."

I rummaged around in the drawers, looking for a larger round cutter.

Finally, the first batch of scones was in the oven.

"I'm going to check how it's going outside," Josh said. "Keep filming."

He left, and Eddie, the cameraman, said to me, "Never mind Josh. He can be a perfectionist at times."

I rolled my shoulders to release some of the tension. I had one batch of scones in the oven, and I was already tired enough to call it a day. "I thought this competition was about baking and restaurant service and ambiance. Not whether I use scales or measuring cups."

"This is called reality TV," he said. "In reality, it's anything but. The show's not concerned about the quality of your food or the arrangement of the flowers on the table. It's about creating drama and interest. Reality's boring."

I didn't agree, but I didn't say anything. I think baking perfect scones, tarts, cupcakes, and other delicious things and watching people enjoy them are very exciting.

Josh didn't return, but Reilly came in and took the director's place. "What's up next?"

"Scones made with the slightest touch of orange peel. I serve them with our royal tea, that's the one with sparkling wine."

"Boring. Josh said you've already been making scones. What else have you got?"

"Macarons?"

"Perfect. Do that."

And I did.

While I worked, Reilly jotted notes on his iPad. "I'm coming up with questions we want the judges to ask you," he explained.

"Do I get them ahead of time?"

"No, that wouldn't be realistic. We want you answering off the cuff."

"I thought reality TV wasn't about reality."

He grinned at me. Reilly was in his early thirties, lightly

tanned, with nicely muscled arms and chest beneath his T-shirt, softly curling brown hair, and intense hazel eyes. "Lily, this show is all about what we want it to be. Nothing more and nothing less."

My rooster timer crowed to tell me the scones were ready to come out of the oven. I slipped on my oven mitts and took the baking sheet out. The cameraman stepped closer and focused his camera. The scones looked good, I thought, high and round and beautifully golden.

When he had the shot, Eddie helped himself to a scone. The sound guy and the clapper-board woman did so, as well.

I needed those for tomorrow, but I didn't say so.

"The macarons need to rest for thirty minutes," I said. "What do you want me to do while that's happening?"

"They need to rest?" Reilly said. "Why?"

"The shells have to dry out so as not to create bubbles when they bake."

He made a note on his iPad. "Sounds like a good time to take a break. I want to see what's happening outside."

I have to admit, I was also curious. The building that houses Tea by the Sea is made of stone, so I can't hear much of what's going on out front when I'm in the kitchen at the back. I took my apron off, hung it on the hook, and followed Reilly and the crew out. I'd been in the kitchen for three hours, but everyone was still in place outside, and Marybeth and Cheryl were still serving.

"How's it going?" I whispered to Cheryl as she passed me with a stack of used dishes. Not a scrap of my baking remained.

"Weird. We've been told we can't serve the tea or food until someone says to, so a few tables are still waiting. They're getting impatient, but trying not to look it in case the camera turns their way. I've been giving them water, so they have something."

"They were told the process can take a long time and not to come if they couldn't devote most of the day."

"Every time I turn around, there's a camera stuffed in my face. I got such a fright, I almost dropped a full tray the first time it happened. I'm afraid Marybeth's face is going to crack if she keeps smiling like that. She's either smiling or threatening to burst into tears. The director cursed her out for looking unnatural. I don't know what he expects. We're not actors."

"Have the judges eaten anything?"

"They were served first."

"Did they like it?"

"Impossible to tell, Lily. They kept their faces totally impassive. Now they're visiting tables, admiring the place settings and food arrangements and talking to people."

"Otherwise everything going okay?"

"Gary Powers caused a bit of a stink earlier. I'm surprised they didn't throw him out."

"What happened?"

"He came over all flirty with Scarlet McIntosh."

I rolled my eyes. Gary Powers had a reputation. Come to think of it, his wife, the mayor, did also.

"No, *flirty* isn't the word," Cheryl said. "More like lecherous old man."

"Gary's not that old. Forty-five maybe."

"Around that. But he acts like an old lech. Anyway, Tommy Greene stepped in and got right in Gary's face. Told him to back off and sit down and shut up, or he'd be thrown off the set. Gary looked like he was going to stand his ground, but then he gave in. Said something about not meaning any offense, just wanting to meet the, and I quote, star. He cracked a joke to the crowd, but no one laughed. Susan puts up with a lot from him, but I'd say that pretty much took the cake, no pun intended."

"Was the incident filmed?"

"Oh, yeah. Much to Susan's dismay. Josh told her they wouldn't use the footage, but I don't know if you can believe that. Scarlet blushed and giggled and tossed her hair and told Tommy not to make a fuss. The guy was only trying to be friendly. More giggling. She's an idiot. Claudia D'Angelo, on the other hand, is super nice. She's been so polite to Marybeth in particular. She knows what it's like working as a server."

I glanced around the patio. The cameramen walked between the tables, the giant black machines on their shoulders so out of place in my oasis of old-fashioned gentility. Guests pretended to sip tea or nibble on fresh baking and chat, while watching the cameras out of the corner of their eyes. One elderly man checked his watch as I passed, and said, "Can we go now?" His table had been cleared, and his teacup was empty.

"Of course you can."

"That fellow"—he nodded to Josh—"said we can't leave until he says so. He doesn't want empty tables."

And I didn't want unhappy customers.

"I think they're almost finished. Perhaps wait a few more minutes, if you don't mind?"

"It's all right, Harold," said the equally elderly woman across from him. "It's not as though we have anything better to do today."

Their tablemate laughed. "I can't wait to get online and tell everyone Tommy Greene admired my hat." She proudly touched the spray of feathers on her straw hat and threw a longing look at the English chef.

The man himself had taken the spare chair at Rose, Bernie, and Matt's table, and I went to join them.

"No point in talking to this bunch," I said to Tommy. "They're my grandmother and my friends. Not exactly impartial observers."

"They're the only interesting people here." Tommy jerked

his head toward the rest of the patio. "How many times can you say, 'Very good' or 'The scones are too dry'?"

"I hope no one said the latter."

"Sure they did. People like to complain. They think complaining will get them more airtime than compliments will. And they're right."

"That hardly seems fair," Bernie said.

"Fair? You think TV's ever been fair? Don't worry," he said to me. "We don't pay attention to what any of them have to say."

"Isn't that part of the judging process?" I asked. "You take their opinions into account in making your final decision?"

"That appears to be part of the judging process." He gave me a long look, which I couldn't decipher. "I have my own criteria for picking a winner."

I shifted uncomfortably.

"I'm just teasing," he said. "All I'm interested in is the quality of the food, and you've done a first-class job today, Lily."

"Find yourself a chair, love," Rose said. "Mr. Greene's a native of Halifax. In Yorkshire."

He gave her a genuine smile. "The moment I heard that accent, I knew I wanted to talk to this lovely lady."

"Listen up, everyone," Josh bellowed. "That's it for today. You can go now."

"We haven't been served yet," a woman protested.

Josh shrugged, not much caring.

I caught Cheryl's eye and nodded toward the woman who'd spoken. She understood and hurried to assure the guest her afternoon tea would be out shortly.

Josh walked away without another word.

Reilly said, "Thanks for coming, everyone. We have most of what we're after, but we'll call if we need you again."

Everyone had been required to fill out a permission form before being given access to the patio.

Gary Powers stood up. "Hey, I haven't spoken to the judges yet. I have some ideas they'll be interested in. The scones were too dry."

"As I said," Reilly said, "we have what we need for now."

"My wife's the mayor." Gary raised his voice to be heard over Susan's attempts to shush him. "Aren't you going to speak to her?"

"Does being the mayor give her special insight into running a professional kitchen?" Tommy laughed. "I think not."

Gary's face tightened. Susan hissed at him, he hesitated, and then he dropped back into his chair.

Tommy smirked and whispered something to Rose that made her laugh.

The crew began shutting down their equipment, rolling up the cables, and loading the trucks and vans.

"We're done?" I said to Reilly. "It's not even two o'clock."

"We got what we want for today. What you want, too. Happy customers enjoying your food in this nice garden." He pointed east, across the narrow landmass of the Outer Cape, in the direction of the open ocean. "Clouds are moving in. You might get rain sooner than expected. Josh'll want to see the footage from today, and then we'll decide if we need to gather all the customers again, even if we have to do it inside. Take advantage of the time off, Lily. The judges will be in your kitchen tomorrow, watching you work, and then they'll eat what you've made. The stress of that can be intense. On Wednesday you'll bake for them one more time, and they'll give you their opinion. We've booked you all week. Depending on how it goes, we might be done on Wednesday, or we might need to shoot more on Thursday and Friday."

While we'd been talking, I'd kept my eye on my surroundings. Most of the guests were getting up to leave, chatting excitedly. Full of apologies, although the tardiness wasn't her fault, Marybeth brought out the last trays of food and full teapots and served the remaining grumbling guests.

A cluster of giggling women had gathered around Tommy Greene, and he was cracking jokes and signing autographs. Edna and her friends, including Susan, our mayor, were chatting to Claudia D'Angelo. Gary had cornered Scarlet again, and he was talking to her in an uncharacteristically low voice. Her eyes scanned the patio, seeking escape. Still, she was a professional, and she kept her smile fixed on her face.

My personal guests also prepared to leave. The light wind blew Bernie's red curls around her face as she stood up. Matt helped Rose to her feet, and Bernie gestured to me that she'd see my grandmother up the driveway to the house. I nodded my thanks.

"Looks like they're done," a voice with an English accent said behind me. "That was early."

I turned to Simon. "I expected to be here all day. But they seem to move at their own pace. I have to be back on set, bright and bouncy and ready to go, at seven."

"No B and B breakfasts again tomorrow, then?" Sand was trapped in his fair hair, and a streak of dirt crossed his cheek. He'd put in most of a day's work already, and the stubble on his face was coming in thick and fast, outlining the sharp cheekbones. The sun sparkled in his ocean-blue eyes. His gardening gloves were stuffed in the pocket of his grass- and dirt-stained overalls, and heavy boots, also grass and dirt stained, were on his feet.

The gardens at Victoria-on-Sea are one of the highlights of the property and part of the reason Rose can charge as much for a night's stay as she does. It's not easy maintaining an English-style country garden on the bluffs over-looking Cape Cod Bay, and we were lucky to have snagged Simon at the beginning of the season, when our regular gardener up and quit with no notice. Simon's a professional gardener and horticulturalist; he'd come to America for the summer on a special work visa, but the job had fallen through, leaving him with no prospects for the season. It had worked out all around.

"Rose explained to the guests what's happening," I said, "and they understand. We're doing a scaled-down break-fast tomorrow. I'm going to make muffins and coffee cake in the morning and prepare a breakfast casserole for Edna to heat after I've left."

"You were expecting to be filming all day here and then making breakfasts in the B&B?"

I smiled at him. "Sleep's vastly overrated. It's only for a few days. I didn't want to do this show in the first place, but now that they're here, I can't not do all I can." I dug in the pocket of my white capris and pulled out a hair elastic. I reached behind my head and twisted my hair into a high ponytail. I immediately felt more comfortable.

"If I may be frank," Simon said, "all that makeup doesn't suit you, Lily."

I found a tissue and wiped at my lips. "I don't have to bake tonight for the tearoom. I'm going to take advantage of it and enjoy a partial afternoon off."

As we chatted, the guests continued dispersing, many of them calling their good-byes and thanking me. A giant white SUV idled in the driveway. To my surprise, I saw Bernie help Rose climb inside it. Scarlet finally broke away, abandoning Gary Powers in mid-sentence, and hur-ried to join them.

"Claudia, Tommy, ride's leaving," Reilly called.

The two chefs left their circles of admirers and also got into the vehicle. Reilly slammed the door behind Tommy, and it drove slowly away, up the long driveway to Victoria-on-Sea.

"Nice of them to offer Rose a ride home," I said. "Although she walks that route regularly."

Matt and Bernie joined us. "Didn't you know?" Bernie said. "They're staying at the B and B for a week. Rose told us over our tea. Four of them, the three judges and the director."

"They are?"

Bernie chuckled. "Rose hopes that, to quote, the gracious hospitality of Victoria-on-Sea, combined with the bracing sea atmosphere and the delicious homemade baking, will further inspire the judges to award Tea by the Sea the *America Bakes!* trophy."

I groaned. "Oh, great. Now I have to produce TV cooking show–quality muffins and coffee cakes?"

"Pretty much." Bernie patted her flat stomach. "It'll be tough finding any more room in here, but I'll suffer for your art, Lily, if you need any tasting done."

"As fun as this has been, I have to be off," Matt said. "I'm expecting a load of lumber to be delivered shortly." Matt had bought the decrepit house next door to us and was slowly and diligently knocking it into some sort of livable shape. "You still up to giving me a hand later in the week?" he asked Simon.

"I'll be over."

"Hey!" Bernie said. "I've had a great idea. Maybe we can get you on one of those home renovation shows." She pointed up the driveway to Victoria-on-Sea. The SUV had stopped at the bottom of the veranda steps, and passengers were unloading. "I wonder if those people have any contacts in that line."

Matt threw us a wave and headed to his own property.

"As long as I'm giving Matt a hand later, I'd better get

back to my own work," Simon said. "If you need any help, Lily, you know you can count on me."

"I'd love it. But the contract for the show says only the owner and head baker's allowed to be doing the cooking. I guess that's so we don't bring in a ringer. Plus, it keeps restaurant chains out of the competition."

He touched the lock of sandy hair tumbling over his forehead, flicked his finger, and said, "Cheers."

"Is it my imagination," Bernie said, "or does Simon's accent get sexier every time he speaks?"

"It's your imagination," I replied.

"Might be. Tommy Greene's English, too, and far from being sexy, I found him a bit creepy."

"What do you mean?"

"Too much charm maybe? Laying it on too thick."

"Part of his job, I'd say."

"Maybe."

We watched Simon amble through the gate and cut across the lawn at his usual slow, gentle gait. I liked Simon. I suspected he liked me. But he was going back to England in the fall, and this summer I had to devote every bit of attention to getting Tea by the Sea established. I had no time for romance. On the other hand . . .

"Did Matt enjoy joining you for tea?" I asked Bernie.

"He likes Rose. He likes sparring with her. You know that."

"He enjoys sparring with you, too, Bernie. As dates go, it was like something out of *Pride and Prejudice*, with Rose in the role of chaperone."

Beneath her freckles Bernie's face turned various shades of pink. "It wasn't a date, Lily. You get the strangest ideas sometimes."

"If you say so. How was the non-date?"

"It was fun. I hope the camera ran out of film and no one noticed, so they need to do it all again."

"Do they still use film?"

"You're missing the point. Anyway, while we were sitting and waiting for something to happen, I had time to think about my book. A formal tea scene would be good, don't you think? Maybe I can make it humorous. Rose—my Rose—and Tessa have tea with Rose's stuck-up mother, and the mother tries to trip up working-class Tessa's manners, but . . ."

Bernie was writing a novel. She was, to say the least, having trouble concentrating on what she wanted it to be about. She'd quit her job as a forensic accountant at a major Manhattan law firm, cashed in her savings, and come to the Cape to spend the summer writing her book. Bernie had talent—real, genuine talent—and I wanted nothing in the world as much as I wanted her to succeed. But she simply couldn't settle down and just write the thing. Every shiny object that crossed her path gave her a new idea, and she went haring off in all directions in pursuit of it. She'd already changed the entire plot and the setting, both geographical and historical, at least twice. Twice of which I was aware. Thankfully, I knew who Rose and Tessa were—partners in a nineteenth-century Boston detective agency. At least that hadn't changed recently.

"If you want to include the tea scene, add it to your formal outline, and then I'll see it. Otherwise," I said, as I always did, "when you have something for me to read, I'll be ready."

Bernie had anything but writer's block. Her problem was that she had too many ideas. She'd wasted months leaping from one great idea to another. She didn't want to show me her work, not until it was finished, and I respected that. After all, I never give anyone a taste of my unbaked bread dough. But finally, realizing that if she was ever going to get anywhere with it, she had to settle down, come up with a concept, and simply write, I suggested she draw up character sketches and a rough outline to show me. She'd enthusiastically agreed to the idea and then kept hedging about why it wasn't ready. But last week, at last, she presented it to me, and I read her concept. I liked it, I liked it a lot, and I believed the book could be a big success. If ever it got finished. I was pleased my suggestion seemed to have worked and she was getting some good writing done.

"Patience, Lily," she said. "The creative process cannot be hurried. Before I go, I'm going to pop up to the house and say good-bye to Rose. I want to hear what she thought of how the day went." Bernie strolled happily away, the skirt of her colorful summer dress flowing around her long legs.

I headed toward the tearoom to tidy up the kitchen prior to playing hooky for the rest of the afternoon. Only two tables of guests remained, lingering over the last of their tea and the sweets offering. Cheryl was clearing off the tables while small birds hopped about the flagstone floor, searching for crumbs.

Before going inside, I stopped to talk to Cheryl. "Once you've tidied up, you and Marybeth can go home. I should do more baking to get in the freezer, but I'm beat. All that smiling is exhausting!"

Cheryl laughed. "Gosh, yes. How do you think it went?"

"I've absolutely no idea."

"I've seen both seasons of that show," she said. "The judges can be pretty mean. Not Claudia. She always tries to find something nice to say. But Tommy and Scarlet, oh yeah. Mean."

After finding out I was going to be on *America Bakes!*, I'd caught a few episodes. Tommy Greene appeared to delight in being as critical as possible, and Scarlet McIntosh seemed to think she was in possession of a scathing wit. Instead, she came across as just plain nasty.

"Let's not give them anything to be mean about," I said. "They want me at seven tomorrow, so I'd like you here by eight. Is that okay?"

"Fine. We warned our families we wouldn't be doing regular hours this week. Marybeth's kids wanted to come today. They said they'd drink tea and be polite. I put a stop to that. There's no way those two could have sat still for three hours." Marybeth was Cheryl's daughter. "My Jim's away. He's been helping a buddy with his charter business in Nantucket this week."

I turned to head inside and saw a woman standing alone on the other side of the gate, watching me. She was in her late forties, short and stocky, with black-rimmed eyeglasses, a nose like a hawk's, thin lips, and dyed blond hair, secured to the back of her head by a big sparkly clip.

"I'm sorry," I said, "but we're not open today. There's a sign . . ."

"I saw it."

I smiled at her. She did not smile back. "Can I . . . help you?" I said at last.

"Nope. Just having a look around. Nice place you have here. You're Lily Roberts."

It was not a question, but I answered, anyway. "I am. And you are—"

"Afternoon tea. Isn't that too fancy for Cape Cod?"

"My customers don't think so."

"Maybe. Maybe not. These novelty things never last, do they?"

"Considering that afternoon tea was first served in eighteen forty, I'd say it's lasted very well."

"You know what I mean. It's English, right?"

"I'm sorry, but as I said, we're closed. If you'd like to make a reservation, we accept them online. TeabytheSea-dot-com."

"I don't need a reservation."

The door opened, and Marybeth came out of the restaurant carrying an empty tray to help her mother finish cleaning up. Her eyes widened when she saw whom I was talking to; she sucked in a breath and came to stand next to me. "Allegra," she said, her voice as cool as the prosecco I keep in the fridge to accompany the royal tea.

"Marybeth." Equally cool.

I glanced at Marybeth. Behind us, I felt as much as saw Cheryl stop what she was doing.

"Everyone's left," Marybeth said. "You're too late."

"I'm never late. I didn't come earlier, because I have a business to run, but I wanted to check the competition."

Comprehension started to dawn. "You must be from North Augusta Bakery," I said. "Allegra Griffin."

Allegra's nose wasn't her only hawklike feature. Those black eyes reminded me of a bird of prey about to dive for its quarry. "I am," she said at last. "And I don't appreciate an upstart outsider coming to my town to try to show me up."

"I'm just a baker chosen to appear on a cooking show. I'm not trying to show anyone up."

"We'll see." She turned away. I started to let out a breath when she turned again. "You shouldn't wear red. It doesn't suit you."

Chapter 3

I attended to my forgotten macarons while Cheryl and Marybeth put the patio to rights and prepared the indoor tables for the following day, when the three judges would take tea with me.

The encounter with Allegra had unsettled me more than I'd expected. She hadn't made any overt threats, but she didn't have to. Her stance, her tone, her attitude had been threatening.

Marybeth placed a full teapot on the table and sat down. I'd made a few extra sandwiches in case of mishaps, but we hadn't needed to dip into them. Cheryl, Marybeth, and I were dipping into them now.

Cheryl selected a sandwich made from chicken poached in Darjeeling. "The nastiest woman ever to grace North Augusta and environs was Noreen Griffin. The second nastiest is her daughter, the ill-named Allegra."

"I briefly worked at the bakery a couple of years ago." Marybeth poured the tea. "A high school summer job. How long did I stick it out, Mom? Three days?"

"If that," Cheryl said. "She started working there soon after Allegra took over from her mother. Noreen was never a kind person, but she knew how to keep her temper under control when she had to. Some people actually thought she was rather nice. She owned the bakery, and when she was no longer able to work all day, her daughter stepped in. Most of the staff fled."

"Thus the need to hire new staff," Marybeth said.

"I haven't been there," I said. "What's it like?"

"I've only ever had better baking at one place." Marybeth gestured toward the kitchen with her chicken sandwich. "And that's here."

"Rumor has it," Cheryl said, "Allegra's like the witch in some fairy tale. She sold her soul in exchange for baking skills. Fairness forces me to admit that wouldn't have been necessary. Noreen was a legend in her own time, and she taught her daughter everything she knew. Their baking is practical, traditional, middle American. Heavy on fruit and cream pies, chocolate cakes, chocolate chip cookies. Her specialty is donuts."

"They are to die for," Marybeth said.

"Don't tell me you still go there?" a shocked Cheryl said.

"Of course I do." Marybeth ducked her head. "Sorry, Lily, but you don't make donuts, and they're my favorite. My kids love them. Allegra never comes out front, so no danger of running into her."

"Apology accepted." I selected an herbed cucumber sandwich. "Not a donut fan myself, but to each her own. Hmm, this sandwich needs more chopped herbs. It's too pale."

"Tastes good, though," Cheryl said.

"TV's about pictures," Marybeth replied. "Lily's right."

"It sounds as though the bakery isn't competition for us," I said. "Do they do sit-down meals?"

"Sandwiches, soups, and the like. All plain and practical and homemade, and all absolutely delicious. At least that's what people say," she added quickly.

I put my sandwich down and picked up my teacup. I sipped at the contents. Creamy Earl Grey, my favorite, a delicious full-bodied Earl Grey with notes of bergamot and vanilla and a hint of dulce de leche for creaminess. I let the warm, aromatic, flavorful liquid linger on my tongue for a moment. I always feel better over a cup of fragrant tea, and today was no exception. "I didn't want to be on this stupid TV show in the first place, never mind making an enemy out of a longtime local business owner I'd never even met before today."

"Don't worry about it," Cheryl said. "Most of the North Augusta Business Improvement Association members are Allegra's enemies, and even if they aren't, she regards them that way."

"She'd have been run out of town years ago if it wasn't for her sister," Marybeth said.

"Do I know her?" I asked.

"You sure do, Lily," Cheryl said. "Allegra's younger sister is Susan Powers, mayor of North Augusta."

It was absolutely lovely to lock up the tearoom and head home in the middle of the afternoon. I could kick my shoes off, drop into a chair, and simply relax. I had a bottle of wine chilling in the fridge, and a book I'd been looking forward to getting into. Before going back to my little cottage overlooking the bluffs to take my labradoodle, Éclair, for a walk, I detoured to the veranda that runs the width of Rose's house.

Victoria-on-Sea was a huge, gorgeous house built in 1865 to be a vacation home for a Boston banker and his family. Situated on a large property on a stretch of bluffs looking out over Cape Cod Bay, the house was sparkling white, with a gray roof and gray accents, adorned with miles of intricate gingerbread trim, dormer windows on the upper level, and a wide covered veranda running the width of the house. It boasted eight guest bedrooms and suites, all en suite, and a set of rooms for Rose's own accommodation.

Most of the chairs on the veranda were occupied. B & B guests sipped drinks and pretended to read or to chat while keeping an eager eye on the TV people.

Rose occupied the center of the circle of TV people—Tommy Greene, Josh, Scarlet, and Claudia—proudly holding court. Her black cat, Robert the Bruce, aka Robbie, was curled up on her lap. A thick hardcover book and a pitcher of icy lemonade rested on the table next to her. "Lady Frockmorton was very particular about her afternoon tea. Oh, yes, she had an eagle's eye for detail. I taught Lily everything the head cook at Thornecroft Castle taught me."

"Fancy digs, Thornecroft," Tommy chuckled. "How the mighty have fallen. They do tea in the conservatory now for the paying public, April to November."

"You should mention that on the program," Rose said. "Afternoon tea is all about tradition, and . . . Here she is now." My grandmother beamed at me.

Josh said, "Hey there, Lucy."

"Lily," I said.

"Sorry. Are you ready for tomorrow?"

"Yes, I am. Looking forward to it," I lied.

Scarlet grunted something that might have been, "Hi," and continued scrolling through her phone.

Tommy jumped to his feet and offered me a sweeping bow. "Can I get you a chair, Lily?"

"No, thank you. I'm heading home. I hope everything went well today?"

"Well enough," Josh said. "Could have been better. Could have been worse."

"Pay him no mind, dear," Claudia said to me with a warm smile. "Josh is never happy unless he's unhappy. If you get my meaning. I found it was all quite delightful. Your guests raved about the food and the service, and your lovely stone building and beautiful patio might have been built specifically to be on TV."

"Thank you." I flushed with pleasure. Never mind the TV program. Claudia D'Angelo liked my cooking!

"Afternoon tea is one of life's great pleasures, and you do it to perfection."

"What a load of rubbish." Tommy, I noticed, wasn't drinking lemonade. His glass contained an amber-colored liquid and a single square of ice. "Afternoon tea gives the rich and the posh something to do before they dress for the ball. Gives the common people belowstairs nothing but a lot of extra work."

"It provides me with a living," I said. "As you saw this afternoon, plenty of people who also work hard for a living seem to enjoy it."

"Never mind him." Scarlet studied her nails. "Tommy likes to pretend he's all for the working classes. He reads all sorts of strange books in the library of his beach house in Malibu."

"You should try reading someday, Scarlet. They say it broadens the mind. If you need anything else broadening, that is." He gave me a wink, which I didn't return. The comment might have sounded as though it was good-natured joshing between friends and coworkers, but Scarlet's mouth narrowed, and she stabbed at the buttons on her phone with renewed energy.

"What time is it? Where the heck's Reilly, anyway? I'm about ready for a nice glass of wine."

"You're always ready for a nice glass of wine," Josh said.

She threw him a poisonous glare. Tommy laughed and leaned back in his chair. He lifted his glass in a salute.

"You're sure the Wi-Fi works in my room?" Claudia asked Rose. "I didn't have a chance to check when we arrived, since Reilly hustled us out in such a rush. I have work to do later."

"It reaches everywhere in the house," I said. "As well as on the veranda."

At that moment Reilly came out of the house. "I've been on the line with the network. They've had a complaint."

"What is it now?" Josh groaned.

Reilly jerked his head toward Rose and me.

"Spit it out," Josh said.

"It's inappropriate for you to be staying here. At this B and B. The complainant said it will give Tea by the Sea an unfair advantage."

"And that's a problem how?" Tommy said. "All's fair in love, war, and reality TV, don't they know?"

Reilly gave me a sideways glance as he said, "That's not true, Tommy. We run an honest competition."

Scarlet snorted and continued scrolling.

"Who's this so-called complainant?" Josh asked.

"The network didn't say."

"One of the other competitors obviously," Josh said. "Who's up next?"

"North Augusta Bakery. That's in the town nearest here. Homey sort of place. Gingham curtains on the windows. No tablecloths on the tables, picnic table–type seating. Does bread, rolls, breakfast pastries, donuts, cakes, cookies, that sort of thing. Breakfast sandwiches for breakfast, and sandwiches and soup for lunch."

I decided not to mention that the owner of North Augusta Bakery had been lurking around Tea by the Sea earlier.

"Sounds more your sort of place, Tommy," Scarlet said. "You can pretend to be a member of the working classes having your lunch break."

"Probably them complaining," Josh said. "Tell the network if they can find suitable accommodations for four people in Cape Cod in July with no notice, we'll go there." He leaned back, crossed his legs, and finished his drink. "Meanwhile, we're staying here. I'm not moving into a motel on the highway, and I'm pretty sure none of you want to, either. Tommy, pass me that bottle. I've had enough lemonade. Are you ready for us in there?"

"Yes," Reilly said. "Mrs. Campbell was kind enough to offer us the use of her drawing room as a meeting room."

I threw a questioning glance at my grandmother. She tried not to smirk. The drawing room at Victoria-on-Sea is not quite as private as it first appears.

Josh stood up. "Okay. Let's see what we got today. Claudia, you're with me and Reilly. Scarlet and Tommy, find something to amuse yourselves."

"Reilly," Scarlet said, "did you arrange to have a bottle of wine put in the fridge in my room?"

"Yes."

"Then I will be amused." Scarlet got to her feet and sailed into the house without another word.

"As for me," Tommy said, "I'll escort this lovely young lady home."

"I don't think—" I said.

"No problem at all." He picked up his glass as well as the bottle.

"Actually, I need to talk to my grandmother," I said.

He pouted dramatically. "I guess that means me and my bottle will retire to our room. Josh, I hope we don't have to all go out to dinner together."

"Command performance," the director said. "I've made a reservation. We want the locals excited about our show coming to their town, and that means you need to show your ugly face. And that also means you have to try to pretend to be a nice guy."

"I'm always a nice guy," Tommy said. "Can I help it if everyone around me's an inconsiderate jerk? And that, Josh, includes you."

Tommy went into the house and slammed the door behind him. Reilly rolled his eyes at me and he and Claudia followed Tommy.

I dropped into a chair. "I hate group dynamics. Even worse when you have mega egos attached."

"Reminds me of the quilting guild in Grand Lake, Iowa," Rose said.

"You're always full of surprises. I didn't know you quilted. I've never seen anything you've made."

"I don't. Because one week as a member of the quilting guild of Grand Lake, Iowa, was quite enough for me, thank you very much." She sniffed and picked up her glass of lemonade. "It's early, but everything's off kilter today. I might have my G&T now."

Robbie stretched and yawned.

"What did you want to talk to me about?" Rose asked.

"Talk to you? I didn't want Tommy Greene's company, that's all. His charm's as false as his teeth."

Rose shrugged. "Exaggerated for dramatic effect most likely. I'm sure he's very nice underneath. He is from Yorkshire, after all."

"Where everyone's perfectly lovely. A county of pussycats."

Conscious of the non-TV guests still relaxing on the veranda, Rose dropped her voice. "Are you aware that Scarlet's a former Miss Louisiana?"

"Josh mentioned that. Does it matter?"

"Only if you're concerned about her qualifications to judge baking. Of which she has exactly zero. I'd be surprised if Scarlet's the name on her birth certificate. Her qualifications to be on TV, however, are obvious." Rose snorted, and Robbie, still on her lap, curled his lip. Those two really did look alike sometimes. My grandfather's heritage is Scottish, and Rose's cats had always been honored with the name of one Hebridean hero or another. "Claudia's perfectly lovely," Rose said. "I'll enjoy getting to know her, if I get the chance. They're here for more than a week, until next Wednesday."

"You should have told me they're staying here."

"Didn't I?"

"No, you didn't."

"No reason I should have. You don't involve yourself with the day-to-day running of the B and B, love. If you'd like to take a more active part—"

"Definitely not."

"As you keep telling me."

"Because," I said, "I have more than enough to do." I smiled to soften my words as I stood up. "I'm going home. Do you want me to make your drink first?"

"Thank you, but no. I've decided to wait a while longer. Everything is better with anticipation." She picked up her book with one hand, stroked the cat with the other.

I went into the house. The main door opened onto the front hall, where we'd set up a reproduction antique desk for reception. A wide sweeping staircase with a red carpet and solid oak banisters led to the second floor, and the ground-floor hallway continued along the length of the house. Guest bedrooms ran off the hall, and Rose's suite was at the end. The drawing room was at the front of the house, overlooking the veranda, the guest parking area, the formal gardens, and the long driveway leading to the main road. Doors to the dining room were across the hall, and turning left led to the kitchen.

I pay the B & B housekeepers a bit extra to let my dog out a few times during the day and ensure her water bowl's refreshed, but today I was glad for the opportunity to have a short romp with her. I took one step across the hall, intending to duck through the dining room and out the French doors, but an angry shout from the drawing room had me stopping in my tracks.

"Yes!"

"I said no, and that's final."

My ears perked up. The rest of the house was quiet, as it usually is in mid-afternoon.

"I don't know how many times I have to tell you, Josh," Reilly said, "our audience is mostly women. Women watch for the food, not to look at younger, prettier women."

"That redhead comes across so well on screen. What would it hurt to include the shots of her talking to Tommy?"

"No, the old woman's much better. That English accent's a hoot."

I assumed the old woman was Rose and the redhead, Bernie.

"Moot point, both of you," Claudia said. "The old woman, as you call her, is the cook's grandmother, and the redhead is her friend. They're hardly impartial observers."

"So what?" Josh snapped. "No one knows that, Claudia. No one cares."

"I know. I care," Reilly said. "And that's final. What I want to include are the shots of that jerk leering at Scarlet, and Tommy giving him what for."

"That has nothing to do with the cooking," Claudia said.

"It provides dramatic interest," Reilly said. "Okay, what about using the old guy with the loose dentures? Claudia, do you think he's too old?"

I slipped into the dining room and shut the double doors behind me. *Interesting*, I thought. I didn't know anything about the TV business, and I didn't want to know, but it seemed strange to me that Reilly, who'd been introduced as the director's assistant, was telling the director what they were going to do.

Chapter 4

If my kitchen had been crowded yesterday, it was *really* crowded today. So crowded there wasn't room for the clapper-board woman or the assistant director. The woman had to stand in the open doorway leading outside, and Reilly shouted at us from the entrance to the dining area.

Bernie and Rose had been banished entirely.

I'd been in the B&B kitchen before six to get muffins and a coffee cake in the oven along with a quickly-prepared breakfast casserole for Edna to serve to our guests, and I arrived at the tea room promptly at seven and been told to wait. I took a seat in the garden and watched the activity as the sun rose over Cape Cod. Crew bustled around as equipment was unloaded and carried into the tearoom. First Scarlet, then Claudia, and finally Tommy went into the makeup trailer, and after various degrees of time had passed, they came out camera ready.

Bernie's car drove past and parked at the steps of Victoria-on-Sea. Rose emerged from the house, Bernie took her arm, and they walked down the driveway, past the trucks and trailers, through the gate, and took seats at my table.

"What brings you two here?" I asked.

"I'm acting as your agent," Bernie said. "It was Rose's idea."

"Agent? I don't need an agent."

"Sure you do," Bernie said.

"Even supposing I did, what makes you qualified?"

"You know many agents, do you?" Rose asked me.

"No, but—"

"Until you do have a proper agent, we decided Bernadette will act on your behalf."

"When did *we* decide this?"

"Yesterday at tea. Matt agreed," Bernie said. "You need to have someone representing your interests in all this. That person will be me. I worked at a law firm, remember, and I know plenty of lawyers I can call for advice at a moment's notice."

I refrained from rolling my eyes. "Whatever. I'm not being paid for this, although they are paying for the use of the property. The publicity's supposedly enough, although I have my doubts." I grimaced at Rose and Bernie.

They smiled back.

"Whatever," I said again.

"Lily," Melanie, the makeup artist, called from the steps of the trailer. "You're next."

I stood up. I'd spent a lot of time deciding what to wear for my big day of baking. The kitchen is my happy place, so I eventually decided to look happy in a sundress splashed with blue and yellow.

"That dress has too much pattern in it," Bernie said.

I looked down at myself. "What do you mean?"

"You look like an abstract painting."

"I want to stand out."

"No, you don't," Bernie said. "You want your food to stand out."

"Good morning, ladies. Lovely day, isn't it?" Tommy Greene's false teeth flashed at us. "Mrs. Campbell, right?

Late of Yorkshire and greatly missed there, I'm sure. And the lovely Bernadette."

Rose tittered. Bernie vacillated between looking pleased and offended. I left them and went to have my hair and makeup done.

I sometimes wonder if the reason I like baking so much is that I'm not at all an impulsive person. Cooking's an art, but baking is a science. There's room to experiment, of course, to try new things, and the sky's the limit when it comes to decorating, but the principles of baking are constant. The ingredients have to be weighed or measured accurately, balanced perfectly one to the other, and baked precisely at the time and temperature required.

I love nothing more than to be alone in my kitchen, measuring, stirring, folding, and then admiring the fruit of my labors when the end product emerges from the oven or the refrigerator. I can't make a living working alone in a private kitchen, so I have to work at restaurants or bakeries, and now that I have my own place, I still need staff and customers, some of whom are more demanding than they should be.

Baking while a room full of critical people questioned my every move, and a camera filmed it happening, was not my happy place.

But, I told myself, I'd decided to do this show, and so I would do it willingly, cheerfully, and professionally. After all, wasn't introducing people to good food, well prepared, one of my joys in life?

Yesterday I'd baked while the camera filmed me. Today the three judges would talk to me and ask questions while I worked. I'd given them advance notice of what I intended to prepare so they could have their questions ready.

I started with scones, which is what I make the most of every day. Can't have afternoon tea without freshly baked scones.

"Tell me about afternoon tea, Lily." Claudia gave me an encouraging smile. Tommy stood behind the cameraman, watching. Scarlet had disappeared. "Why does it appeal to you?"

I added the premeasured butter and dry ingredients to the mixing bowl and kneaded them together with my hands. "Afternoon tea's all about tradition. About hospitality and taking time to gather with friends to enjoy the finer things in life. Afternoon tea, in my opinion, anyway, is a delicacy, an indulgence, and it should be treated as such. What can I say? I love treating people."

"I've been told your grandmother worked as a kitchen maid in an English castle in her youth. Did she teach you about the proper serving of tea?"

I patted the dough together and held up my sticky hands to show them to Claudia (and the camera), and then I dumped the contents of the bowl onto a floured sheet of parchment paper and began combining and folding. So natural and comfortable was the rhythm, I could talk easily. I was far less nervous than I'd been yesterday, and I hoped that came through. I wouldn't have thought it possible that I could almost ignore the giant black lens of the camera following my every move.

"Despite its name, Thornecroft Castle isn't a castle, but rather a stately home. My grandmother started working as a cook's assistant there when she was fourteen."

"Very *Downton Abbey*," Claudia said with a light laugh.

"According to my grandmother, it was. One day she ran into, literally, a young American soldier named Eric Campbell on the streets of Yorkshire, married him when he got out of the hospital, and came to America as a young bride."

I patted the dough, cut the circles, and laid them on a prewarmed baking sheet.

"Those look quite delightful," Claudia said as the scones

went into the oven. "They were quick and easy to make from ingredients most people have at hand. I've worked long enough in this business to know that what looks quick and easy often isn't."

"That's true," I said. "But in this case what you see is exactly what you get. Scones really are amazingly simple and require no special ingredients or equipment."

"I can't wait to try one. I see you're using a French-style wooden rolling pin, but a solid marble one is on the shelf over there." The camera focused on my hands and then lifted to the marble rolling pin displayed in front of a row of different sized mixing bowls. "Do you have a preference?"

I decided not to tell her that I didn't use the marble rolling pin anymore, the one I'd carried from job to job around New York City, since I'd wielded it to defend myself from a deranged killer. "This style fits comfortably in my hands, and the scone dough doesn't need as much pressure as chilled pastry does."

"Okay," Reilly said. "That was good."

The cameraman lowered his camera and gave his back a good stretch while I washed my sticky hands at the sink.

I next prepared lemon tarts, while Scarlet chatted about her mother, who was apparently the best pie maker in all of Lafayette, Louisiana. I'd made the pastry yesterday and kept it in the fridge overnight, so now I rolled it out and cut the circles to fit into individual tartlet pans as I explained how pastry benefits from time to chill. I prepared the lemon filling and added it to the shells prior to popping the gorgeous little tarts into the oven.

Scarlet said, "That's it?"

"What do you mean?"

"Isn't *tart* an English word for *pie*? I thought you were making pie. My daddy would have laughed to see those teeny tiny little things."

I stumbled for something polite to say.

"Thing is, Scarlet"—Tommy stepped forward—"this type of cooking isn't for men who've put in a hard day's work. Men like your dad and mine. It's for people—bored, spoiled society women mostly—who want to dress up and gossip with their friends and pretend they're aristocracy."

I put the mixing bowls into the sink and ran water over them. When the tarts were ready to be served, I'd pipe a generous dollop of whipped cream on the top of each one. I decided this wasn't the right time to mention that.

"Lily?" Reilly said. "Have you got anything to say about that?"

"You want me to reply?"

"Uh, yeah, honey," Scarlet said. "That's kinda the point. I talk. You talk."

"We all talk." Tommy threw me a wink.

The day dragged on. The judges took turns talking to me, and occasionally arguing among themselves, while I prepared shortbread, pistachio macarons, and an Earl Grey chocolate tart and tried to make intelligent conversation. Baking done, it was time to make sandwiches. I'd be serving chicken poached in Darjeeling, herbed cucumber, and roast beef on crostini. Today I'd decided to add additional herbs to give more color to the cucumber sandwiches.

"You call that a sandwich?" Tommy said as I cut the crusts off the thinly sliced white bread containing the cucumber slices. "My dad would have had more than that stuck between his teeth after his lunch."

I refrained from sticking my tongue out at him.

"Nice image, Tommy," Scarlet said. "Not."

At last, I was done. Nothing left but to serve afternoon tea to the judges. Marybeth and Cheryl had spent most of the day in the dining room, allowed into the kitchen only between one batch of baking and the next to do the dishes and tidy everything up in order for me to make a mess again. Occasionally, I'd heard the voice of my agent, aka Bernie, asking Reilly or Josh how everything was going and whether I needed anything. They always replied, "Fine," and "No." Rose, I guessed, had gotten bored and gone home.

The judging would take place in the dining room, and the judges would enjoy a properly served afternoon tea. We'd set the table with my personal set of Royal Doulton Winthrop, white china with a thin red trim adorned with delicate gold leaves, which had been my sixteenth birthday gift from my maternal grandparents. Fresh flowers in crystal vases and stiffly ironed red linens completed the table setting.

If Tommy made a crack about his mother not being able to afford Royal Doulton, or if Scarlet commented that my macarons wouldn't feed her father and his family of twenty-seven children, I'd smack them.

We took a long break while everyone had their makeup refreshed, the crew helped themselves to the contents of the catering table set up beside the driveway, and the cameras and other gear were moved into the dining room. As I crossed the patio, heading for the makeup trailer when it was my turn, I saw Reilly and Josh huddled together next to an equipment truck. Their voices carried on the wind coming off the bay, and I could tell they were arguing, although I couldn't hear the words. Reilly threw his hands in the air and stalked past me with angry strides, his face set into hard lines.

"Lily? I'm ready," Melanie called.

As I turned to go into the trailer, I glanced back to see that Josh had a satisfied smirk curling around his lips.

We enjoyed a proper tea party, other than the presence of the cameras, the jumble of lights and cables and other equipment, and the circle of people watching us, some with headphones on and some with clipboards or iPads in hand. Bernie gave me an enthusiastic thumbs-up. Reilly leaned against the wall, arms crossed over his chest, scowling. Josh, on the other hand, looked pleased with himself. To my surprise, Allegra Griffin hovered in the background, next to Gary Powers. Before sitting down, I waved Bernie over.

"That woman, the one by the vestibule, standing next to Gary, is from North Augusta Bakery. Can you ask Reilly if she's allowed to be here?"

Bernie whispered in Reilly's ear. Reilly glanced over at the woman in question and nodded.

"Yes," Bernie told me. "She's allowed to watch, and in turn, you'll be permitted to visit the set when they're filming at her place. Reilly isn't happy about Gary being here but said if he minds his manners, he can stay."

I took my seat at the table with the three judges. Marybeth came to take our orders for tea. Claudia studied the tea menu and then put it aside and asked me which brew I'd recommend. Scarlet said, "I don't like hot tea." Tommy informed us that where he came from, tea was tea, the thicker and the stronger and the more sugar added, the better, and you were happy to have it.

"I enjoy a Creamy Earl Grey at this time of day," I said to Claudia. "So refreshing for a break after a hard day at work."

"I'll have that, then, please." She handed her menu to Marybeth with a smile.

Marybeth's own smile was so wide and so frozen in place, I feared it would be stuck there permanently. The camera, I noticed, never focused on her or Cheryl's face, just their hands as they brought the full teapots—a larger one containing Creamy Earl Grey for Claudia and me, a smaller pot with English breakfast for Tommy, and a glass of iced tea for Scarlet. I keep iced tea and lemonade on hand as part of the children's menu. I considered telling her that, then decided she might take offense.

Next came small bowls containing strawberry jam, clotted cream, and butter, which Marybeth arranged in the center of the table. Scarlet asked me what these were for, and I explained that they went with the scones. I made sure they knew the jam was made by a woman I knew personally, from fruit grown by a Cape Cod berry farmer.

The food was served on two three-tiered stands, arranged in the traditional manner: perfectly cut sandwiches on the bottom, plump scones in the middle, delectable desserts on the top.

"May I?" Claudia said to me, with a nod toward the larger teapot. I nodded, and she poured for us both. Tommy served himself tea, adding a generous glug of milk and two heaped teaspoons of sugar, and the judges tucked into the food.

I held my breath, my stomach in knots. Claudia admired the texture of the scones and explained to Scarlet and Tommy that the flaky layers were perfect for holding jam and cream. Scarlet admitted that the lemon tarts were yummy. The judges tasted everything, while I tried not to watch their faces for signs of what they were thinking. The judges made polite but vague conversation as they ate. No one offered an opinion on the quality of the food. Scarlet nibbled at everything before demurely tucking the residue aside to be whisked out of sight. Tommy tried everything and consumed it all, while Claudia enjoyed a scone, a selection of sandwiches, and a single piece of shortbread.

"The presentation of afternoon tea is very formal, isn't it, Lily?" Claudia said as she dabbed her lips with her napkin, indicating she was finished. Tommy leaned back in his chair, a satisfied look on his face. I dared to hope that meant he'd enjoyed it.

"It doesn't have to be," I said. "Anyone can enjoy a cup

of tea and a homemade scone, even a store-bought scone, in the middle of the day, but here at Tea by the Sea, I want to provide my guests with a truly extraordinary experience, to pamper them, if you like."

Marybeth brought a second pot of Creamy Earl Grey. She had to slip behind Tommy's chair to get to Claudia's place. As she did so, Tommy turned slightly; Marybeth stumbled and lurched forward. She let out a yell of surprise, and the pot went flying. She grabbed it and managed to keep it from hitting the floor, but hot liquid spilled from the spout, spraying Tommy's lap. He leapt to his feet with a bellow of shock.

"Oh, my goodness," Marybeth cried. "Are you okay?" She put the teapot down and grabbed a napkin.

"No, I'm not okay," Tommy yelled. "What's the matter with you? You can't carry a teapot?"

"I . . . I'm sorry."

"Sorry doesn't cut it." He snatched the napkin out of her hands and dabbed at his lap. "Call yourself a waitress? You'd be better out in the fields, picking the food, not serving it. I could have been seriously burned, would have been if I were a woman wearing a skirt, with bare legs, like Scarlet there. As for you, Lily," he snarled at me, "you need to get yourself competent staff if you want your business to be in the big leagues."

"Bummer," Scarlet said.

I'd been momentarily shocked by the strength of Tommy's reaction, but I finally found my wits and leapt to my feet. "That's completely unfair. Accidents can happen to anyone, as any chef should know. Marybeth, are *you* all right?"

Her eyes brimmed with tears; her lower lip trembled. For the first time, the camera was pointed directly at her, but I didn't think she noticed. "I . . . I'll be . . . I'm fine."

"You'd be on your way out the door if you worked for me," Tommy yelled. "You stupid—"

His anger was way out of proportion to what had been a minor incident. Marybeth's face crumbled, and she burst into tears. I was about to tell Tommy to get out of my establishment, that I wouldn't tolerate the bullying of my staff, but someone beat me to it.

Cheryl pushed herself between her daughter and Tommy. Her eyes blazed fire, her fists were clenched, and her jaw was set. I thought of a mother cat defending her kittens. "How dare you! You tripped her. I saw it happen."

"Rubbish."

"You stuck-up English jerk. You might think you're a fancy chef and a big-name TV star, but you're nothing but a bully, and I don't know why anyone stands for it."

The camera closed in. It swung between Cheryl's face and Tommy's.

"And who might you be?" he sneered. "Another waitress working the tourist season in a small town? At least you look like you've been around the block a few times, pet, so you might not be totally incompetent."

Marybeth lifted her hands to her face and sobbed. Cheryl was struck silent. But only for a moment. "You are a very nasty man. I wonder how you can sleep at night."

"Oh, my dear. I have no trouble sleeping at all. If you're asking if you can join me, sorry, but you're too old for my taste."

I glanced around, expecting someone to intervene. When I saw the look on Reilly's face, I realized that wasn't going to happen. He looked about as happy as a child cavorting on the beach on a sunny summer's day. Josh was nowhere to be seen.

I took Cheryl's arm. "Enough, please. Don't give them what they want. Let's go."

Cheryl's mouth opened. It closed. It opened again, and she said to me, "You're right." She put her arm around Marybeth's shoulders. "Come on, honey. Let's make ourselves a cup of tea. Off you go." She gave Marybeth a gentle push, and Marybeth headed for the kitchen. Cheryl moved to follow her, but she stopped inches away from Tommy. She looked directly into his face. "Someone, someday, will put a stop to you and your bullying."

"Probably," he said.

"And it might well be me." She followed her daughter.

"We're done here," I said when the kitchen doors had swung closed behind them.

Reilly stepped forward. "I'd say we have what we need for today."

"Permanently. I don't want you back."

"You signed a contract, Lily. The judges will consult amongst themselves here in your restaurant, over scones and a nice pot of tea—glass for our Southern belle—and then they'll call you in to tell you their decision. That'll happen tomorrow. If we need to shoot any more scenes, we will."

"I don't want you people here."

"I don't much care what you want," Reilly said.

"What's going on here?" Josh stepped between us. "Never mind. Like the woman said, we're done here for today."

Bernie, who'd been watching the whole thing from the sidelines, crossed the room with rapid strides. "Come on, Lily. Let's go. We need to consider our options."

She was right, I realized. I'd accomplish nothing more by getting angrier. I looked at Tommy. He returned my stare with a duck of his head and a surprisingly bashful smile. Almost, I thought, as if he were offering me an apology.

Bernie and I went into the kitchen to find Marybeth drying her eyes and Cheryl trying to comfort her. Bernie opened the back door. "We need air even more than we need tea. Come on, ladies. Outside."

We stood in the shade of the big old oak shading the entrance to the kitchen. Traffic passed on the road, and we could hear the voices of the TV crew packing up their equipment.

"I'm sorry," Marybeth said. "I shouldn't have lost my cool."

"You were perfectly entitled to lose your cool," I said. "He was playing for the camera the whole time."

"He tripped me. I'm sure of it. You know I'm not clumsy."

"I believe you. It was a setup." I wondered if that was what Reilly and Josh had been arguing about shortly before we gathered for the judging.

"Someone should put a stop to it," Cheryl said. "Professional bullying for entertainment's not right."

"No," Bernie said, "but it brings in the audience."

I checked my watch. "Look, it's almost three. Marybeth, you go on home. Put your feet up for a little while, maybe have a glass of wine before your kids get home."

"We have to clean up," she protested. "That TV crew won't do it. Besides, I came with Mom."

"I'll give you a lift," Bernie said. "I have to get home, anyway. I've had a great idea for the villain in my book. I'm going to call him Thomas Yellow."

We burst out laughing.

"Thanks," Marybeth said when she could talk again. "I accept your offer. Both of your offers. I have to go to the washroom first, Bernie. Then I'll be right out." She went into the kitchen.

"As your agent," Bernie said, "I'm thinking of putting a hardship clause in your next contract."

"I shouldn't have risen to the bait," Cheryl said. "I've seen that show. At least once a season Tommy turns on some unsuspecting schmuck simply trying to do their job. All the better if he can get the tears to flow or lots of words they have to beep out."

"You protected your child, and that was the right thing to do," I said. "No matter how old that child might be."

"How'd it go?" Simon came around the building, stuffing his gardening gloves into his pocket. "Looks like they're wrapping up for the day."

"Don't ask," Bernie said.

"You're proof not all Englishmen are jerks," Cheryl said.

"What does that mean?" he asked.

"It went well, until the very end." I told him about the day, leaving out the dramatic finale. "They seemed to enjoy the food. They ate plenty of it, anyway, and I think Claudia, at least, liked the presentation. They'll meet with me tomorrow, have tea again, and then tell me what they liked and what they didn't, and give me a rating out of ten. Then they're on to North Augusta Bakery. The highest score goes through to the next stage."

"Marybeth's been a long time," Bernie said. "Do you want me to check on her?"

At that moment Marybeth came back out. She'd taken her apron off and was carrying her bag. I was pleased to see that her face and eyes were clear, the tears had dried, and she even had a slight smile on her face. "I'll give you a call later, Mom. See you tomorrow, Lily."

We waved good-bye, and then Cheryl and I went inside to clean up. Simon followed, asking if there were any leftovers.

Chapter 5

The event at teatime left me feeling unsettled and cranky. Josh could insist that I had to continue with filming the show the following day, but he couldn't make me look happy about it.

I'd made a mistake agreeing to this, when I'd known better in the first place. And now I was, I realized, stuck with it. I'd lost most of a week's income, and that over the busiest time of the year, in the hopes of some future promotional opportunities for Tea by the Sea, as well as Victoria-on-Sea. If I boycotted the show now, those promotional opportunities would never come about, and the income would still be gone.

Simon went back to his gardens, clutching a thickly buttered scone and a fistful of pastries while Cheryl and I tidied up the most recent mess. That done, I started more baking while Cheryl prepared sandwich ingredients to put in the fridge. As I kneaded and folded and mixed and tasted, I felt some of my anger fading, but I could tell by the set of her shoulders and the look on her face that Cheryl's wasn't.

I popped a batch of vanilla cupcakes into the oven and

washed my hands. "That should do it. Thanks for staying and helping out."

"Not a problem. Might as well take advantage of Jim being away for the night and earn myself some overtime. Has anyone ever told you you're a good boss?"

"Not that I recall."

"I'm telling you now." She took off her apron and threw it into the hamper in the back room to join the rest of the day's laundry. "If I wasn't concerned about ruining your business, I'd be tempted to slip a little poison into that Tommy Greene's tea tomorrow."

"Don't even joke about that."

"I'm not joking. Good night, Lily. Are we closed to the public all day tomorrow?"

"Yes. The judging's supposed to be in the morning, which is what some of this food's for, but if it goes longer than expected, I can't have customers with reservations hammering on the door. And then, I sincerely hope, we'll be done and *America Bakes!* can go on to torment North Augusta Bakery."

"Allegra Griffin and Tommy Greene. A match made in heaven." Cheryl left, and the back door swung shut behind her.

I waited until the cupcakes were out of the oven and cool enough to put into containers before I also left for the day. I went through the dining room, checking everything was ready for the morning. I switched out lights as I went, and then I locked the front door behind me.

I often put in long nights baking for the following day, but tonight I wanted to get home early. I was dead beat. All that smiling and making polite conversation was difficult enough, never mind knowing professionals were judging my efforts. And then the incident between Tommy and Marybeth. I've worked in the restaurant industry for a long time, and I've seen plenty of temperamental cooks.

My ex-boyfriend, a Michelin-starred chef, came to mind. Verbal abuse might be common, but there's never any excuse for it. Cooking is a high-stress career, but so are a lot of careers. So is life.

I walked slowly up the long driveway toward the lights of Victoria-on-Sea. The sun was lowering itself into the calm waters of the bay, and the sky was a blaze of red, deep gray, and pink. The petals of the daisies and white roses glowed in the dusk settling over the flower beds. A flock of birds flew overhead, seeking refuge for the night.

Only two people were sitting on the veranda. Rose and Tommy Greene. Rose had her nightly gin and tonic and was regaling him with stories of her days at Thornecroft Castle as she gently stroked Robbie, snoozing on her lap.

I hesitated, decided not to approach, and turned away, but I was too late.

"Lily! Come and join us," Rose called.

I reluctantly climbed the steps. Tommy stood politely, and I gave him a stiff nod. He smiled a greeting, but I did not return it.

"All finished, love?" Rose asked. Robbie opened one eye, saw it was only me, and closed it again.

"For tonight."

"Why don't you get yourself a drink and join us? Tommy and I are having great fun trying to find out what families we both know."

"I'm tired," I said. "It's been a long day. If you don't need me for anything, I'll be off."

"Are you all right, love?" she asked.

"I'm fine." I looked at Tommy. "It's also been an emotionally difficult day. Where's the rest of your merry crew?"

"They went out for dinner," he said. "I didn't feel like making merry, as you put it, so I stayed behind. Besides, your tea was more than enough."

"Good night, Rose."

"Your grandmother tells me you live on the property," Tommy said. "Let me walk you home."

"That's not necessary."

"No, but I'd like to see more of the garden."

"Garden's open anytime." I walked away.

I heated a frozen dinner in the microwave, ate it without tasting it, and then took my book and a glass of wine out to the porch. I didn't read for long: by eleven o'clock my eyes began closing and my head nodding. I put the book down and got up. I took my things into the cottage and got Éclair's leash. She's a labradoodle, energetic, and highly intelligent, with floppy ears, intense dark eyes, and masses of curly beige fur. She's named for the French pastry because of the streak of cream fur running under her belly. She didn't need to be told we were going for a walk and danced at my feet.

I let us through the gate, and she began running in circles, following her nose, chasing scents only she could detect. I breathed in the warm, soft night air, full of the scent of the sea and of the gardens. Éclair headed for the big house, and I trailed along behind. It was a clear night, the moon was bright, and the lamp over the veranda was on, as were some of the lights in the guest rooms. Rose's windows were dark.

A man was in the rose garden, examining the bushes, and Éclair hurried to greet him. I called to her sharply, but I was too late. Tommy Greene straightened and turned around. He saw me, and then he bent down and gave the dog a hearty pat. Pat over, Éclair ran back to me, and Tommy followed.

"Good evening," he said. "I've been admiring your garden. It's quite special."

"Thank you. Good night." I turned around and started to walk away. He fell into step beside me while Éclair ran on ahead.

"Nice place you have here," Tommy said. "You and your grandmother. This garden must take a lot of work." His accent slipped, some of the rough edges fell away, and his tone was softer and lighter.

"It does," I said. "We have a good gardener. He's English."

"As the best are. I was admiring the roses. Some nice varieties, and several that are not at all common."

"That's down to the previous owners and their gardener. They were collectors, I understand."

"It shows."

I looked at him. "You . . . know about roses?"

He smiled at me. I was so startled I almost froze in my tracks. The smile was genuine, and even kind. "Love of my life. Apart from my wife and the kids, and sometimes my wife complains she's in third place."

"Where does cooking rate?"

"Pretty high up there, I will admit, but I wouldn't say I *love* it. I've been cooking since I was a wee lad helping out in my parents' pub in Halifax. It's a job, you know. Not a passion, although I do enjoy it. I did enjoy it, anyway, when I was cooking. It's a job I've been lucky enough to do very well out of indeed."

We rounded the house, and the waters of Cape Cod Bay came into sight.

"I miss England sometimes," he said. "Yeah, a beach house in Malibu's nice, but it's not a two-bedroom flat over a Yorkshire pub, now is it?"

"I . . . uh . . . guess not."

"I miss cooking. Cooking's my roots. You might say it's in my blood, and I've not been doing enough of it lately."

"You own what? Five restaurants?"

"Six. Three in Manhattan, one in New Orleans, one in Vegas, and two in LA. I think that makes six."

"Seven."

"Oh. Right. The Vegas one's new. I forget about it some-times. Yeah, I own those places, and I've designed the menus, worked out the major details, anyway. But I don't *cook* there. I don't cook much at all anymore."

My cottage is situated not far from the main house, but I didn't head immediately toward it. I followed Tommy as he walked to the edge of the bluffs. He was showing me another side of him, and although I was wary, I was also curious. He leaned on the railing and stared across the water.

"What would you think about a Cape Cod version of Greene's Pub?" he asked.

"You'd get plenty of customers. The nice places in North Augusta have lineups all summer long. Some of the not-so-nice places, too. It can be quiet in the off-season, though."

"I might scout around while I'm here. Would you like a job?"

I turned and faced him. The soft breeze ruffled strands of hair that had escaped from my ponytail, and a piece drifted into my mouth. I plucked it out. The salt-and-seaweed scent of the sea was strong, and far below us the tide crashed against the rocky shore. The beach was empty; the tide coming in.

"I have a job. If you mean, would I like a job working for you, I don't think so."

"You're angry about what happened today."

I stared at him. "Of course I'm angry. I'm furious. You bullied one of my staff. You're a big-shot TV personality, a wealthy man, a business owner with six, no, seven restau-rants, and you bullied a young woman working as a wait-ress. You wanted to have her fired from a job she needs to help provide an income for her family. Yes, I'm angry, but I think you're the one who needs anger management lessons." I threw up my hands. "For all that it would help." I started to walk away.

"For what it's worth," he said, "I'm sorry. I told Marybeth that. If it matters to you, and I hope it does, she accepted my apology."

I stopped and turned around. "You did? She did?"

"That's my TV shtick, don't you know? I'm the brilliant but bad-boy chef, rough around the edges, hardscrabble childhood, fought my way to the top with my fists and plucky determination and hard work."

"Is that right?"

He leaned against the railing and looked out over the dark water. "Nah. Maybe some of it's a grain of truth, but not about my childhood. My parents owned a pub, but it was a nice pub in a nice area. They were good people, still are good people. I got in a few scrapes when I was a lad— what boy doesn't?—and I had some what you'd call anger management issues when I was starting out. No more than any other family-taught cook from the North of England trying to make it in the London culinary world. But somehow I got that reputation, and it stuck. The foulmouthed genius, they called me. Still do. On the show I'm expected to throw a temper tantrum every now and again. He wanted me to get in an argument with you about putting extra stuff, like orange peel, into scones, but I figured you wouldn't be drawn, and I told him that."

"So you turned on innocent little Marybeth. I can't forgive you for that."

"Maybe you shouldn't," he said. "I was surprised, truth be told, when she started to cry. I figured she'd know it was all part of the show. Reality TV—"

"Has nothing to do with reality. But people aren't always aware of that, are they?"

"No."

"If you don't like being known as a bully, why don't you stop?"

He turned to face me. His eyes were dark and serious, and he pondered my question for a long time. "I've been thinking of doing that, but maybe I'm addicted. To the fame, the money most of all. Plenty of good chefs are out there who'd do a better job than me of being a TV personality. So I stick to being the bad boy, and I give the director and his producers what they want."

"That's sad."

"The price of success. I meant what I said."

"About what?"

"You can have a job with me anytime. Your baking's good. Top notch. Made with skill and love."

"And Cape Cod ingredients, grown locally by local farmers."

He chuckled, the sound surprisingly warm and gentle. "Can't forget the importance of good ingredients, and I never do. I haven't had such a good scone as I had today since my gran died, and I mean that, too. I hate the stuff these yanks make. Hard as rocks and as dry as that patch of sand down there. Never mind chocolate chips. The devil's invention, those are."

"I make chocolate chip cookies for the children's tea."

"My point exactly. Great for the kiddies. You think about it. The offer's there. As for the show, I'm going to give you ten out of ten."

"You are? Uh . . . thank you."

"You've achieved exactly what you set out to achieve, and everything about your place is perfect. I can't say what the other judges are going to give you, and I won't say I won't find the next place just as good, but I wanted you to know."

He turned to his left and pointed toward the stairs leading down to the beach. "Is it safe to go down there, do you know?"

"Not at night. Even with the moonlight, it's too dark, and the beach isn't lit. The tide's coming in, and although it doesn't cover the beach completely, it does create some tricky spots, which you need to be nimble of foot to get around. Save it until tomorrow. When the tide's out, you can walk a long way."

"I'll do that." He gave me a wave and left me.

I stared after him. The man was full of surprises.

Chapter 6

The next time I saw Tommy Greene, he was dead.

Yesterday I'd been determined not to participate in the show any longer, but as my anger receded, particularly after my conversation with Tommy, I realized I couldn't just not show up. A lawsuit would ruin me. I'd signed a contract, and I could be pretty sure that CookingTV and their backers had a heck of a lot more legal firepower than I could assemble.

I'd make nice and continue with the show today and hope never to see them again. If by any chance I did win this round, I'd try to find a way to get out of continuing.

We'd have a slightly later start today, so I'd been told to be on set at nine for makeup and the rest. I'd serve afternoon tea and sit at a table on the patio, weather permitting, with the judges and listen to them criticize me and my place.

What fun. Not.

Rose had once again explained to her guests that the individually cooked breakfast offerings would not be available. Despite that, I got up at my regular time of a quarter to six, let Éclair into the enclosed yard while I showered, fed her breakfast to enjoy while I dressed, and we left my cottage at six o'clock, as usual.

I walked slowly along the cliffside, enjoying the early morning warmth and clear air, while Éclair sniffed at every bush and blade of grass, checking the overnight news from the neighborhood. The bay was busy with charter fishing boats and early whale-watching trips heading to the animals' feeding grounds in the open ocean.

Éclair spotted a familiar figure leaning on the railing also watching the activity, and she hurried to say good morning. Simon turned with a smile for me and a hearty pat for the dog, and I let us into the small, dark, outdated B & B kitchen. Every room in this house is decorated as though it were in a grand nineteenth-century English country house, except for the kitchen, which hasn't been updated since the 1950s at the latest. It was dark, poky, crowded, and badly laid out.

I put the coffeepot on and began assembling ingredients for a breakfast bread and butter pudding.

"Not doing the full English again today?" Without being asked, Simon rummaged in the fridge for fresh fruit for the morning's salad and put berries and melons on the chopping board, along with bananas.

"No time. I have muffins and a coffee cake in the freezer, and I'll put this in the oven for Edna to slice and serve. I'm not due on set"—I put quotation marks around the words—"until nine for makeup and all that nonsense, but I want to go up as soon as I'm done here to make sure everything's perfect in the dining room as well as on the patio, if they decide to shoot outside."

"The rain that had been predicted seems to be holding off. When I'm finished here, I'll pick today's flowers and bring them up."

"Thanks." I poured a mixture of eggs, milk, sugar, vanilla,

and cinnamon over the cubes of day-old bread I'd arranged at the bottom of a large baking pan. "All I want is for this to be over. I hate having my space invaded. I hate being judged. I suppose I'm judged all day, every day, every time someone puts a crumb in their mouth, but I hate having it said out loud to my face. Most of all, I hate having my staff upset."

"What happened yesterday? It was obvious something had, but you didn't want to tell me."

"I still don't. I don't know what I think about it." I remembered my talk with Tommy yesterday evening. How . . . nice . . . he'd seemed.

"They did some filming in the gardens yesterday afternoon, after finishing in the restaurant," Simon said.

"That's good. I think. Do you think it is?"

"I do. It's all part of the atmosphere of Tea by the Sea, and any mention of Victoria-on-Sea's good, too. Josh wasn't there, but his assistant, Reilly, showed the camera crew what he wanted. He even got some shots of me admiring the roses. The English guy, Tommy, was there, too. He had some surprisingly knowledgeable questions about the plants."

"Turns out he's a keen gardener. Hardly goes with his tough-guy image, does it?"

"I don't know 'bout that." Simon put on a rough-and-tumble Cockney accent and held up the knife he was holding. He narrowed his eyes and bared his teeth. "We gardeners can be a bunch of mighty tough blokes, you know, mate. We regularly get into fights to the death over who has the best petunias or camellias."

I laughed. "I'm *sooo* scared. Maybe I'm being pessimistic. Hopefully, it'll all work out. Rose is excited about her friends and family in Iowa seeing the show."

Simon sliced the last banana into the glass bowl containing the rest of the fruit, put the paring knife down, and stood up. "On that note, it's back to work I go. Catch you later, Lily."

He passed Edna coming in. I told Edna what I wanted her to do and let her know that I'd be available before nine if she needed me.

"I drove past the bakery in town," she said. "They've gone to a lot of trouble to spruce the place up. Flower baskets lining the windows, two big planters on either side of the front door, windows washed, door freshly painted. I suspect they even scrubbed down the awning. I don't think that's happened since Noreen first opened the place."

"Can't fault them for that. I got out my good china and asked Simon to pay particular attention to giving me the best flowers."

"Are you going to mind if you don't win? It seems as though all sorts of things come into the judging on this show, not simply the quality of the food. Clean awnings could be the deciding factor. They might dock you because Gary Powers was being such an obnoxious loudmouth on Monday."

"I'll mind, sure. Probably more than I think I will. I've gone to a lot of trouble over this. We all have, and we've all been highly inconvenienced. I'd hate to trip at the finishing line. I don't know if I want to keep going up the ladder, though. I do have a business to run, and at some point, the time I devote to the show is going to stop balancing the publicity value and start having a negative impact. At this point, it seems to be out of my hands."

I took Éclair home, told her to have a nice day, and headed up the driveway to Tea by the Sea.

I did love this commute: in less than three minutes, I was unlocking the front door and stepping into the vestibule of the tearoom. I'd told Marybeth and Cheryl to come to work today at the normal time of 10:00 a.m., if they didn't hear from me otherwise. As I hadn't heard otherwise from Reilly or Josh, I hadn't called my staff with an update. Marybeth had been extremely upset yesterday. Tommy told me he'd apologized to her, and I hoped the apology had been truly sincere.

The dining room was hushed, the alcoves wrapped in shadow. I'd decided to use different china today to provide variety in the décor, so the tables had been laid with dishes I'd bought specifically to match the *by the Sea* part of our name: white china with an edge of navy blue and gold trim. Blue linen napkins were at each plate, along with sterling silver cutlery. All of which might not even be needed if Josh decided to film on the patio today. As I went into the kitchen, I debated what pattern would show up best on TV if filmed outdoors as well as provide the image I wanted to project for the tearoom. I'd decided to serve the royal tea today: a flute of sparkling prosecco at each person's place would look nice.

I was so occupied considering place settings that for the briefest of moments as I entered the kitchen, I didn't understand what I was seeing.

A man lay on the floor, facedown, arms outstretched. I recognized the dyed blond hair and thin back and shoulders as those of Tommy Greene.

Chapter 7

I waited in the kitchen for the emergency services to arrive. Like most restaurant people, I have some training in first aid, and I'd fallen to my knees next to Tommy Greene to check for signs of life. It was immediately obvious he had none. His skin was cool to the touch, and he wasn't breathing. Blood, a lot of it, matted his yellow hair. My stomach rolled over, and I pushed myself to my feet. I looked around me. All was as I'd left it last night, everything in its place, ready for another day of baking and serving tea. Everything except—

My marble rolling pin lay on the floor, half under the fridge. I instinctively took a step toward it to pick it up and put it back in its place on an upper shelf. I froze. My stomach rolled again, and I left the rolling pin where it was.

I could hear the roar of the sit-down lawn mower in the background, so I knew there'd be no point in phoning Simon and asking him to come and wait with me. He wouldn't hear the phone ringing.

Instead, I called Rose. The phone rang for a long time before a muffled, sleepy voice said, "Victoria-on—"

"Rose, it's Lily. I'm at the tearoom. There's been an . . .

accident. I'm perfectly fine, but the police have been called." As if to emphasize my point, the sound of sirens rapidly approaching grew louder. "You'd better get up and see to our guests. The police will have questions."

"Who? Why? Is someone hurt?"

"Gotta run." I hung up.

I opened the back door and stepped outside, thinking about the last time I'd spoken to Tommy Greene. He'd revealed a great deal of himself to me in that brief conversation as we watched the tide coming in, and I'd left liking the man, believing I'd come to some understanding of him. I could have been wrong, of course. Reality TV, as I'd been reminded, has nothing to do with reality.

Something niggled at the back of my mind as I waved to the first police car that swung off the highway into our driveway. I fought to get the outline of a thought into focus. An ambulance followed the cruiser. Lights flashed and sirens screamed, doors flew open, and men and women in uniform leapt out.

Doors opened.

I hadn't had to unlock the kitchen door when I ran out. The last thing I do every night before leaving is check the doors. The tearoom has two entrances. The rear one for staff and deliveries, which opens directly into the kitchen, and the front door off the patio, which opens into the vestibule, where guests check in and we display our menu and show off some place settings. Had I not checked the locks last night?

I struggled to remember, but nothing came to mind. The entire hectic day had been such a blur. I looked down. The lidded bucket containing the day's kitchen scraps, which Simon puts in the compost bin, was where I'd left it, but putting it out hadn't been my last task of the day.

"In there." I indicated the kitchen as people in uniform arrived. "He's in there."

"Are you all right, Ms. Roberts?" the young police-woman asked as her partner and the paramedics ran past me. I've had dealings with the police before, unfortunately, and most of them know my name. I know theirs.

I swallowed and nodded. "I'm fine, Officer Bland. You'll want to call the detectives, I'm afraid. I don't think it was an accident."

"They're on their way," she said. "I heard a TV show's been filming here. How's that going?"

"It's . . ." I swallowed. "Difficult."

"Must be interesting, though."

I didn't reply. She was, I realized, staying with me and chatting politely to ensure I didn't collapse into weepy hysterics, but rather to ensure I didn't bury evidence under a bush or in the compost bucket.

"You should tell your colleague not to touch the rolling pin on the floor by the fridge. It wasn't there last night."

More police vehicles were arriving. Bernie's car slowed as it made the turn, and my friend's freckled face stared out the window at me. I lifted my hand in acknowledgment, and she continued up the driveway. Rose must have called Bernie, probably the moment she and I hung up.

I realized the sound of the lawn mower had stopped, and a moment later, Simon rounded the building at a run. "Lily! What's going on?"

"Tommy Greene." I nodded toward the kitchen. "Dead."

He touched my arm lightly and stared into my eyes. The scent of fresh mowed grass clung to him like a perfume, and his attractive blue eyes overflowed with sympathy and kindness.

Detectives Williams and Redmond arrived together, and Simon stepped away from me.

"Nice of you to call us at a reasonable hour this time, Lily," Chuck Williams said.

He and I never did get on.

"Dispatch said you found a body in your restaurant kitchen when you arrived for work," Amy Redmond said. "Did you recognize him?"

"Yes, I did. His name's Tommy Greene, and he's here with the TV show. Do you know about that?"

"Talk of the town," Williams said.

"He's also a B and B guest. I have absolutely no idea what he'd be doing in my kitchen hours before opening."

"Did you kill him?" Williams asked.

Simon bristled. "What kind of a question's that, mate?"

"A pertinent one, I'd have thought," Williams said.

"No, Detective," I said. "I did not."

"You say the dead man's a guest at the B and B," Redmond said. "Is he with his family or with others from the TV group?"

"Some of the people from the show are staying here."

Redmond and Williams exchanged glances. Williams opened his mouth to say something, but Redmond got it out first. "Why don't you check the scene here, Detective, and I'll go up to the house and break the news to the man's colleagues?"

Williams pulled a face.

"Before we do that," Redmond said to me, "anything we should know?"

"My rolling pin, a big marble one, is on the floor under the fridge. It doesn't belong there. I mean, obviously, it doesn't belong there. It usually sits on a high shelf. I don't use it much."

"Anything else disturbed?" Williams asked.

"Not that I noticed, but I didn't check. I think the back door might have been left unlocked."

Redmond cocked one expressive eyebrow. "You think?" She was about my age, early thirties, slightly taller than me, with olive skin and intense, dark eyes. Trim and attractive and as coiled as a spring. Williams, by contrast, was counting down the days to retirement. Flabby jowls, bulbous red nose crisscrossed with fine lines, round belly, and thin, greasy hair plastered to his scalp in a failed attempt to pretend he wasn't going bald.

"I'm pretty sure," I said. "I don't need a key to unlock it from the inside, but I don't think I had to turn the lock. I'm not entirely sure. I was upset, I called nine-one-one, and I ran out here to get some air and to wait for you. I'm sorry. I can't be positive."

"That's fine," Redmond said. "Do you normally lock the door when you leave for the night?"

"Always. It's part of my end-of-the-day routine. I don't remember doing so yesterday, but I don't remember not doing so yesterday."

Williams snorted in disapproval, but Redmond said, "That's quite normal with things we do so routinely, they're virtually automatic."

"Like when you can't remember if you switched off the cooker, and you go home to check, and every single time, it's off," Simon said.

"Precisely." Redmond smiled at Simon. Simon smiled back, and I felt a totally unexpected, and unwarranted, stab of jealousy. When they'd met other times, I'd suspected she liked him. He was a good-looking man. He was also nice, friendly, and could cook. Amy Redmond was about the same age as us, and single. What more would a woman want?

I mentally kicked myself for thinking about such an inappropriate subject when a man lay dead a few feet from us.

Redmond turned from smiling at Simon and focused her attention on me. "Who else has keys to that door?"

"Marybeth and Cheryl, my employees. No one else. A spare's kept on the key hook in the kitchen of the B and B."

"Check the key's there, will you?" Redmond asked me

as Williams wandered into the tearoom, pulling on a pair of blue latex gloves.

"Sure," I said.

"Officer Bland, you're with me. We can walk to the main house. Simon, you can go back to work, unless you have something to tell me, but first, I do have a question. I assume you were working in the garden this morning. What time did you start?"

"I was at the door to the house kitchen at six, as usual, when Lily arrived. Had a coffee, helped Lily with getting breakfast ready, and I was in the garden shed before six thirty. I didn't see anyone around. Couple of cars went by on the highway, but nothing moving here."

"Thanks."

We headed for the driveway and the big house at the edge of the bluffs.

"My mom loves that show," Officer Bland said. "She was so excited when she heard they were coming here. She's not going to be able to decide if she's happy Tommy Greene's dead or upset about it."

"Why's that?" Redmond asked.

"He's the sort of personality people love to hate. He was, I mean."

"Is that so? I've never seen the show myself."

I said nothing, as at that moment we heard a shout as Matt Goodwill sprinted across his sand- and weed-choked property toward us. He was dressed for a day of writing, not construction, in casual pants, a short-sleeved T-shirt, and sandals. Matt was a highly successful true-crime writer. "Lily! Simon! Detective Redmond, what's happened?"

"A person died on this property last night or early this morning," the detective said. "Do you know anything about that?"

"No. Who?"

"You'll be informed in due course. In the meantime, if you gentlemen have nothing to add, thank you for your time." We'd reached the steps to the veranda.

"You know where to find me." Simon walked away. He didn't get far before he stopped to pluck dead foliage off the geraniums in the bed lining the guest parking area.

"Is that Bernie's car over there?" Matt asked ever so casually. Matt liked Bernie. Bernie was still pretending not to like Matt.

"Yes," I said.

"I'll come in with you and check if she needs anything."

"If she needs anything," Redmond said dryly, "I'm sure she knows where to find you."

Most of the guests, including the TV people, had gathered in the dining room at the B & B. No doubt the sound of sirens and the sight of police cars and ambulances screeching onto the property had curious guests rising from their beds. Edna was laying out breakfast pastries next to the boxes of cereal, cartons of yogurt, and the bowl of fruit salad, and Bernie was pouring coffee.

Rose had taken a seat at the head of the largest table. She hadn't had time to apply her full makeup this morning, and her clothes were an uncharacteristically dull combination of beige sweater and black pants. I could tell by the way she was sitting that Robbie had taken his rightful place on her lap. Edna and I regularly, and fruitlessly, warned Rose that the health department would shut us down if they knew a cat was allowed freedom of the kitchen and the dining room, but Rose firmly ignored us. Booking information about the B & B made it plain a cat was in residence. Anyone who didn't care for cats, according to Rose, was welcome to find accommodation elsewhere.

The buzz of conversation, full of questions, filled the room. It stopped the moment we stepped through the door, and everyone turned to face us.

Officer Bland was in her uniform, and Redmond was not, but anyone could tell instantly who was in charge here. The detective was an attractive young woman, but her entire demeanor screamed cop.

I glanced around the room, searching for signs of guilt. What those signs might be, I didn't know, but I looked for them, anyway. Josh and Claudia had taken seats at a table for four, coffee and muffins in front of them.

I pointed them out to Redmond and whispered, "The third person who's staying here doesn't appear to have come down yet. The rest of the crew are being put up someplace else."

"Can we use your drawing room?" she asked.

"Of course," I said.

Redmond took a step forward, but the buzz of her phone stopped her. She glanced at it and turned her back to take the call. She kept her voice low, but I heard her say, "Tell them no work today. Send whoever's in charge up here." She put her phone away. "Lily, check for that spare key, please."

"Right." I hurried out of the dining room as fast as I could without actually breaking into a run. A quick glance at the hook by the kitchen door showed me the tearoom key was in place, hanging next to the spare key for Rose's car. That didn't necessarily mean anything: if someone had taken it, they'd had time to put it back. It was unlikely anyone from outside, including our guests, would know where I kept a key to the tearoom, and if someone had searched for it, they would have left signs. Not that I'd necessarily recognize those signs, but I hadn't seen anything out of place in here this morning.

By the time I got back to the dining room, Redmond was standing at Josh and Claudia's table, Bland slightly behind her, and every eye in the place was on her.

"It's there," I said. "The key. Where it should be. Everything seems in order."

She nodded in acknowledgment and then spoke to Josh and Claudia. "Good morning. I'm Detective Amy Redmond. North Augusta PD. I understand you're here filming a TV show?"

"*America Bakes!*" Josh said. "Are you wanting a role, Detective? I'm sure we can find you a spot." The joke fell flat, and he grimaced. "Sorry. Is something wrong?"

I heard the front door open and steps cross the hallway. Reilly came into the dining room. He threw a questioning look toward Josh, and Josh shrugged in answer.

"Are the other members of your party not up yet?" Redmond asked.

"Scarlet isn't one for rising at the crack of dawn," Claudia said with a dismissive sniff. "Or even the crack of noon, unless she has to. As for Tommy, he's not usually late for breakfast. We were supposed to meet here with Reilly at seven thirty to go over plans for the day. It's after that now. What's happened?"

"Who's Reilly?"

"Our assistant director. That's him now." She waved, and Reilly hurried to join them.

"Detective?" Josh said. "You haven't told us why you're here."

Redmond indicated the room full of eavesdroppers. "Why don't you come with me? We can speak privately."

Rose put Robbie on the floor and stood up. "You may use our drawing room, Detective."

"Thank you," Redmond said.

"What's going on?" Josh repeated. "Reilly? Do you know what's happening here?"

"I haven't got a clue," Reilly said. "The whole place is crawling with cops, and we've been told not to unload the trucks."

The guests, the ones who had not been invited for a private chat, chittered with excitement. I could tell by the expression on Edna's face that Rose had given her the news. Edna's husband was the longtime editor in chief of the local newspaper. She knew how to keep a secret.

Rose gripped her cane. "Allow me to show you to the drawing room, Detective."

"I know the way, thank you."

"Nevertheless, it would be my pleasure. Edna, carry on with what you're doing."

"I have no intention of doing otherwise, Rose," Edna said.

Slowly, ever so slowly, my grandmother tapped her way across the room. Claudia and Josh exchanged worried glances and then stood up. They, plus Detective Redmond and Reilly, fell into step behind Rose. Robbie ran on ahead.

Bernie put down the coffeepot, and Rose said, "Bernadette, you may continue to assist Edna."

"But—" Bernie began.

"Thank you so much, dear." Rose sniffed the air. "Is something burning?"

Bernie got the hint and headed for the kitchen.

"I have a full crew cooling their heels down by the tearoom," Reilly said. "I need you to tell your people to get out of their way and let them get set up. Time is money, Detective."

"Is it? Then I thank you not to waste my time with foolish demands. Lily, will you find the missing guest? Scarlet, is it? Ask her to join us."

"Sure. Rose, what room's Scarlet in?"

Rose fumbled in her pocket for her keys to open the desk drawer and get out the registration ledger.

"Two-oh-two," Josh said. "I mean, I think she's in two-oh-two."

"You think, do you?" Claudia snickered.

"Call your people," Redmond said to Reilly, "and tell them no one's to leave the property until they've been spoken to."

Josh threw up his hands. "Will someone tell me what's going on?"

"In due course," Redmond said calmly.

Reilly took out his phone and sent a quick text.

"I can't fail to notice," Claudia said, "that no one is being sent to fetch Tommy."

"Tommy?" Reilly looked around. "Where is Tommy?"

"After you've got Scarlet, love," Rose said to me, "the linens need sorting. I'll sit right here to keep the curious out of the way of the police."

I got the message and ran up the stairs. I knocked on the door of room 202, and a voice said, "All right, all right. I'm coming. Give me a minute, will you!"

"It's Lily Roberts. I'm sorry, but you need to come down immediately."

A moment later the door cracked open and a pale face peered out. Scarlet's face was clean of makeup, her long hair hung limply around her shoulders, and she was still in her nightgown. "What do you want?" Not prepped for the cameras, she was, I thought, almost unrecognizable.

"The police are downstairs, and they want to talk to you."

"The police? Don't be ridiculous."

"Not being ridiculous."

She stepped away without opening the door fully. I pushed it open and stood in the entrance. She'd been given one of our best rooms, with a view over the bay and a small private balcony. All the rooms at Victoria-on-Sea, except for the kitchen, are decorated as though Queen Victoria might drop by at any moment in search of a place to spend the night. This one was very feminine in shades of peach and sage green. The decorative pillows and the thick duvet had been tossed onto the floor, the French provincial dresser was covered with pots of makeup, and the dress Scarlet had been wearing yesterday was tossed over a chair. The sheets on the king-sized bed were a total jumble, and the pillows thrown haphazardly on the floor.

"I'm not exactly dressed." She indicated her nightgown, a sleek floor-length satin sheath in an attractive lilac shade with a deeply plunging neckline trimmed with yellow lace.

"Pull that on and come down." I pointed to the dress on the chair.

"I'm not wearing the same dress I wore yesterday, and I'm not going downstairs without my makeup on and my hair done. I have an image to protect, you know."

"The police don't care what you're wearing or about your image. I'm pretty sure there won't be any filming today."

"You have no idea what you're talking about. Is Reilly making a fuss because I'm late for his little breakfast meeting? Too bad." She plopped onto the small stool in front of the dresser and studied her face. Clearly, I was dismissed.

"Scarlet," I said, refusing to be dismissed. "I'm not kidding. The police are here, and they are not known for their patience. If you don't come down with me, an officer will be the next to come and get you. He's unlikely to say please."

She swung around. "You are serious, aren't you?"

"Yes. I am."

She sighed heavily, letting me know what an imposition this was. "Very well. If I must. Lead the way."

"Aren't you going to put some clothes on?"

"Why should I? Everything's covered, isn't it?"

"I suppose it is." I've seen plenty of evening dresses substantially more revealing.

She swept her phone off the night table, stuffed it into the bodice of her nightgown, and followed me.

Downstairs, Rose had taken her seat at the registration desk and was pretending to consult the computer. The double doors to the dining room were closed, muffling the conversation coming from within. The drawing-room door was open, and I indicated to Scarlet to go ahead. She took a deep breath, lifted her head, straightened her shoulders, and marched in. I followed.

"Here I am," she said. "What nonsense is this that I can't even be allowed time to get decently dressed?"

"Are you Scarlet McIntosh?" Redmond asked.

"I am. And who, may I ask, are you, darlin'?" The Louisiana accent was very strong.

Redmond didn't answer. Instead, she said, "That's all, Lily. Thank you. Please shut the door as you leave."

I did as ordered.

I looked at my grandmother. She gave me a nod. No one else was in the hallway, so I slipped into the linen closet and pulled the door shut behind me. My ears alert for the sound of approaching footsteps or Rose's discreet cough, I pulled place mats, tablecloths, and napkins off the bottom two shelves and dumped them on the floor. I lifted the shelves off their brackets and propped them against the wall, and then my probing fingers found a lever at the back of the closet. I pulled it, and a small door swung silently open. I crouched down and waddled into the space revealed.

Rose and I hadn't built the secret room, but we'd discovered it during renovations after she'd bought the place. Other than the contractors, no one but she and I knew about it, not even Edna or Bernie. The room had obviously been built specifically to listen in on conversations in the drawing room, as the adjoining wall was much thinner than other walls in the house. Not only that, but discreet holes had been drilled through the wall, and a painting hung over them. The house had been built in 1865 as a private home. The owners before Rose had also run the house as a B & B, but the secret room predated them. I'd love to know why someone living in a family house would feel the need to creep into the walls and listen to private conversations, but it was unlikely I'd ever find out.

We had never intended to use the room to eavesdrop on our guests, but it had turned out to be surprisingly useful when the police commandeered the drawing room. We'd furnished the room with an old wingback chair, a small table, and a lamp with a dim bulb. I switched on the lamp and settled comfortably into the chair to listen. The sound came through the wall perfectly. Rose would stand—sit?—guard outside and let me know when it was safe to emerge.

"I'm sorry," Amy Redmond was saying on the other side of the wall, "but a man who I've been informed goes by the name of Tommy Greene was found dead this morning."

A moment of stunned silence followed her words before everyone began speaking at once.

Scarlet: "Tommy's dead?" She burst into tears.

Claudia: "Nonsense. Man was fit as a fiddle."

Josh: "Clearly you're mistaken. Reilly, call him again. He's slept in. Probably went out on a bender last night."

Reilly: "I have to call the studio. We need to get someone down here ASAP to take his place." A chair creaked as he stood up.

Redmond: "You, sit down." Another creak of the chair, and she continued, "Was Mr. Greene a heavy drinker, sir?"

Reilly: "No. Not at all. Josh doesn't know what he's talking about."

Josh: "Don't take that tone with me. Tommy likes his

beer. Man's an Englishman. You know how they love their pubs."

Claudia: "I can assure you, young lady, that Tommy isn't, despite what some may say, the type to go on a *bender*."

Scarlet, through her sniffles and blowing nose: "Can I go now? I have to call my agent."

Redmond: "No."

Josh: "That baker was with you when you came in. The young, pretty one."

When I realized he was referring to me, I felt rather pleased. That feeling didn't last long.

Josh: "She's useless in front of the camera. Too nervous and doesn't smile enough. I've been wondering if we can substitute the redhead for the blond one. More of a presence."

Reilly: "You can't do that. You know what the rules of the show are. The owner or head baker has to do all the baking for us by themselves."

Redmond: "That is neither here nor there."

Josh: "Yeah. Okay. Did you find her with him, the blonde? Did she kill him?"

Claudia: "You're not thinking straight, which comes as no surprise to me, Joshua. If Lily had killed him, she wouldn't be freely wandering the property, now would she?"

Scarlet: "Who said anything about killing? It was a heart attack, wasn't it, Detective?"

A long, uncomfortable silence followed Scarlet's questions. I imagined Amy Redmond studying them all, one at a time, them fidgeting in their seats, averting their eyes from her penetrating stare when it fell on them. Then Redmond said, "It's early yet, but indications are that foul play might have been involved."

Reilly swore. Josh muttered. Claudia murmured what might have been a prayer. Scarlet wept with increased gusto.

"One at a time, please, can you tell me where and when you last saw Mr. Greene?"

"We went out to dinner together last night," Josh said. "The three of us. Claudia, Scarlet, and me. Tommy didn't come. We took a taxi into town and met up with Reilly and some of the crew. We must have left here around six, or shortly after."

"Why did Mr. Greene not join you?"

"He just said he didn't want to. Tommy wasn't a man who felt he had to explain himself to anyone. We got back here, at a guess, around nine, maybe slightly after."

The women muttered agreement.

"I didn't see him again. No reason I should have," Josh said. "We were in different rooms, and we had no business to discuss until this morning."

"Same with me," Claudia said. "Josh, Scarlet, and I caught a cab back here after dinner, and then we went our separate ways. I retired early, as is my custom before an early call and a day of filming."

"And you?" Redmond asked.

"I stayed in my room and watched TV," Scarlet said. "Nothing else to do in this joint. Some of the crew were talking about going to a bar after dinner. What about you, Reilly? You were with them, as I recall."

"That's right. We hit a couple of bars in town. I was back at my hotel by midnight. Can't say what the rest of the crew got up to after that. I didn't see Tommy after the day's filming ended around four. We shot some footage in the garden after we finished in the tearoom. Turns out Tommy liked roses. Who knew?"

"I'll be speaking to this crew," Redmond said. "I have to ask if you know of any reason someone might have attacked Mr. Greene?"

Silence again.

Claudia broke it. "Tommy could be, shall we say, temperamental. He was a perfectionist, but people he worked with understood that about him. He only wanted everyone to do their best. Any enemies he might have made over the years didn't have anything to do with us or our show. You need to cast your net further afield, Detective. Tommy owns . . . owned . . . a chain of successful restaurants. The restaurant business, particularly in certain cities, can be a highly competitive one. He recently opened a new place in Las Vegas, I heard. Is that correct, Josh?"

"Yup," the director said.

"I'll keep that in mind," Redmond said.

"One thing did happen yesterday." Reilly dragged the words out slowly, almost reluctantly.

"What?"

"Like Claudia told you, Tommy could be temperamental. He demanded the best of everyone and got angry when he didn't get it. He had an incident with a waitress in the tearoom. She spilled tea on Tommy, and he overreacted."

"Oh, yeah," Scarlet said. "He, like, flew into a total rage. He told the blond baker chick to fire her."

"What did Ms. Roberts say to that?" Redmond asked.

"Nothing," Reilly said. "She didn't have a chance to say anything. The other waitress, the older one, stepped in. She was in a right fury, so much so I thought her reaction was way out of line. Tommy hadn't said anything to her. She was like a mother bird if someone threatened her nest."

"I assume you're talking about Cheryl Wainwright and Marybeth Hill," Redmond said. "They are mother and daughter."

Reilly laughed. "That explains it. She, the mother, let Tommy have it. The look on his face when this short, chubby, middle-aged, small-town waitress dared to give the great Tommy Greene what for was priceless. What did she say, Dad? That someone needed to put a stop to his bullying once and for all. And it might well be her."

"Words to that effect," Josh said.

"You were witness to this?" Redmond asked.

"Oh, yeah," Reilly said. "We all were. Even better, I have the whole thing on film."

Chapter 8

I was so startled by what Josh and Reilly had to say about Marybeth and Cheryl, implying they had reason to kill Tommy, that it took a moment for me to realize Reilly had referred to Josh as Dad. I decided to think about that later. For now, Tommy had told me he'd apologized to Marybeth and she'd accepted his apology. That may or may not be true, but until I learned otherwise, I'd assume he'd told me the truth. That's the problem with eavesdropping on conversations you're not intended to be party to. It would be difficult for me to tell Redmond what Tommy had told me without her wondering why I was mentioning it.

Redmond then asked the group if they had any idea why Tommy would have been in the tearoom kitchen after hours last night or early this morning. They all claimed to be surprised to hear he was. The judges had been told to be on set at nine this morning, following a quick breakfast meeting with the director and assistant director. They had no reason to go to the tearoom before that. Scarlet giggled and wondered if Tommy had plans to meet up with the "blond baker chick," who I assumed was me, but Claudia said Tommy didn't have a reputation as a womanizer and had never been known to want to make friends with any of the competitors.

"Doesn't mean he wasn't up for trying," Reilly said, to which Redmond didn't reply.

She asked them about Tommy's private life and if they'd seen anyone hanging around the set yesterday who shouldn't have been there, or if they knew of anyone or anything that had been bothering him lately.

"He'd been moody since we arrived in Massachusetts," Claudia said. "It's hard to tell with Tommy. He was always moody, but I thought more so than usual lately."

"Do you have any idea if something was bothering him?"

"No. Sorry. We weren't friends. I don't think he had any friends in the crew. I don't mean people didn't like him, just that he had no interest in making friends with any of us. We have a job to do, and when it's over, we go back to our own lives without so much as another word."

"I like making friends," Scarlet said.

No one replied.

I heard the door open, and Chuck Williams said, "How's it going in here, Detective?"

"These people have been very helpful. We're almost finished. For now."

"Good. Good. Have any of you ever been in the kitchen of Tea by the Sea?"

"We all have," Reilly said. "As well as most of our crew. We've been filming in there over the past two days."

"How'd you get in?"

"How'd we get in?" Josh repeated. "Through the door, of course. How else would we get in? We didn't climb in the windows."

"I mean," Williams said sharply, "who unlocked the door for you?"

"No one," Claudia said. "It's a restaurant, and that means it's open to the public. The doors aren't locked during service hours. Even when we were filming outside and the guests were all on the patio, they had to be able to go to the restroom without a staff person escorting them in and out."

"How about the kitchen? Was that door locked?"

"What are you asking us?" Reilly said. "We had the run of the place, as is part of the contract for the duration of the filming. Doors were open when we needed them to be. I don't know or care who handled that."

"What about after hours?"

A chair squeaked. "I have no idea what goes on in that place after hours," Claudia said, "nor do I care. Now, if you'll excuse me, Detectives, I've told you everything I know. This has all been most upsetting. I need to go upstairs and rest. Josh, when do you expect to need us on set?"

"Your set," Redmond said, "is closed until further notice."

"Moot point," Josh said. "I have to talk to the network, see what they want to do now that . . . uh . . . we're short a judge."

"That's one way of putting it," Scarlet said. "As we're not working today, I'd like to hit the beach. Where's the best place near here, Detective Redmond?"

"I am not a tour guide."

"Whatever."

"Before you go, please give your contact information, including phone numbers, to Officer Bland," Redmond said. "Thank you for your time."

The group left the drawing room, and the door shut behind them. I was about to text Rose and ask if the coast was clear when Williams spoke. I thought he and Redmond had left with the others.

"Get anything?" he said.

"Not much. They all claim not to have seen the dead

guy since around six last night. They went to dinner together, but he didn't go with them. So they say. Might be
true. Might not. We need to ask the other guests if anyone
saw him last night or early this morning, and we need to
talk to the rest of the crew. They're still outside?"

"Yeah. I spoke to them. No one knows anything. They
all said they saw nothing. Bunch of them went out to dinner in town last night, but Greene didn't come. They say
that was normal. He didn't usually hang around with the
crew."

"I assume," Redmond said, "because you were asking
about the locking of the doors, you didn't find any sign of
forced entry. Lily Roberts says the spare key's where it's
supposed to be, and it didn't look to have been disturbed.
I'll have it checked for prints."

"Forced entry? Doesn't look like it. Roberts said the
door might have been left unlocked overnight. Funny way
to run a business. You'd think she'd be more careful."

"Unlocked this morning," Redmond said, "doesn't
mean it wasn't locked when she left yesterday. The dead
guy might have come with someone who has a key. Or met
them there. I need to talk to Lily again."

Oops.

I sent Rose a quick text. **Cops looking for me. Send them
to the kitchen.**

Rose: [*thumbs-up emoji*]

I left the secret room and crouched in the dark, confined
space in the linen closet.

"Everything all right, Detectives?" my grandmother
said in a voice pitched to carry to the far corners of the
property.

"No need to shout, Mrs. Campbell," Williams said. "I
can hear you well enough."

"Was I shouting?" she shouted. "So sorry. Hearing aid not working properly." Nothing, I knew, was wrong with Rose's hearing.

"Where's Lily?" Redmond asked. "We'd like to speak to her next."

"She's in the kitchen. That girl never stops baking."

"I'll find her," Redmond said. "In the meantime, perhaps you can tell Detective Williams what you know about the deceased."

"Uh . . . no."

"No? What do you mean, no?" Williams asked.

"Lily might not be in the kitchen, after all. You'll both have to go in search of her. She might have finished up and gone home. Or perhaps she went up to the tearoom to see what's happening."

"Call her and tell her we want to speak to her," Williams said.

"She doesn't answer her phone during the day."

"Funny way to run a business."

"I have no idea what you're up to, Mrs. Campbell," Redmond said. "Rest assured, I will find out. In the meantime, I'll go in search of her. Detective Williams, someone needs to ask the non-TV people if they saw Tommy Greene last night or early this morning."

"Why don't I interview the rest of the guests?" Williams said, as though it was his idea. "And you can play hide-and-seek with Lily Roberts. Where did Bland get to?"

"She went into the dining room with the TV people," Rose said.

Muttering about the possibility of laying charges for wasting police time, Detectives Williams and Redmond walked away. A moment later I heard a light tapping on the door behind which I crouched. While they'd been talking, I'd replaced the shelves and the linens.

"All clear, love."

I slipped into the hallway, shut the door behind me, and trotted quickly toward the kitchen. "I'd better find Redmond before she tears the place apart looking for me."

Bernie was in the B & B kitchen, facing Redmond, when I came in. "I haven't seen . . . Oh, there she is now."

The detective turned and frowned at me. "Where have you been?"

"Busy, busy. We have a full house today, and murder or not, people need to be fed."

"Coffee, Detective?" Bernie said. "Pot's fresh."

Redmond looked as though she was about to refuse out of principle, but she gave in and said, "Yes. Thanks. That would be nice." Her gaze wandered to the platter of bran muffins on the counter.

Matt Goodwill sat at the kitchen table, looking very comfortable as he enjoyed his coffee and muffin, and Edna was putting dishes in the dishwasher. I was about to ask how breakfast service had gone, but at the last moment I remembered I was supposed to have been working in here.

"You were looking for me, Detective?" I asked innocently.

"I need to interview you. Let's go back to the drawing room."

Bernie pointed to the coffeepot and raised one eyebrow. I nodded, and she poured me a mug. Edna arranged the coffee and two muffins on a tray and handed it to me.

"Might as well enjoy breakfast while we chat," I said.

We ran into Detective Williams coming out of the dining room. He eyed the tray I was holding and followed us into the drawing room. Reluctantly, I surrendered my coffee and muffin.

"No one saw Greene at the time in question," he said to Redmond as he settled himself in Rose's favorite chair, coffee and muffin in hand. "Or so they say. A couple of the guests left early this morning, before we arrived, to go fishing, so we'll need to get to them when they return."

"Are the TV people making noises about leaving?" Redmond sipped her own coffee.

"They say they have to wait for instructions from the network. Whoever they are."

"The people who hold the purse strings," I said.

"They can't be considering continuing with the show," Redmond said.

Williams shrugged.

"Did you learn anything from the crew?" I asked. "About Tommy Greene, I mean."

"No one confessed, if that's what you're asking," Redmond replied. "Tell us about yesterday's incident between Mr. Greene and Marybeth and Cheryl."

"I'm not sure what you mean." I pretended to think. "Oh, did you hear about that?"

"Why don't you tell us," Williams said.

"Nothing much to tell. Marybeth had a minor accident and spilled hot tea on Tommy. He got mad and yelled at her, and she was upset. That was it. He wasn't hurt. Accidents happen in a busy restaurant. All part of the job."

"Her mother intervened," Redmond said.

"Cheryl? I suppose you could say that. She yelled at him and called him a bully. And then it was over. Everyone went their separate ways." I smiled at the two detectives.

"I hear she threatened him," Williams said.

"I wouldn't say threatened exactly."

"What would you say exactly?" Redmond asked.

"I forget her exact words, but it was the sort of thing we all say when someone annoys us. Means nothing."

"Means nothing," Williams said. "Unless the man shows up dead less than twenty-four hours later."

"Tommy apologized to Marybeth. She accepted his apology. It blew over."

"How do you know that?" Redmond asked.

"He told me."

"He told you?"

"Yes."

"Perhaps, Lily, you need to tell us when you had this conversation with Mr. Greene," she said.

As I related the talk we'd had when walking through the garden and then standing at the edge of the bluffs, I realized I might have been the last person to see Tommy Greene alive. The last person, that is, other than the one who killed him. "I told him not to go down to the beach, with it being dark and the tide coming in. And then I left him. I didn't see where he went."

"What time was this?"

"Around eleven maybe. I took the dog for a walk before turning in, and we came across Tommy in the garden."

"Did you see Mr. Greene again that night or early this morning?"

"No."

"Aside from the incident with Marybeth, did you see any other signs of dissent or disagreement between Greene and the rest of the cast and crew? Or anyone else?"

"I got the impression none of them got on all that well with anyone else. They seemed to snipe at each other a lot, but I wouldn't read too much into that. I don't have any experience of working on TV, but it's a high-pressure situation, made worse by competing egos."

"Thank you for your time," Redmond said. "Oh, one more thing. We will not be needing the assistance of you or anyone else in this matter. Do you understand?"

"I'm always happy to help," I said.

"We expect you to help when and if you're asked questions. Not otherwise."

"Okay." That was fine with me. I'd never wanted to be involved in those other cases.

"Before you go, give me Cheryl Wainwright's address," Williams said.

"I don't know it off hand. It should be in my employee files."

"Where are they kept?"

"In my house. I forgot to call Cheryl and Marybeth to tell them not to come in today." I checked my watch. Quarter to ten. "They should be here soon."

"I want to talk to her, Cheryl," Williams said. "We might be able to wrap this one up quicker than we first expected."

I didn't care for the sound of that. I threw Amy Redmond a panicked look, which she pretended not to notice. Redmond and Williams didn't get along at all. She was young, ambitious, newly arrived in North Augusta from working on the force in Boston. He was middle aged and lazy. He had never lived or worked anywhere other than North Augusta, and he wanted to cruise into his retirement as easily as possible. I knew from past experience that he'd latch on to the first subject he tripped over, and from then on, he'd be reluctant to consider any other possibilities. Redmond would keep an open mind, and she'd keep investigating, but Williams's intransigence served only to complicate things and slow everything down.

In this case I should have nothing to worry about. Cheryl was hardly the sort of woman who'd stalk a man and kill him because of a mild insult to her daughter, and besides, the man had apologized, and Marybeth had accepted his apology.

The death of Tommy Greene, I told myself with confidence, had nothing to do with us.

Chapter 9

I wasn't invited to tag along with the detectives to hear what Cheryl and Marybeth had to say, but I went, anyway, and they didn't chase me away.

As we walked up the driveway, I checked my phone. I'd turned the ringer off when I was hiding in the secret room. As expected, Cheryl had texted to ask me what was going on and what did I want them to do.

I didn't answer, as I could see them sitting on the tearoom patio, watching the police activity. Marybeth was scrolling through her phone, and Cheryl had pulled her ever-present mystery paperback out of her tote bag. Cheryl saw us come through the gate and nudged her daughter.

The TV trucks and trailers lined the driveway, and men and women milled about, chatting quietly. If they'd started to unload their equipment, the police had told them to put it back. I looked for signs of weeping, but all I could see was shock on many faces, worry on others. Josh stood apart, just watching, but Reilly stood in the center of a cluster of people, talking in a low voice. Claudia and Scarlet were nowhere to be seen. Two uniformed police officers were interviewing the crew, jotting notes in their note-books. Melanie Ferguson, the makeup artist, stood on the steps of her trailer. She gave me a half-hearted wave as I passed, and I grimaced in return. She pointed to the detectives, mouthed, "Cops?" I nodded.

Marybeth and Cheryl were alone on the patio, sitting at a table for two. Cheryl stood up when we approached. She eyed Detective Williams warily but spoke to me. "What's going on, Lily? We got here a few minutes ago and found all . . . this." She waved her hand to encompass the detectives, the TV crew idly milling about, the officers interviewing them, and another officer guarding the entrance to the tearoom. "No one will tell us anything."

"This place is closed for a police investigation," Williams said.

"I can see that, Chuck," Cheryl snapped. "I was asking Lily."

"I hear," Williams said, "that you had an argument with a man by the name of Tommy Greene yesterday."

Marybeth sucked in a breath. "Oh my gosh, don't tell us something happened to him." She looked at me through wide eyes, and I gave her a slight nod. She bowed her head.

"Answer the question, Mrs. Wainwright," Williams said.

"If you're calling me Mrs. Wainwright, Chuck," Cheryl said, "I assume that's an official question, and I'll answer by telling you he and I had a minor altercation yesterday afternoon. The man was rude, and I don't have to put up with that. I told him so." She crossed her arms over her chest and glared at the detective.

"What did you do after this minor altercation?" Redmond asked.

"I went about the end of the day's routine, and then I went home."

"Did you see Mr. Greene again after this minor altercation?"

"Nope. Lily, seeing as to how we're not going to get any work done today, I'll be off. Let's go, Marybeth."

"You're not interested in why we're asking these questions?" Redmond asked.

"All I'm interested in is when I can come back to work. The man was a jerk, and I don't particularly care what's happened to him."

I don't know Cheryl or Marybeth on a personal level. I know the basics of their private lives, mainly from what I overhear as they chat to each other as they go about their tasks. Cheryl isn't what I'd call warm and friendly, not to me or the customers, but she's reliable, hardworking, efficient and, I thought, honest. Her dismissive, uncaring attitude toward Tommy Greene and whatever had happened to him seemed to be out of character. The man had gotten under her skin. She might pretend to be unconcerned, but the tightness to her lips and the pulse in the side of her neck told me otherwise.

Marybeth, on the other hand, had pulled a tissue out of her pocket and dabbed her eyes. "You're not saying, but it's easy to guess why you're here and asking these questions. He . . . died?"

"Yes," Redmond said.

"I'm sorry to hear that."

"Are you?"

"Of course I am. I'm sorry if anyone dies, but particularly someone who'd been nice to me recently."

"Nice to you!" Cheryl said. "The man was a total and complete jerk. He was so rude to you, you had to leave work early."

"He said he was sorry."

"Rubbish," Cheryl said. "He said nothing of the sort."

"He told me he'd apologized," I said.

Cheryl still looked doubtful. "When did this supposed apology supposedly happen?"

"I told you, Mom."

"You told me nothing of the sort."

"Didn't I? When I went inside to wash my face and get my purse before going home, he came up to me. He apologized, said he was way out of line, and asked my forgiveness. I gave it to him, and he invited me and my husband to come to his restaurant in New York City one day."

Cheryl threw up her hands. "You can be so naive, honey. That was no apology. You can't afford a trip to New York City, never mind eating at his fancy restaurant."

"But he was going to pay for the entire meal, a night in a hotel nearby, even give us train fare to get there. Plus, a thousand bucks to cover my expenses."

Cheryl snorted. Redmond and Williams watched the exchange with interest.

"He did, Mom," Marybeth said. "He sent me an e-transfer right there and then for the thousand dollars. I don't care about that. He apologized, and he was sincere, and I liked him for it. I told Bernie in the car. I guess I forgot to tell you."

"If you received an electronic transfer, you'll have a record on your phone," Redmond said.

"I do," Marybeth said.

Cheryl looked abashed for a brief moment, and then she lifted her chin. "Well, I didn't like him, and I still don't. Nothing but a bribe to keep her from taking her story to the gossip rags or putting it out on Twitter." She scooped up her book and stuffed it into her bag. "I'm going home. Lily, you'll call me to let us know when you want us back." She took Marybeth's arm. "Let's go, honey."

"Don't be in such a rush, Mrs. Wainwright," Williams said. "What did you do yesterday evening, after leaving here?"

"What did I do? I don't have to tell you, Chuck, but I will. I went straight to my house."

"Was Jim at home?"

"No, he was not. He's helping a friend in Nantucket run his charters while one of the regular crew's off sick, so he's been away for a couple of days. Whatever I was doing, I wasn't sneaking around here under cover of darkness and bashing Mr. Fancy Chef over the head."

"What makes you think he was bashed over the head?" Redmond asked.

"Nothing. It's an expression."

"Do you have a key to this place?" Williams asked her.

"Yes, I do. Marybeth and I often arrive before Lily finishes at the B and B, and we have to let ourselves in to get started on the day. If we're done here . . ." She started to walk away.

Williams cleared his throat. "Not so fast. Cheryl Wainwright, I am—"

"We'll be in touch, Mrs. Wainwright," Redmond said quickly. "I'd advise you not to leave North Augusta, but if you plan to do so, please notify our office."

"It's summertime in Cape Cod. I have a job to do. When you folks let us get back at it, that is." Cheryl marched away, back straight, head held high.

Marybeth threw me a look. I shrugged and nodded, and she scurried after her mother.

When they'd gone, Williams turned on Amy Redmond. "What are you playing at, Detective? I was about to arrest her, and you knew it."

"Yes, I knew it. That would have been premature."

"And what makes you think that? She practically confessed. The man was bashed over the head."

"She's right in that it's a common expression. She was angry at him at the time of the incident, but several hours, at least, passed before Mr. Greene was attacked. She had plenty of cooling-off time."

"Cheryl Wainwright, or Cheryl Dowd, as she once was, doesn't take advantage of cooling-off time."

"What does that mean?" I asked. "Do you two know each other? Apart from the times you've been here, I mean."

"I've known Cheryl since we were in high school. She's the same age as my sister. She was a wild one. Cheryl, I mean, although my sister was, too, as I recall."

"I know you like to believe you're far younger than you are," Redmond said, "but that has to have been more than a few years ago."

"More than a few, yes. But that doesn't matter. Some women never change. Thank you for your time, Ms. Roberts. If I need anything more from you, I'll let you know."

"When can I have my kitchen back?" I asked, although I feared I knew the answer. *When I say you can.*

"When I say you can," he replied.

I glanced at Amy Redmond. She raised one expressive eyebrow, telling me to run along now.

"I'll run along now," I said.

"You do that," Williams said.

I turned and walked away. I moved about as slowly as was humanly possible without dropping into a crawl. I stopped next to a terra-cotta pot overflowing with sweet potato vines and purple and red petunias and plucked dying leaves and dead flowers off the plants with great care.

"Mark my words, Detective," Williams said. "Cheryl

did it. Still so sure of herself, still that cocky attitude that says, 'You can't catch me.' "

"If you have proof, *Detective*," Redmond replied, "we'll charge her. But I'm not railroading a woman based on her high school reputation."

"More than high school, I'm sorry to say," he said, sounding not at all sorry. "Far more than that. Time was—"

They went into my tearoom, and I heard no more.

Chapter 10

I returned to Victoria-on-Sea, intending to talk to Bernie and Rose. I didn't have any trouble finding them, as they'd taken seats on the veranda to watch the activity in the driveway and on the restaurant patio. I was pleased to see that none of our guests had joined them and the guest parking area was empty except for Bernie's car.

"Another fine mess," Rose said.

"Has everyone gone out?"

"The guests got bored waiting for a takedown or a raging gun battle," Bernie said. "I'm getting bored myself. Police work isn't as exciting as it seems on TV."

I dropped into a chair. "I saw Josh down at the tearoom with the crew. What about Scarlet and Claudia?"

"I didn't see them leave," Rose said. "So they must be in their rooms, although they might have gone out the back for a walk on the beach or along the bluffs to enjoy the lovely day."

"It's difficult, in writing crime fiction," Bernie said, "to make detecting seem exciting when it's mostly asking a lot of useless questions while hoping to uncover that one important nugget. Speaking of which, if you're okay here, I'll be off home. While watching nothing happening over there, I came up with an idea for a new character. A bumbling, misogynistic, bigoted cop."

"Not based on anyone you know, I hope," I said.

"Certainly not."

"What happened to Matt? Did he go home?"

"He had to. He has a Zoom interview scheduled with a research subject he couldn't put off." She stood up.

"Sit down," I said.

Bernie sat.

Rose stroked Robbie's ears.

"We have a problem," I said.

"Other than one of TV's hottest reality stars being murdered on the premises and the ladies and gentlemen of the press gathering and nervous guests wondering if it's safe to stay here?" Bernie said.

"At least he wasn't poisoned, not like the last one," Rose said. "So the police shouldn't need to confiscate your food and nail a public health warning notice emblazed with a skull and crossbones to the door."

"There is that," Bernie agreed. "What is it, Lily? I was thinking we had no reason to be involved in this. Either someone followed that guy, Greene, here and they got into an argument, or one of the cast or crew did it."

"Williams wants to arrest Cheryl."

Bernie laughed. Rose didn't.

"Oh," Bernie said. "You're not joking."

"I am not. You drove Marybeth home yesterday afternoon. Did she say anything to you about Tommy Greene?"

"Yeah. She told me he'd apologized to her and offered to make it up with dinner at his restaurant in New York for her and her husband. So she'd know he was serious, he gave her some money to help with the expense. She was pleased, not about the dinner or the money he'd given her, but that he'd gone to the trouble to seek her out and genuinely apologize. It was a real apology, too, not something lame like, 'I'm sorry if you were offended.' "

"What happened that he had to apologize for?" Rose asked.

I filled her in quickly.

"Not nice," she said. "But such behavior's common enough, unfortunately. Some people still think they can act like the lord of the manor dealing with the peasantry. I can tell you some stories. Not about Thornecroft, mind, as Lord and Lady Frockmorton were nothing but kind to all the staff, but some of their relatives—"

"Perhaps a tale for another day," I said.

"If Marybeth was fine with the apology," Bernie said, "what does that have to do with Cheryl?"

"Marybeth didn't tell Cheryl that Tommy had apologized, and Chuck Williams seems to think the threat Cheryl made against him means she came back later and killed him."

"Stuff and nonsense," Rose said. "Detective Williams reads too many mystery novels."

"It's got to be more than that," Bernie said.

"I fear it is. It would appear they knew each other in their youth. Not a stretch, as North Augusta's a small town in terms of permanent population, and it would have been even smaller decades ago. Cheryl, according to Williams, had a reputation as a troublemaker in high school. He started to imply that that reputation continued after school, but I didn't hear the rest. He wanted to arrest her on the spot, but Redmond intervened and said not without proof."

"Oh, dear," Rose said.

"Do you think that's possible, Lily?" Bernie asked. "That she did it, I mean?"

"Absolutely not. Cheryl was furious at Tommy for the way he behaved toward Marybeth. I was furious enough myself that I tried to tell them their film shoot was over and done with. I soon calmed down, and I can't see Cheryl sneaking back here after hours to get her revenge. I mean, really, why would she? She'd have to be insane to carry a grudge to that extent. I have to admit I don't know Cheryl on a personal level, but I hope I know her well enough after working with her almost every day for the past several months to know she's not nuts."

"If Williams has her at the top of his suspect list . . . ," Rose said.

"There she will remain," I said. "No matter what evidence to the contrary comes to light."

Bernie got to her feet. She leaned over and lifted Robbie off Rose's lap. "Once again, my book is going to have to wait. Let's see what we can find out about the people involved."

"This time," I said, "I have to agree with you. If Cheryl isn't the woman I think she is, and she killed Tommy Greene, we'll let justice take its course. But if she is innocent, we might be able to help her. Do you think I should ask her what she got up to in the past that makes Williams distrust her?"

"Not yet," Rose said. "Let's see what we can find out first. Bernadette, you take the TV people. See if anyone has a past they might want to keep hidden. I'll tackle the North Augusta grapevine. It might be possible this wasn't our Mr. Greene's first visit to North Augusta and someone didn't like having him back."

"What do you want me to do?" I asked.

Rose pointed up the driveway. "It looks as though the police are leaving, love. You go and bake. It's what you do best. We will reconvene here at"—she checked her watch—"three o'clock. I'm thinking a meeting over a late lunch. A late lunch at a nice place in town."

*   *   *

The police indeed were leaving. They rolled up their crime-scene tape and packed up their equipment and told me I could have my restaurant back. Josh, they said, could do whatever he wanted.

I listened in as the director assembled his crew and told them that until he got word from the powers that be, they'd have to sit tight. No more filming would happen at Tea by the Sea, and tomorrow's scheduled move to North Augusta Bakery was on hold.

"Surely the network isn't going to continue with this?" I said once everyone except Josh and Reilly had dispersed. "Not after the man's death."

"Money is money," Reilly said. "A lot of money's been invested in this season. It's not cheap, you know, bringing an entire crew to the Outback."

"This is Cape Cod. Hardly the Outback."

"Not a studio in Hollywood, either. We can use the footage we got here, so you might still get your shot at fame."

"I don't want a shot at fame. Airing that would be in extremely bad taste."

"Good thing you're not making the decisions, then, isn't it?"

"But—"

"No buts. I'll check your contract again, but I don't recall that there's a clause giving you a chance to back out because your notions of good taste are offended."

I sputtered. I looked at Josh, hoping for some support, but he merely shrugged.

"The show must go on and all that," he said.

"Can you manage without Tommy?" I asked.

"We'll have to, won't we?" Josh said. "For now. But we'll have to find a replacement for him, and fast. Tommy was the star of the show. Not many people tuned in to watch an empty-headed beauty queen and an out-of-date cookbook writer make polite conversation. The audience liked Tommy's aggression and that rude fighting spirit."

"No one's irreplaceable," Reilly said. "Plenty of up-and-coming young chefs would kill for a chance at getting themselves on TV. Okay, bad choice of words, but you get the point. Some people at the network were thinking it might be time for a change, anyway."

I started to walk away, and then I remembered something and swung back. "When you were talking to the police earlier, Reilly, you called Josh Dad. Is he your father?"

They didn't look at all alike, so I assumed Reilly took after his mother, but there was something about the way they tilted their heads when they thought, and the shape of the chin was much the same.

With a flash of horror, I realized what I'd said, but it was too late to take the words back. I hadn't been in the room when Josh and Reilly were interviewed by the police, but hiding and eavesdropping. Fortunately, neither of them seemed to have noticed my slip.

"Yup," Reilly said. "We have different surnames because my parents never married. They didn't even stay together for long. Josh and I reconnected after I finished school."

Josh said something impolite about his ex-girlfriend, and Reilly slapped him on the back with a guffaw.

Chapter 11

It's hard enough running a restaurant without a TV shoot on your property, never mind an ongoing police investigation. I hesitantly opened the reservations page to start accepting bookings for tomorrow and the remainder of the week, and then I plunged into my sugar, flour, butter, and mixing bowls. Bernie once said baking was my happy place, and it usually is, but today I couldn't settle as easily into that happy place as I might have liked. As I worked, I couldn't stop thinking of Tommy Greene and of Cheryl Wainwright.

By quarter to three I had a satisfyingly hefty number of scones in the freezer and pastry dough and sandwich fillings in the fridge, enough to give us a start on the next day. I shook out my hair and retied it, threw my apron into the laundry bin, and left by the back entrance, taking care to ensure the door was locked behind me. I'd struggled to recall if I'd locked it on leaving yesterday or not, but my mind remained blank. The detail was important: If the door had been locked and no signs of forced entry were to be found, then someone had let Tommy Greene in, and that someone had almost certainly killed him. If the door had been unlocked, anyone, absolutely anyone, could have come in.

Such a minor detail—a matter of absentminded forget-fulness about a routine task—yet so critically important.

All the TV equipment was packed up and gone; the parking lot of Tea by the Sea empty. At the B & B, a single car—a shiny white Lexus SUV—sat out front, next to Bernie's aging, battered Honda Civic.

Rose and Bernie waited for me on the veranda. Robbie was nowhere to be seen, Rose clutched her cavernous purse to her chest, while Bernie impatiently tossed her keys from one hand to the other.

"What took you so long?" Rose asked. "We were about to leave without you."

I glanced at my watch. "It's two minutes after three."

"Meaning you're two minutes late. Punctuality is a virtue. Besides, our destination closes at four." She picked up her pink cane and descended the steps.

Bernie hurried to open her car's front passenger door for Rose. I shrugged and hopped into the back.

Thick as thieves, those two.

I might look like my grandmother, but I'm nothing at all like her in personality. Bernie and Rose, however, are as alike as two eggs in a mixing bowl. Each is as stubborn, single-minded, and adventurous as the other. Rose had lived in Iowa after she married my grandfather and came to America. She might have lived in Iowa, where she loved her husband, helped him run his construction business, and raised their five children, but as a true Englishwoman, she'd missed the sea, and she tried to vacation on the East Coast whenever possible. To the family's horror, following my grandfather's death, she moved to the Cape and sank the proceeds of her house and all her savings into a Victo-rian monstrosity. Once she had possession of her dream home, she realized she couldn't afford the taxes or the upkeep on such a huge house, and so she turned it into a B & B to provide her with some extra income. Rose hated running a B & B, but for reasons I never entirely understood, she wanted this house so much she put up with having strangers constantly tramping through it.

The moment she was old enough, my own mother had fled both her mother and Grand Lake, Iowa, for the freedom and adventure of New York City. Until coming to the Cape this past winter, I'd lived in Manhattan my entire life. Bernie and I have been best friends since grade school, and Bernie got to know Rose when she visited us. Bernie and I are also total opposites. I consider her impulsive and foolhardy; she calls me overly cautious and timid. Maybe I care for her so much precisely because she reminds me of my beloved grandmother.

"What's happening with the TV people?" I asked as I fastened my seat belt. "The ones staying here, I mean. Whose car's that?"

"Reilly," Rose said. "He's inside meeting with Josh. Scarlet and Claudia have gone out. Scarlet asked me for recommendations for a spa, and Claudia has gone shopping. I called them cabs. Plural. They took separate ones, although they left around the same time, both of them going into town. They couldn't be bothered to coordinate their activities enough to share a lift."

"I didn't get the feeling they were one happy family," I said.

"Quite," Rose replied. "Reilly and Josh were pacing up and down at the top of the bluffs earlier, waving their arms, yelling, quite obviously arguing about something. Regretfully, I couldn't get close enough to hear."

"That surprises me," I said. "I would have expected you to casually wander by, enjoying a breath of fresh sea air and accidentally eavesdropping."

"I tried," my grandmother admitted. "As soon as I got within hearing range, Josh stalked off, and after throwing him a filthy look, Reilly politely asked me how to access the beach."

"You think it means anything?" Bernie asked. "That they were arguing?"

"Probably not," I said. "Reilly told me a lot of money's been spent on this season of the show already. Tensions have to be running high if they don't know if they're going to continue with it. I'd assume not continuing with it means job losses all around."

No one had told me where we were going, but I didn't have to be a detective to figure that out. "You think the people at North Augusta Bakery might have had something to do with this?" I asked. "Did you learn anything of interest this afternoon?"

"I have some feelers out," Bernie said. "These things take time."

"Early days yet," Rose said. "I signed up at the last minute for the duplicate bridge tournament beginning tomorrow. I loathe duplicate tournaments, but needs must." She emitted a martyred sigh.

"Allegra Griffin, owner of the bakery, was at Tea by the Sea both Monday and yesterday," Bernie pointed out. "She was witness to the altercation between Marybeth and Tommy Greene."

"There was no altercation," I said. "Tommy yelled at her, and she ran away. Which is not really the point. Lots of people were witnesses to that."

Bernie pulled onto the stretch of road that winds its way along the coast toward North Augusta, North Truro, and Provincetown. To our left, long sandy laneways led to large houses overlooking the waters of Cape Cod Bay, sparkling in the distance.

"And they are all," Bernie said, "present company excepted, to be considered suspects until they can be eliminated."

"Surely the TV people are far better suspects than anyone from North Augusta."

"Unfortunately," Rose said, "I have no contacts in the world of television, and neither does Bernie, so once again, needs must. If we can eliminate some of the suspects, then the police can concentrate their attentions on the most viable."

"Not that the police care one whit who we eliminate or not," I said.

"Not having contacts in those circles is bad enough," Bernie said, "but they're all based on the West Coast, and few of my financial connections reach that far." She lifted her hands off the steering wheel and flexed her long fingers. I did not want to know what Bernie meant by financial connections. She'd been a forensic accountant at a major Manhattan criminal law firm. She knows how to sort through mazes of shell companies; she can parse a set of books as high as a mountain down to one important line and uncover that single monetary indiscretion that will send a man to jail for the rest of his life. Or not. A few minutes on the computer, and Bernie can come away with information about people that I suspect wasn't obtained within the strict bounds of legality.

"Therefore," Rose said, "we have to focus our efforts on where we can learn things."

"What about the restaurant business?" I asked.

"What about it?" Bernie said as she steered the car off the coast road and headed toward the business district of the small town of North Augusta.

"Tommy was a chef. Remember?"

"And?"

"And? I know people who work in New York City restaurants."

Rose twisted in her seat and gave me a big smile. "So you do. Bernadette and I forgot about that. Bernie, perhaps Lily can be of help to us for once."

I rolled my eyes, but my grandmother had already turned away.

North Augusta's a busy place in summer, and today was no exception. The sidewalks were crowded with shoppers, and every parking space on the main street and in the parking lot next to the pier was taken. People went into the charming tourist and artisan shops and came out with big smiles and bulging bags. Lines were long outside the ice cream and coffee shops lining the boardwalk, and patrons waited for tables on the shaded restaurant patios. Brightly colored flowers and variegated foliage spilled out of baskets hanging from lampposts, and dappled sunlight broke through gaps in the tree canopy to fall on slow-moving vehicles.

Somehow a parking space always appears when Bernie needs one, and as we approached North Augusta Bakery, a BMW convertible with the top down and New York license plates slipped into the traffic in front of us and Bernie maneuvered into its spot.

I'd not paid a great deal of attention to the bakery before, so today I stood on the sidewalk, checking it out. I'd never been inside, and although Bernie had encouraged me to investigate the competition prior to the arrival of the TV show, I hadn't. I knew we were completely different establishments, and I also knew that if I saw something they did better than me, I'd be tempted to change my entire menu. Better not to know.

As Edna had reported, the flower boxes in the windows

and the urns on either side of the door overflowed with fresh blooms. The glass in the windows sparkled in the sunlight, and the bright red paint on the window frames and the door looked fresh.

Nothing wrong, nothing at all, with sprucing up your place for the cameras. I'd done the same myself.

Bernie held the door for Rose and me, and we went inside. It was quarter after three and the bakery closed at four, so the open shelves lining the back wall were mostly empty, but my nose twitched at the scent of freshly made bread rising from the unclaimed loaves. They looked fabulous, varying between plump, round, crusty sourdough; long, thin, pale baguettes; light white bread dusted with seeds; and hearty whole wheat. A chalkboard behind the counter displayed the day's meal offerings of soup, sandwiches, salads, and desserts. Of the three soup offerings, two were crossed out. Groups of people occupied about half of the picnic table–style benches. Paintings covered the walls, all of them with little stickers indicating they were for sale. Most of the paintings showed typical Cape Cod tourist scenes, and the quality was, I thought, good.

Rose led the way to a table for four tucked into a quiet corner. She eyed the bench suspiciously. "Not a suitable seating arrangement for a lady in her later years," she mumbled as she laid her cane on the table and tried to maneuver herself onto a seat. The voluminous skirts of her purple and orange dress fluttered in the wind coming from the air-conditioning vents overhead.

"What would you like?" Bernie asked her.

"Just a cup of tea, love. I had lunch earlier."

"I'll get you a tart to go with it," I said. "The lemon ones look nice."

Bernie and I took our place in front of the clerk and studied the chalkboard. The glass display case beneath the counter held a picked-over selection of donuts, tarts, and slices of cake, all that was left at the end of a busy day.

"Help you?" said the clerk, the right age to be a high school student with a summer job.

"I'll have a roast beef on rye and a slice of red velvet cake," Bernie said.

"I'll try the sweet potato soup with half a ham sandwich," I said. "And a lemon tart and tea, please."

"What type of tea?"

"What do you have?"

"Chamomile, lemon, green, black. Iced too."

"Black tea. Hot. With milk."

"We'll bring your order over." She handed me a tent-shaped card with the number twenty written on it.

"Nice enough place," I said as I climbed over the bench seat.

Rose sniffed. "A veneer of recent and hasty improvements."

"The food has to be good if it was chosen for the show," I said.

"Not necessarily," Bernie said. "They want conflict, remember? Conflict and contrast. No one criticized your cooking, not to your face, anyway, so they might have been saving all the nastiness for the next place. You were probably lucky you were chosen to go first in this round."

A boy dropped a mug onto the table.

Rose recoiled. "What may I ask is this?"

He blinked. "Tea. Didn't you order tea?"

"This is tea the way a single tomato is pasta sauce." She picked the tea bag up between her thumb and index finger, as though displaying a particularly dangerous sort of insect. "Tea needs to be—"

"Thank you," I said. "It's fine."

He threw Rose a look, gave his head a shake, and walked away.

Bernie chuckled.

"How long," I asked, "have you lived in America, Rose?"

"I believe you know the answer to that, love."

"Long enough to know that Americans are not always familiar with the fine art of preparing tea." I indicated the stout white mug containing lukewarm water and the tea bag on a saucer, next to a single-serve plastic container of cream.

"Well, they should be," Rose said, not for the first time. And, despite any intervention from me, unlikely to be the last.

The boy brought the rest of our order. He eyed Rose warily as he put the plates on the table, and then he slipped away.

"Sort of like this lovely slice of cake." I pointed to the red layers separated with a thick layer of vanilla butter-cream, and more buttercream spread on the top and sides. "Not a speck of jam to be seen. I loathe jam on cake, and I can't understand why the English use it so much. Next time I'm in England, I'll tell everyone I meet that. I'm sure they'll appreciate hearing from me."

Bernie wiggled her eyebrows, and Rose pretended not to have heard me.

I leaned over the bowl of bright orange soup and breathed deeply. It was thick and creamy and smelled wonderful, fragrant with roasted vegetables and strong spices. The pieces of bread holding the sandwiches together were thickly sliced, obviously made in-house, and packed with filling.

"There's a time for a doorstop of a sandwich like this one," Bernie said, "and a time for a delicate little one, such as Lily serves."

I lifted my sandwich to my mouth, but it didn't make it all the way.

"Look what the cat dragged in." The owner and head

baker emerged from the kitchen. She did not look happy to see us.

"Good afternoon, Allegra," I said politely.

She stood by our table, hands on her adequate hips, glaring down at us. She wore an askew hairnet and a gray apron with greasy fingerprints on the sides and a smear of chocolate across the bib.

"You should ask Lily to show you how to make a proper cup of tea, dear," Rose said, not at all helpfully.

Allegra ignored her and spoke directly to me. "What are you doing here?"

"Having lunch," I said.

"Why?"

"Because I've been told you make a nice lunch."

"See?" Bernie held up her sandwich as proof.

"I'd like you to leave." Allegra called to the young woman behind the counter, her voice booming off the walls. "Lola, refund these women their money."

People at adjoining tables froze mid-bite or mid-sip and stared. Bernie put down her sandwich. Rose had pushed her mug to one side and was nibbling on her lemon tart.

I spread my hands. "We'll leave if you want us to, but I don't know what we've done."

"Done! What you've done!" Allegra's voice began to rise. Patrons exchanged worried glances. The boy who'd served our food came out of the kitchen. "You ruined my big chance. I was going to beat your foolish little whim of a so-called bakery, and I was going to go on to win the whole competition. And you"—a short, blunt finger stabbed the air in front of my face—"you ruined it."

Bernie slowly got to her feet.

"I didn't do anything," I said, trying to keep my voice low and under control. "A man died at my place, yes, and that's terrible, but it wasn't my doing."

"With the *All-America Bakes!* trophy in the front window, I'll finally . . . finally . . . be able to sell this place my mother saddled me with and get out of this dump of a town. You had to put an end to that, didn't you? Well, this isn't over, mark my words."

"Lily has no words to mark," Bernie said. "The shoot hasn't been canceled, far as we know. The higher-ups still have to decide."

"Without Tommy Greene, who knew good, solid, practical American baking when he saw it, not a fancy lady's whim."

The four people at the table by the window threw a few bills down, hastily gathered up their belongings, and scurried away, glancing nervously over their shoulders as they went.

"It's okay, Auntie A." The waiter put his hand hesitantly on Allegra's shoulder. "These ladies are leaving." His eyes pleaded with me, and he jerked his head toward the door.

"We'll leave, but I'm sorry you feel that way," I said. "I wanted to take the opportunity to see your place and try your food. That's all. It is very good. What I had of it, anyway."

"Don't try to make nice to me," Allegra said.

"Okay." Bernie took one step toward Allegra. She towered a good eight inches over the other woman. When we were kids, I called Bernie the Warrior Princess—come to think of it, I still do—with her lean, near six-foot frame, flaming red curls, and flashing green eyes. "We won't make nice. Instead, I'll ask you straight out why you're accusing Lily of having had anything to do with the death of Tommy Greene, when she didn't have the slightest reason to do so. You, however, are severely overreacting, so overreacting I have to wonder if you're trying to deflect responsibility."

"That's not fair," the server said.

"Keep out of this, Larry." Allegra shook off the boy's hand and stood her ground, her pointed chin tilted, staring up at Bernie. "I'm not saying she wanted Tommy Greene to die, but it worked out well for her. Now she won't have the humiliation of losing to the likes of me."

"As has been said, the show's not canceled yet," I said. "This is a useless conversation. Rose, let's go."

"But I haven't finished my tea, love. You can't rush a nice cuppa." Rose smiled at me.

"You English people stick together, don't you?" Allegra said. "You think I didn't hear the old lady and Tommy chatting about the good old days back in the old country?"

"I've never called England the old country in my life." Rose's accent thickened and broadened so much, I could almost see the steep, narrow streets and verdant green hills of Yorkshire spreading out behind her. "I'd be more than happy to stop by one day and teach your staff how to make a proper cup of tea. We *old ladies* are still good for something, you know."

Angry red splotches stood out on Allegra's pale face, a vein pulsed in her neck, and her eyes were narrow with rage. Her nephew shifted nervously next to her. Another group of diners had departed posthaste.

I took Rose's arm and pulled her to her feet. Bernie grabbed the mug to keep it from falling to the floor. No doubt if it had, we would have been presented with a bill for the broken china. "We're leaving." I handed Rose her cane.

"You might not have killed the man yourself," Allegra spat at me, "but that Cheryl Dowd did, and she works for you. You should have known better than to hire the likes of her, but there's no talking to outsiders, is there?"

When Rose finally had both feet on the floor and cane in hand, we headed for the door. I propelled my grandmother across the room, and Bernie fell into step behind us. We stumbled out of the bakery into the warm sunshine. Bernie, as usual, had to have the final word.

"You've got a screw loose," she called behind her.

The door slammed in her face.

"Loose screw is right," I said when we were safely back in Bernie's car and heading out of town as fast as traffic would permit.

"I assume Cheryl Dowd's your Cheryl," Bernie said.

"That's her maiden name. Williams told me that. Cheryl's been married long enough to be a grandmother, so I'd say either Allegra hasn't seen Cheryl for decades or she hasn't forgotten old grievances." I remembered the outright hostility between the two women when Allegra came to my tearoom on Monday. The outright hostility on Allegra's part, at any rate. "I'm still not entirely sure what happened back there, or why she'd even think I wanted Tommy dead. Does she think I ordered Cheryl to make a hit on the man? Unbelievable."

"Her reasoning is somewhat confused," Rose said. "First, she implied Tommy would prefer her bakery to yours because he liked practical food. Fair enough. Then she thought he and I were in cahoots because we're both from Yorkshire."

I stared out the window, watching the coastline pass. The houses here were set back far from the road, marked by long sandy driveways and verges of tough seagrasses. "I'd say we were the unfortunate recipients of years, decades, of pent-up frustration. Allegra considers herself to be trapped in her family bakery. She needs to sell it for a good price to make a new life for herself. She saw being on the show, particularly if she won, as a way of getting that good price. Now she's afraid that's not going to happen, and someone, anyone, has to be blamed. That someone was first me and then Cheryl."

"If she hates the place that much," Bernie said, "I'm surprised her baking's so good. I hardly had the chance to enjoy my lunch, but everything looked good, and what I did have was great."

"The lemon tart was superb," Rose said. "Better than yours, Lily. You should ask her for her recipe."

"I'm sure that will be forthcoming."

"Reactance," Bernie said as she turned into the driveway of Victoria-on-Sea.

"What's that?" I asked.

It was late in the afternoon—teatime—and the sun was shining. My tearoom looked so sad, the tables unlaid, the chairs empty, the gate locked, the only sound made by cracked teacups tinkling cheerfully in the light breeze. A group of women leaned over the fence, taking pictures of the patio. Probably a garden tour group. Victoria-on-Sea was listed as the number one garden attraction in North Augusta, according to Tripadvisor. It was also the only garden attraction in North Augusta.

"Reactance is when one accuses someone else of doing either what they themselves have done or wish they could do.," Bernie explained.

"You think Allegra killed Tommy Greene?" I asked.

"I think the possibility's there. If we'd had a nice lunch, made polite conversation with her employees without knowing they're her relatives, we would have left none the wiser. Instead, with her temper tantrum and accusations, she placed herself at the top of my . . . our . . . suspect list." The car came to a screeching halt at the bottom of the veranda steps. A few cars were in the B & B lot: guests back from their day at the beach or whale watching or fishing, resting up before dinner. Reilly's SUV was gone.

Scarlet and Josh had taken chairs on the veranda, glasses of wine in hand, a bottle in an ice bucket. A platter of cheese and crackers and bowls, the type to contain nuts or olives, rested on the table between them.

We made no move to get out of the car. "What reason would Allegra have for killing Tommy?" I asked. "Assuming they didn't have a past history. Did anyone see her and Tommy together on Monday or Tuesday?"

"They might have exchanged a word or two," Bernie said. "Allegra showed up after the filming was over on Monday, but the judges were lingering, remember, and she was watching the tea being consumed yesterday. I can't say I noticed anything at all out of the ordinary. But that doesn't mean they didn't have a history. Just means they didn't perform it in public."

"I don't think that's it," Rose said. "She was counting on Tommy preferring her type of food to yours, Lily."

"That shouldn't matter," I said. "Judging is supposed to be on the merits of the food, atmosphere, decor, and service. On how well the bakery achieves what it intends to achieve, rather than personal preference, right?"

"You are so naive, Lily," Bernie said.

"Why does everyone keep saying that?"

"Because you're so naive, Lily." Rose turned to me with a smile. "Don't take offense. It's a positive trait."

I muttered something rude.

"Whereas," Bernie continued, "Scarlet and Claudia might be more the types to prefer a nice ladylike tea in a pleasant English-style garden. If Allegra had been counting on Tommy to swing votes her way, and then she saw him being friendly with Rose and enjoying Lily's tea . . ."

"She bumped him off," Rose finished.

"That makes not the least bit of sense," I said. "There's no guarantee the show will continue with our segment or, even if it does, that the replacement judge will have Tommy's tastes."

"It doesn't have to make sense to us," Bernie said.

"Only to the killer. Did Allegra overhear Tommy apologizing to Marybeth?"

"I don't know. I was outside. None of us heard what was said between them."

"I wonder if he told Marybeth he was giving you high marks as part of his apology. Or, even if he didn't, if Allegra interpreted it that way. It would be worth knowing if Allegra has a history of . . . shall we say, overreacting. And if she considers Cheryl to be her enemy for any particular reason or just that everyone's her enemy."

"Good thing I've signed up for tomorrow's bridge tournament," Rose said. "Bridge players can always be counted on to be up to date on the latest town gossip."

"Out you two get," Bernie said. "I'm off home to see if any of my feelers produced results."

"I'll make a call to some of my friends in New York," I said. "Maybe we can learn something about Tommy himself."

Rose and I got out of the car, and Bernie pulled away, spraying sand and gravel everywhere.

Josh and Scarlet watched us as we climbed the steps.

"Good afternoon," Rose said. "Is it still afternoon?"

"For a while yet," Josh said. "Please, won't you join us. Can I offer you a glass of wine?" He indicated the bottle in the cooler.

Scarlet's smile stretched her dark red lips without reaching her eyes.

"Not for me, thanks," I said. "I have to get back to my kitchen and do some prep for tomorrow."

"A cook's work is never done," Josh said. "I learned that early, directing this show."

Scarlet studied her fingernails. The polish was bright red, and it matched the color on her toes as well as her lipstick. Her bare feet peeked out from beneath a floor-length blue-and-white beach dress.

"Any news about the show?" I asked as Rose settled herself into a chair.

"Nothing yet," Josh said. "It can take the powers that be a long time to make a decision."

Scarlet drank her wine.

"Aren't you the lucky ones," Rose said. "You're able to bide your time in such a pleasant place."

"Your home is lovely," Josh said.

"Thank you, but I meant the Outer Cape. Is Claudia around?"

"I invited her to join us, but she had some business to conduct. Unlike you"—Josh gallantly tipped his head in my direction—"Claudia no longer cooks at her own place, but she does have her restaurants and her line of cook-books to manage."

"So nice to have a hobby in your old age," Scarlet drawled.

Rose's eyes widened at the nastiness of the remark, but Josh gave Scarlet a smile.

I excused myself and headed for my cottage. It was after four o'clock on a Wednesday in July, and not a chef in New York City worth his or her salt would be able to answer any of my emails, but I wanted to get them sent while I was thinking about it.

Éclair greeted me in her usual overjoyed manner when I came in. I gave her a hearty rub and then let her into the enclosed yard, promising her a walk before I went back to the tearoom. I settled myself at my computer and sent texts and wrote emails to my restaurant friends. Briefly, I asked if they knew of any trouble Tommy Greene had been in, financial or otherwise, or if they'd heard any rumors surrounding his death. I didn't have to go into any detail about why I was asking. His death was a big story in the national media. Twitter overflowed with tributes to the man. Tea by the Sea was, unfortunately, mentioned by name and location. I groaned and put my head in my hands. Word that a man had died in my place was all I needed after being closed for several days, and now the uncertainty as to whether or not the show would continue filming.

I flipped quickly through the online papers, searching for the story. Several showed pictures of Tea by the Sea, including a couple that had obviously been grabbed off my web page. Detective Chuck Williams's name appeared in many of the reports, some accompanied by a picture of him attempting to look tough and in command. He had nothing worthwhile to say. *A shocking crime. North Augusta remains a safe place for your family's vacation. An arrest is expected shortly.*

Neither Amy Redmond's picture nor her name appeared anywhere, and that was the way she liked it. Let Williams have the spotlight.

That done, I decided I'd better return the text my mother had sent me this morning. Words along the lines of *Another murder! What sort of place is your grandmother running there?* I assured Mom all was well and the police had the matter in hand.

I was closing my computer and was about to call to Éclair when my phone rang. I answered immediately when I saw Cheryl's name. "Everything okay?"

"Depends on what you mean by okay, Lily."

"I don't know what I mean by okay."

"Have you checked the reservations book?"

"Not since I opened it up for tomorrow. Don't tell me we're going to be empty! I was afraid that would happen."

"Not exactly. As I was home early, anyway, I checked the voice-mail box this afternoon." Because I'm occupied in the B & B kitchen in the mornings, Cheryl checks the voice mail once at night and again in the morning, before coming in, and she answers reservation inquiries.

"And?"

"It's been ringing off the hook, if it had a hook to ring off. We're completely full from online bookings. I've had trouble catching up to return calls and turn down reservation requests. I tell people we leave some tables free in the garden in case of a change in the weather, and I fear there's going to be a rush of walk-ins tomorrow."

"What brought this on? I thought the words *murder* and *police* would keep people away."

"One woman was in tears when I told her I couldn't guarantee her a table, Lily. She lives in Rochester and is prepared to drive all night to get to North Augusta to see the place where Tommy Greene died. He was, she told me, her idol."

"Oh, dear." I remembered the people I'd seen leaning over my garden fence, taking pictures. Perhaps I am naive. I'd thought they were admiring the plants on the patio.

Chapter 12

I heard nothing more from Josh or Reilly, so on Thursday morning I opened Tea by the Sea at the regular time of eleven o'clock. Cheryl, Marybeth, and I stood back to avoid being crushed by the rush.

"I don't know that I have enough baking on hand," I whispered to my employees as I bolted for the kitchen.

After getting off the phone with Cheryl yesterday afternoon, I'd called Rose and suggested she check the B & B reservations and emails. Fully booked for the foreseeable future, she told me, as well as a string of messages begging to be put on a waiting list.

"What about Scarlet, Claudia, and Josh?" I asked. "Are they staying?"

"They've said nothing about any plans to leave early. They're booked here until next Wednesday."

"If they do check out early, remind them of our cancellation policy, and then you can fill their rooms with the desperate."

"Perhaps I should increase my prices," Rose had said. "Let me think about that. I've thought about it. It would be unseemly to take advantage of a man's death, although I am sorely tempted."

I'd then gone to Tea by the Sea and baked until almost midnight. I staggered out of bed this morning at the regular time and went to the B & B to get the breakfasts on. Victoria-on-Sea was full, but I didn't have any special requests, and everyone was served by quarter to nine, so I had time to take a cup of coffee and a blueberry muffin to the privacy of my own front porch, kick off my shoes, and take a few precious minutes for myself. I read the emails and texts that had come in overnight with news from the New York restaurant scene, while Éclair checked under every bush and every blade of grass for the latest news from the neighborhood.

Quite a few of my friends knew Tommy Greene or knew someone who'd worked with him over the years. "Tough but fair" was the general consensus. He had a reputation, well deserved, for forcing his employees to give their best and not letting them off the hook if they didn't. But equally, he was quick to step in and help if a cook was having family issues or other personal or health problems. He paid well and gave generously of his time and money to mentor young chefs who showed promise. If you were tough enough to take the pressure, Tommy's upscale English-style pubs were considered top-notch places to work and learn. In his personal life, there wasn't a whisper of improper behavior, or so I'd been told. He didn't go out drinking after work; he didn't try to pressure his female staff into sleeping with him. He was devoted to his wife and their two young children and complained about missing them when he traveled. He didn't live above his apparent means, which were now substantial but hadn't always been, and there'd never been any rumors of funny money bankrolling his restaurants.

That was that, and I believed it. I'm sure plenty of people have secret lives they manage to keep secret, but the New York restaurant world is a close-knit, gossipy one. No one I knew claimed to be a personal friend of Tommy, they said he didn't have many real friends, but I was confident that if he was involved in things he shouldn't be, someone—probably everyone—would know.

It was a good thing I'd put in extra time in the tearoom kitchen last night. By early afternoon the line for tables stretched out the gate and down the driveway. Fortunately, it was a lovely day, so we could take full advantage of the seating on the patio. I spent all day in the kitchen, rolling, kneading, mixing, folding, stirring, tasting. Marybeth and Cheryl were whirlwinds of activity as they shouted orders, prepared pots of tea, poured prosecco and iced tea, arranged the food, and carried out glasses, teapots, and laden three-tiered stands.

"No publicity is bad publicity," Cheryl said to me at one point when she'd stopped to have a quick glug of water. "Isn't that what they say in show biz?"

"So I've heard."

"When I was cleaning a table on the patio a moment ago, I saw Simon chasing a couple of toddlers out of his flower beds. The parents were too busy taking pictures to notice what the little darlings were up to. Did you know Matt Goodwill's helping out?"

"Helping with what?"

"Directing traffic."

"It's that bad?"

"Oh, yeah. People who don't want to wait for a table or don't want tea are poking around the garden. Several of our guests have asked me if I met Tommy or what Tommy had to eat or what type of tea he preferred. I'm playing dumb, like you told me, which isn't all that hard. I say I'm a part-time waitress and I wasn't working the days he was here." She picked up a tray with fresh china and linens and left the kitchen.

I returned my attention to the tarts I was assembling. This wasn't a day to attempt anything new or overly complicated, and I was sticking to my tried-and-true favorites. Like these lemon tarts. Were Allegra's tarts really better than mine?

At last, the long, busy day came to an end. Marybeth and Cheryl staggered into the kitchen under the weight of trays full of empty teapots and plates containing not much more than a scattering of crumbs. I took a batch of mini coconut cupcakes out of the oven, put it on the counter to cool before packing the cupcakes into containers to go into the fridge overnight, and leaned back with a groan to give my aching muscles some relief.

"A good day," Cheryl said.

"A hard day," Marybeth said.

"How were the tips?" I asked.

"Better than normal," Marybeth said. "I was reading up on Tommy Greene last night, and apparently he was a vocal proponent of good tipping. If you can afford to eat at a Manhattan restaurant, he once said to an interviewer, you can afford to properly thank the person who ensured your evening was a success."

I was dead beat, but the reservations book was full for tomorrow, and I needed to put in a few more hours tonight, particularly if we had the number of walk-ins we'd had today.

I started another batch of scones, while Marybeth and Cheryl quickly and efficiently tidied the patio, the main dining room, and the alcoves to get ready for another day's service.

"Knock, knock." The back door opened, and Simon's tousled head popped around the corner. "Is it safe to come in?"

"Barely," I said.

"You must have been overwhelmed in here today." He wore his gardening overalls, gloves poking out of the pockets, and heavy boots. Sand was trapped in his fair hair, and the T-shirt under his overalls was streaked with mud and sweat. He smelled of freshly cut grass, hard work, and good Cape Cod earth, with perhaps a slight overlay of compost.

"*Overwhelmed*'s the word." Marybeth threw her apron into the laundry basket with a sigh of relief and went to the storage room to get her purse. She came out with her mother's tote bag, as well.

"We were so busy, I scarcely had time to think about what happened last night," Cheryl said, "which is a good thing, and when I was thinking about it, I didn't have a chance to tell you."

"Tell us what?" Marybeth and I asked.

Simon scrubbed his hands under the kitchen sink with vigor.

"Chuck Williams paid a call on me at home yesterday. Not long after I spoke to you on the phone about the reservations, Lily."

"What did he want?" Marybeth asked.

"To go over the same questions he'd asked before. Essentially, did I kill Tommy Greene? To which I replied, 'No, I did not.' He asked what I'd done after work that day, and if I could prove I hadn't come back here. I can't prove what I didn't do, now can I?" Her voice rose, and a twitch started above her right eye. "He asked Jim where he'd been, and Jim said he'd been in Nantucket for a couple of days, working a charter. Jim's no fan of Chuckie Boy, either, and he said if he'd known I'd need an alibi, he'd have stayed home."

"Then what happened?" Marybeth asked.

"Chuck left, saying he'd be back." Tears welled up in her eyes. "I hate this."

Marybeth put an arm around her mother's shoulder. Simon and I exchanged glances.

I shifted my feet. "Cheryl, it's none of my business, but I have to ask. What's the story with you and Allegra? It's obvious you two have a history."

Before I could tell her that Allegra said I shouldn't have hired her, she shrugged Marybeth's arm away, wiped at her eyes, and said, "Nothing. Nothing that matters. It's all water under the bridge." A veil fell over her face, and she said, "See you tomorrow."

I wanted to ask her what Williams had meant when he'd said she'd been a troublemaker in her youth, but as her employer, I hesitated at stepping over that line. Teenage indiscretions and high school animosities were none of my business. I hesitated too long, and by the time I'd decided that a murder in my place of business and my employee being under suspicion for that murder made it my business, the door was swinging shut behind her.

Marybeth gave me a look of apology and hurried after her mother.

"I came by to offer to give you some help," Simon said. "I would have earlier, but I had my hands full keeping future juvenile delinquents out of the shrubbery and politely asking well-dressed ladies not to cut the flowers, thank you very much. 'And no, Tommy Greene hadn't put his foot in that patch of soil, madam, so please don't dig up the bulbs.' I'd never even heard of the man before this week, but by the way some of those women were going on, you'd think he'd been one of the Beatles."

"What brought the Beatles to mind?"

"My mum's a big Paul McCartney fan and has been almost all her life. She has stacks of books about him and his former bandmates, and one of the pictures shows a girl weeping over a patch of grass she pulled out of the ground because he'd supposedly trod on it."

I laughed. It was a good feeling after the busyness of the day, on top of the tension of this week. "Any sign of police activity?"

"Some. Williams and Redmond stopped by a couple of hours ago. They went in the house, came out about half an hour later. No one left with them."

"Probably talking to the TV people again."

"Are you planning on baking tonight?"

"I don't have a lot of time. I'm supposed to be having dinner with Rose at seven, but I'll do what I can until then."

"I'll go and change out of these things, shake off most of the dirt, and be right back." He gave me a soft smile. "If you'd like some company while you work?"

I returned the smile. "I would. Thanks."

He left, and I opened the industrial-sized fridge. When Simon meant providing company while I worked, he didn't intend to pull up a chair, crack open a beer, and chat. Simon knew his way around a kitchen. His mother was a wedding and special events caterer, and Simon had grown up helping her. His father owned a landscaping company. Simon's life choices, he'd told me, had been either cooking or gardening.

I didn't have a lot of time until my meeting with Rose, so I decided to make more scones and ask Simon to prepare sandwich ingredients. I took out a whole chicken and put it aside for him to poach for the filling. I put a large stockpot on to boil and then selected a smaller pot for preparing the eggs for curried egg sandwiches.

I was dumping the wet scone dough onto the flour-covered butcher block prior to folding it and rolling it out when Simon returned. His face was scrubbed pink, his hair wet, and he wore clean jeans and a fresh T-shirt. He rubbed his hands together. "Okay, mate, let me at it."

*   *   *

We worked comfortably together and talked mainly about the subject uppermost in everyone's mind: the death of Tommy Greene. Unfortunately, we came to no conclusions. Simon had been in North Augusta for an even shorter length of time than I had, so he could provide no insights into the community and relationships therein.

At five to seven, sandwich fillings were in the fridge and scones in the freezer. We tidied our work spaces, took off our aprons, and washed our hands. I glanced outside at the sound of a car taking the corner into our driveway faster than was probably wise. Bernie had arrived.

"You're welcome to join us for what passes for dinner," I said. "Bernie and Rose organized it, so goodness knows what we'll be having. Whatever was the specialty of the day at the supermarket, I suspect."

"Didn't you tell me Rose had been a cook in a grand house before her marriage? I'm surprised she doesn't cook for you and her."

"She cooked her entire life. She started work as a kitchen helper in an English stately home when she was fourteen. She married my grandfather and moved to Grand Lake, Iowa, where she raised five children and helped with the raising of numerous grandchildren. Every day of her married life, except for the occasional vacation break, she prepared three delicious, well-balanced, nourishing meals. Sometimes more than three times a day, as family could drop in at odd hours. The day of my grandfather's funeral, she hung up her apron and said no more. She's stuck to that vow, and now she doesn't cook. She reheats. As for Bernie, she never learned to cook and has no desire to do so now."

"I'll pop in and say hi," Simon said. "If it doesn't appear as though there's enough to provide for an unexpected guest, I'll take my leave."

There was enough, more than enough. Bernie had gone to the Indian restaurant in town for takeout. She knows my tastes perfectly well, but unsure of what Rose likes, she got a serving of just about everything. Which was highly convenient, as Bernie and I like just about everything.

We sat around the small Formica table in the kitchen of the B & B. Éclair settled herself on the floor under the table, on guard waiting for something to drop, and Robbie perched on the counter. Once drinks were served and our plates piled dangerously high with onion bhaji, butter chicken, *rogan josh*, spinach paneer, *aloo gobi*, steamed rice, garlic naan, and a variety of pickles and chutneys, Rose said, "Who wants to go first?"

"I will," I said, "as I don't have much to report."

"Report?" Simon ripped a piece of naan into quarters and scooped up butter chicken sauce.

"Didn't I tell you? This is a strategy meeting as well as a dinner. I learned quite a bit about Tommy Greene from my friends who work in Manhattan restaurants, but not much we didn't know." I filled them in quickly as I ate. It was all *sooo* good.

"You're saying it's unlikely someone from the mob followed him here and bumped him off because he owed them money." Rose waved her fork at me.

"Right. The man could be rude in the extreme when he believed someone hadn't met his expectations, but if that was grounds for murder in the restaurant world, there wouldn't be many people still around to cook your food." I knew of what I spoke. My most recent ex-boyfriend, Wesley Schumann, was a Michelin-starred chef, and I'd made the desserts at his popular steak house. I'd left both him and that life when he came after me with one of his butcher's knives when I'd accidentally knocked over a bottle of cooking oil. "It's possible Tommy was rude to someone in other parts of his life, to someone not used to it, like

Marybeth, but I can't see such a person following him here and luring him into Tea by the Sea under the cover of darkness. Or Tommy allowing himself to be lured."

"Under the cover of darkness," Simon said around a mouthful of rice and paneer. "Any chance he was meeting a woman for a secret assignation?"

"Anything's possible, but even if he was the type to fool around—"

"They're all the type to fool around," Bernie interrupted. She dipped her head in Simon's direction. "Present company probably included."

A slight smile touched the edges of his mouth as Simon tore another piece of naan in half, but he didn't reply.

"An assignation in a restaurant, when he has a perfectly pleasant room in a lovely seaside B & B?" Rose said. "Unlikely."

"Maybe he didn't want to be seen." Bernie lifted an overflowing fork to her mouth.

"He had a key to the house for coming in after hours," Rose said. "All the guests do."

"Irrelevant," I said. "As no such woman is on the radar, at least as far as we know."

"Scarlet? Claudia? One of the women on the crew?" Bernie suggested.

"Unlikely. I noticed no secret glances or deliberate avoidance of eye contact between him and anyone. Not that I was watching everyone all the time."

"Still," Bernie said, "they aren't actors, but they are in show business, so they must have learned some tricks."

"If anything," I said, "I'd say Tommy and Scarlet didn't like each other much. And it shouldn't matter, though it usually does, but Claudia's older than he was."

"Which brings us to what or who is on the radar." Rose nibbled at a slice of chicken. "This is tasty. And that's Cheryl."

"Bridge club gossip?" Bernie asked.

"The best and the most reliable. Although I have to say trolling for gossip at a duplicate tournament should qualify a woman for danger pay. Every time I opened my mouth, other than to bid or counterbid or pass, that ridiculous Mabel Thurmond summoned the director." Rose harrumphed. "Woman can't play bridge to save her life, so she has to be a stickler for making sure superior players are chastised and threatened if—"

"What did you learn, Rose?" I asked.

"Nothing worthwhile at bridge, except that Mabel Thurmond likes to bid whether or not she has sufficient points in her hand. The only thing I did learn with relevance to our case is a negative. Before the start of play, as we were taking our seats, several members asked me if I'd met the late Mr. Greene. It was immediately clear that Tommy Greene has no ties to North Augusta. It's unlikely he'd ever set foot in the area before this week."

"Negatives are important," Bernie said. "Helps to keep focus on the positives."

"I had to suggest to several of the ladies, who seemed inclined to want to share what they know, that we go for coffee after the game. Unfortunately, it was after four o'clock by then, so someone suggested a bar instead, and as I'd offered to pay . . ."

I cleared my throat.

Rose got the hint and continued. "Cheryl's a generation younger than most of my bridge companions, but they know her as a schoolmate or colleague of their own children. Cheryl was what passes for a 'bad girl' at North Augusta High. Not in the sense of running around with unsuitable boys, but for getting herself into trouble over things such as shoplifting, being suspected of theft at school, leaving cafés and diners without paying."

"Did that behavior carry on into adulthood?" Simon asked.

"This is confidential, of course," I said, "but when I hired her, I ran a standard records check and found nothing of concern."

"My friends enjoyed relating the old gossip," Rose said, "but they had nothing more recent to add. Cheryl married Jim Wainwright, generally considered to be a good man from a longtime Cape Cod fishing family, and had two children. She never had what you'd consider stable employment, but that's hardly cause for concern in a seasonal, tourist-orientated economy."

"As I suspected," I said. "The idea that she'd suddenly revert to her teenage rebellion years and kill a man is preposterous."

"It might be worth noting that one of Cheryl's boyfriends during those rebellious years was Chuck Williams," Rose said.

I choked on my spinach paneer.

"You have got to be kidding," Bernie said.

"Small towns," Simon chuckled. "Gotta love 'em."

"That was a long time ago, and the women who told me were relating secondhand news, but such appears to have been the case."

"A long time ago," I said, "but old resentments can linger."

"Particularly if one party humiliated the other or carelessly broke their heart or such like," Bernie said. "Did these women know what happened?"

"No. Both parties married other people not long after leaving school, and no one thought another thing about it until my gently probing questions had the memories coming back."

"*Gently* sounds like the right word," Simon said. "Anyone want the last spoonful of lamb?"

"Help yourself," Bernie said.

And he did.

"Did you ask your friends about Allegra?" I said. "She seems to be carrying a substantial amount of anger toward Cheryl."

"More high school rivalry. They're the same age and would have known each other in school, but my friends didn't know any specific details. Something of interest happened much later, however. Marybeth, Cheryl's daughter, took a summer job at North Augusta Bakery when she was in high school."

"Marybeth told me she'd worked there briefly," I said. "Let me do the math. Marybeth's twenty-seven, so that would have been about ten years ago."

"Correct. Allegra's mother had recently relinquished control of the bakery, and Allegra had taken over. Marybeth didn't work there long."

"Three days, she told me," I said.

"She started work shortly before the tourists arrived en masse, so the town didn't have a lot to talk about yet, so the story got around. Marybeth was fired for stealing from the till."

"Wow!" Bernie said.

"Marybeth? I don't believe it," I said.

"No one did," Rose said. "The police were called, meaning none other than our good friend Detective Inspector Chuck Williams, newly promoted from walking the beat."

"Williams isn't a DI," Simon said. "And I've never seen a beat cop in North Augusta. They're always in their cars."

"Rose knows that," I told him. "She likes to pretend she doesn't. It's part of her English airs. Go on, Rose."

"Allegra insisted on charging Marybeth. Nothing came of it, and the case was quietly dropped. Marybeth was either fired or quit, but the result was the same. As you can imagine, she had trouble finding a job for the remainder of that season. Too much of the old 'If there's smoke, there's fire' nonsense."

"Cheryl must have been furious," I said.

"To say the least," Rose said. "My friends remembered it clearly, because she was on the warpath. She marched into the bakery at the busiest time of day, and words were exchanged. The police were called, and Cheryl agreed to leave."

"Okay," Simon said. "I get what you're saying. If Allegra had been killed, it might be possible, at a stretch, to suspect Cheryl. But Allegra wasn't killed, Tommy Greene was, and no one has claimed that he—"

"But he did!" Bernie interrupted. "Tommy Greene told Lily to fire Marybeth. That Lily, unlike Allegra, had no intention of doing so might not have mattered. Cheryl's daughter was bullied, as she saw it, and her job threatened."

The table fell silent.

I studied my empty plate. "I refuse to believe Cheryl had anything to do with this," I said at last. "Cheryl might have been a wild teenager, but she's no longer a teenager, and she's no longer wild. She's a grandmother, for heaven's sake."

Rose sniffed. From his perch on the counter, Robbie also sniffed. "Grandmothers can be wild, love," Rose said. "We don't all take up knitting by the fire in our old age."

I gave her a fond smile. "As you prove to me every single day."

"Although," she admitted, "more often than not the spirit might be willing, but the flesh is weak. The knees and hips in particular." Robbie leapt off the counter and landed on the floor next to Éclair. The dog emitted a startled bark. Robbie curled himself around Rose's legs and purred, and Éclair settled back down with a sniff of disapproval.

"Point taken," I said. "Marybeth might have unfairly lost her high school summer job, and her mother tried to intervene on her behalf, but Marybeth isn't in high school anymore. She's a married woman and a mother. She doesn't need her own mother to fight her battles for her."

My grandmother laid her hand on top of mine. Her warm blue eyes were so full of love, I had to swallow a lump that rose up from nowhere and threatened to choke me. "All mothers, all grandmothers, want to fight their children's battles, no matter how old those children might be. The sensible ones know we can't. The unsensible ones . . ."

"Great," I said when I could speak again. "We've uncovered a motive for Cheryl to have killed Tommy Greene."

"Have to go where the evidence leads, regardless of where we want it to lead," Bernie said. "If you've nothing more to report, Rose, it's my turn."

I stood up and collected the dirty dishes. "First, can I top anyone up?"

Bernie pushed her wineglass toward me. Simon said, "Cheers," meaning he'd have another beer, and Rose said, "No thank you, love."

Éclair stumbled to her feet and hurried to help me dispose of the leftovers, and Robbie returned to his post on the counter to sniff at the empty dishes. I picked him up and put him on the floor, knowing he'd be up again as soon as my back was turned. Rose had never attempted to train Robbie to stay off tables and counters, and it was too late now.

"Okay," Bernie said when the table was clear, I'd served the drinks, made tea for Rose and resumed my seat. "I spent a good part of the day online. Before you ask where online, Simon, don't bother. I never say. Plausible deniability and all that."

He raised one eyebrow at me, and I shrugged in response.

"Gary Powers, husband of our esteemed mayor, brother-in-law of Allegra Griffin, is a part owner of North Augusta Bakery."

"I didn't see that one coming," I said.

"Part owner, and strictly a silent partner. He bought a half interest about a year ago. I don't know why, but at a guess, I'd say the bakery needed an infusion of cash, so Allegra went to her sister and brother-in-law. Unfortunately, I was unable to get a look at any of their banking records." She shook her head, disappointed at her own failure.

"Meaning," I said, "if Allegra needs the money from the sale of the bakery to fund her new, much-desired lifestyle, she needs even more if Gary's to get his share. I wonder if he's considering buying it outright?"

"That would be tricky," Bernie said, "if he lost the head baker at the same time. He's an insurance broker. No evidence of experience either cooking or running a restaurant operation."

"My money," I said, "is on Gary being the one who complained about Josh and the others staying here at Victoria-on-Sea."

"Almost certainly," Rose said.

"What complaint?" Simon asked, and I told him.

"The question I have," Simon said, "is, why would either Allegra or anyone else involved in the bakery want to get rid of Tommy? They hadn't even filmed anything there yet. Maybe he'd love their food and they'd win."

"Motives for murder don't always appear logical to outsiders." I fingered my wineglass. "Although they make perfect sense to the killer. Sometimes. I hate that I know this. There is one other thing . . . I wasn't witness to it, but I heard that Gary and Tommy got into an argument on Monday."

"That's right," Bernie said. "They did. Gary was being

a total and complete jerk all day, and he made some clumsy moves on Scarlet. Tommy told him to sit down and shut up. Tommy might have even said a word they'll have to beep out of the program."

"Do you mean he made moves on Scarlet, as in wanted to get to know her better, or was he playing for the camera?" I asked.

"Hard to say." Bernie looked at Rose.

"He was playing for the cameras for sure. He had that look on his face that means someone knows they're being watched and they're enjoying it. As for his intentions toward Scarlet . . . it's not a secret in North Augusta that Mayor Powers's marriage is not entirely stable."

"Meaning they both fool around, and everyone in town knows it."

"To the apparent obliviousness of the couple involved," Rose said.

"How can she still be the mayor, and on her second term?" Simon asked.

"Rumors of infidelity don't appear to have hurt her political fortunes," I said. "North Augusta people are generally a practical lot, and as long as Susan's doing a good job, her approval ratings remain high. They don't have children, and so far, no families have been destroyed, so what Susan and Gary do in their private lives is considered to be their business."

"What did Scarlet think of this attention Gary was paying her?" Simon asked.

"Again, hard to know," Rose said. "Tommy moved in almost immediately and ran him off."

"What else did you learn, Bernie?" I asked.

"As much as I hate to say it, nothing."

"Nothing?"

"Not yet. I remembered a guy I worked with when I first started at the firm. We went out for drinks one night.

I had a super-fun time, and I was getting to like him. And then he up and quit and moved to Los Angeles. Which is totally my luck, but also totally beside the point. Anyway, he's still doing the same sort of work, but this time for the US attorney's office, so I dropped him a line. I sent a link to a story on Tommy's killing, explaining Lily and my connection, and asked him if he'd mind finding out what he could about CookingTV and the people involved in *America Bakes!*, those who were in North Augusta this week, anyway."

"You think he'll do that for you, even though you had one date and then he moved across the country?" Simon asked. "It must have been quite the date."

Bernie tossed her long red locks, turned her head to one side, lifted her shoulder, gave Simon a flirtatious wink, and said in a deep voice, "Did you doubt it, doll?" She laughed and dropped the pose. "Nah. He talked a lot about what he liked most about our jobs. Digging and digging and digging and following a long and complicated trail to uncover that one salient detail someone has gone to a lot of trouble to hide. That's probably why I liked him so much, because I like doing that, too. In this case, I figured he'd enjoy the challenge."

"Even though he works for a US attorney?"

"Believe it or not, Lily, a heck of a lot of the information that's available to anyone who knows how and where to look is legally out there. All you need is to know how to look and what you're looking for. It's Thursday today, and I might not hear from him until the weekend, when he has some free time. Assuming he gets such a thing as free time in that job, which isn't always a given." She drained the contents of her wineglass. "Do we have an action plan for tomorrow?"

"I'm planning to be open tomorrow," I said. "Regular

hours. I haven't heard anything from Josh about when or if they're going to do the last day of filming."

"When I chatted to him and Scarlet earlier," Rose said, "he made noises about the unexpected chance to enjoy a proper vacation and being in no hurry to return to work."

"What did Scarlet think about that?"

"Judging by the look on her face, not much. I rented out Tommy's room as soon as the police were finished with it, but the TV people have three rooms still booked through until Wednesday. If Josh is in no hurry to leave, I'm happy to accommodate him."

"Do you know what they're doing this evening?" I asked.

"Josh and Scarlet called a cab to take them to town. He said they were meeting Reilly and some of the crew for dinner. Claudia never came down. I get the feeling Claudia prefers her own company to that of her work associates."

"I was hoping to get a chance to talk to her," I said. "Privately, I mean. I want to tell her how much she inspired my career and how much I've learned from her cookbooks."

"Ask Edna to let you know if she's at breakfast tomorrow," Rose said. "Perhaps you could speak to her then."

Bernie stood up. "If that's all for tonight, I'll be off. I can't believe I'm saying this, but it's almost nine o'clock. What time that is for a Manhattan girl to be going home for the night, I don't know. Rose, can you find out if there's been any more trouble between Allegra and Cheryl beyond what you told us? Or between either of them and anyone else? Or about Gary Powers and his shenanigans? Although I don't know what that would have to do with Tommy's death."

"That's an idea," I said. "It might be worth trying to find out if he's ever been in legal trouble because of bothering women who are uninterested in his charms, either from the women themselves or their husbands or boyfriends."

"A follow-up lunch with my bridge ladies would be a good idea," Rose said. "I've jogged their memories, so they might remember additional details."

"Find out what you can about the relationship between Chuck Williams and Cheryl," Bernie said. "If she ended it, and he took it badly, he might not have gotten entirely over it. While I'm waiting for my friend and other contacts to get back to me, I'll continue trying to find out what I can about the goings on at CookingTV and the people involved."

"What do you want me to do?" I asked.

Bernie and Rose smiled identical smiles at me. "Bake, Lily. It's what you do best."

Bernie went home after dinner, saying she needed to get some work done on her book, and Rose and Robbie retired to their room. Simon stayed to help me do the dishes and tidy up, getting the kitchen ready for tomorrow's breakfast service. Then I switched off the interior lights, switched on the one over the entrance, locked the door behind me, and we climbed the three steps to the ground level. The sky to the west was streaked in shades of dark gray, pink, and purple, and the air was soft and full of the scent of the sea. The first of the stars had appeared in the eastern sky. A few B & B guests sat on benches looking over the bluffs to the bay, and their low voices drifted toward us. Éclair trotted happily across the lawn, sniffing at bushes as well as at guests' ankles, and I heard more than one person exclaim in delight over her.

Every nerve in my body tingled in awareness of the proximity of Simon, standing close to me. "Nice night," he said.

"It is," I replied.

My little cottage lies only a few steps past the main house, set back from the bluffs, surrounded by a fence to keep Éclair in and curious guests out. I opened the gate and called to the dog. She came quickly, and we climbed the steps to the front porch. I unlocked the door, and Éclair ran inside, no doubt to check the contents of her food bowl. I turned to face Simon. The light from the lamp over the door threw his face into deep shadows. His blue eyes were dark and serious as he looked down at me. I breathed.

"Good night, Lily," he said. "I'll see you in the morning."

He turned and walked away, and I let out a long breath as I watched him disappear into the darkness. I didn't know what I'd been expecting—if I'd been expecting any-thing—but I felt strangely disappointed.

Chapter 13

As we still hadn't heard if filming would continue, Rose and I decided to resume full breakfast service at the B & B, and the following morning at six o'clock, I was back in the kitchen, putting the coffee on and getting baking ingredients ready while Éclair settled herself under the table.

Simon came in, said good morning, and helped himself to coffee. "No news from the TV chaps?"

"Nothing. I texted Josh last night to ask, but he said the studio hadn't made a decision yet. I get the feeling he's getting as frustrated as I am. Although, I have to admit that judging someone's feelings from a one-line text isn't all that reliable."

"Do you need a hand?" He indicated the sausages I'd laid on the counter. "Looks like the full breakfast is on today."

"It is," I said. "Thanks for the offer, but Edna will be here soon."

"Then I'll be off. All this lovely sunshine is doing my plants a lot of good, but it's doing the same for the weeds, and I plan to get stuck into them with a vengeance before the day gets too hot." He gave Éclair a pat, me a wave, and left, greeting Edna on his way out.

"Someone complained to the TV network about the judges staying here at Victoria-on-Sea," I said to Edna as she greeted Éclair before slipping on her apron. "They said it gave Tea by the Sea an unfair advantage in the competition. Do you know anything about that?"

"It just so happens that I do. The paper received a letter to the editor saying that very thing. Frank didn't print it, as one, it's a private affair, and two, the paper doesn't print anonymous letters. Frank told me because it had to do with this place. I meant to mention it, but then other developments took precedence."

"Understandable," I said. "It was anonymous?"

"Anonymous, meaning Gary Powers didn't print his name at the bottom, but he might as well have. He writes to the paper regularly, complaining about something or other, such as the placement of hanging baskets on the stretch of sidewalk near the bakery. Often his letters are signed, though the ones criticizing the mayor or town council are not, but it doesn't much matter. Frank knows Gary's writing style by now. Even before he married Susan, the guy was a pest. Does it matter?"

"Probably not. I was just wondering, that's all."

Breakfast service passed uneventfully, and I was hoping to get away early when Edna told me Claudia D'Angelo had taken a seat in in the dining room.

"Do you think she'd mind me talking to her?"

"I can't say," Edna replied. "She's on her own and not expecting anyone to join her. Josh was down about an hour ago, and I haven't seen Scarlet, but she doesn't always come in for breakfast. Claudia's having coffee and only wants cereal and fruit this morning."

"I'm sure a quick hello from a fan wouldn't be amiss." I took off my apron, untied my ponytail, and ran my fingers through my hair. Éclair recognized the signs of going home and leapt eagerly to her feet.

"Stay!" I ordered. "I'll only be a few minutes."

The disappointment on her face was positively human. I cringed and bent over to give her an apologetic pat and a mumble of apology.

The French doors in the dining room had been thrown open to admit the morning sunlight and the soft breeze coming off the bay. It was almost nine, and only a few tables were still occupied. Claudia had taken a table for two in a corner. Her gray and black hair was tied in a chignon, and she wore a summer dress of yellow and black stripes. On anyone else that dress would look like a bumblebee costume, but she had the grace and elegance to pull it off. A yellow silk scarf was draped loosely around her neck. She sipped her coffee with one hand and scrolled across the screen of her iPad with the other, peering closely at the screen through her glasses. She did not, I thought, look happy with what she was reading. I assumed it was the daily news.

I put a smile on my face and, feeling unexpectedly nervous, crossed the dining room toward her. "Good morning," I said cheerfully.

She hadn't heard me approach and looked up with a start. She quickly shut her iPad, but not before I caught a glimpse of the screen. Not a newspaper or social media feed, but what appeared to be columns and rows of numbers. The frown disappeared, and she gave me a bright smile. "Lily, good morning. How are you today?"

"I'm fine, thanks. I'm sorry to bother you over your breakfast . . ."

She took off her glasses and tucked them next to her

plate. "Quite all right. I was catching up on the news of the day, hoping to find out that they've caught whoever killed dear Tommy. Have you heard anything?"

"No."

She gestured graciously to the empty chair opposite. "Please, have a seat."

"Thank you." I settled myself into the chair. "I won't keep you, but I wanted to take the opportunity to tell you how much I admire you and your career. You were an inspiration to me when I was starting in this business."

"That's nice to hear," she said.

"I've been to your New York restaurant quite a few times, and I have most, if not all, of your cookbooks. I make some of your pastries in the tearoom. The Earl Grey chocolate tart's a favorite of my customers. I considered mentioning that when I was being filmed, but I thought I might look as though I was trying to influence the judging."

She laughed lightly. "Influencing the judging is the name of the game, dear. Don't be shy about playing every card you have." Her smile was warm and her words gracious, but something dark lay behind her eyes as they constantly flicked toward her iPad. I got the hint and stood up.

"I hope you're enjoying your stay at Victoria-on-Sea, even though the circumstances aren't the best."

"Thank you, dear. Your grandmother has a lovely place, and I'll be sure to tell my friends about it. Although I hope this horrible situation doesn't drag on forever. I have commitments back in the city." She touched the lid of the iPad.

"You'd be welcome to come to the tearoom again," I said. "As my guest."

"I'll keep that in mind." She put her reading glasses on her face and opened the iPad.

Bernie was waiting for me in the kitchen, munching on a blueberry muffin and chatting to Edna, who was loading the dishwasher. "Surprised to see you so early," I said. "I thought you were going to write all night."

"I did. It went well."

"Glad to hear it."

"I've been summoned by Rose."

"Summoned? What about? Did you learn anything new?"

"No. I suspect your grandmother wants us to form a plan of attack for today."

"You're talking about the murder, I assume," Edna said.

"Yup. What's the newspaper know about it? Any scoops you can share?" Bernie asked.

"Frank doesn't know anything the police haven't revealed," Edna said. "There's been a good deal of outside interest in the story, as you'd expect, but no breaking news."

"I'm off," I said. "See you two later."

"Walk with me," Bernie said.

"Walk where? To Rose's suite? Why?"

She waggled her eyebrows at me, jerked her head toward Edna, and said nothing.

"Sorry," I said to Éclair, who'd once again hurried to the door, tail wagging. "Be right back."

The dog's face and tail fell.

"Give me a piece of that muffin," I said to Bernie.

She peered at the unfinished treat in her hand. "Are you that hungry?"

"Not for me. All I seem to have done today is disappoint Éclair. I hate to create a precedent, but this one time only, I'll slip her something."

"Better if I do it, so she doesn't start expecting to be fed in here." Bernie broke off a bite and handed it to Éclair. It disappeared in a flash. Bernie tossed the last piece into her own mouth, and she and I went into the hall.

"I thought you might want to talk about what happened last night," my friend said.

"Last night? Nothing happened last night. You were here, remember?"

"Yes, I was here. I mean after I left. The delectable Simon, I couldn't help but notice, lingered."

"Linger was all he did. We cleaned up. He went home. Sorry not to have more exciting news for you."

Bernie's face fell in exactly the same way Éclair's had. "Drat. I was sure he was about to make his move."

"No moves." I said no more. I'd told Bernie on more than one occasion that I wasn't looking to start a relationship with Simon or anyone else. This summer had to be all about getting Tea by the Sea up and running, and helping Rose keep Victoria-on-Sea thriving and, hopefully, profitable. I had no time for complications such as romance. Besides, even if I was so inclined, Simon was due to return to England in the fall.

I had no time for complications of any sort, and that included this TV show and a murder. But somehow, there I was. Mired in complications once again.

"Change of subject. Are you sticking to the plan?" I said, referring to the outline of her book she'd written to show me.

"I am. Thanks for suggesting it. It is helping, knowing where I'm going and how I have to get there."

The housekeeper clattered down the stairs, carrying a laundry basket full of sheets and towels. "Morning, Lily, Bernie," she said.

"Morning, Jean. Are people checking out today?" I asked.

"Two rooms turning over. One of them left first thing this morning, so I could get started on cleaning it."

"You heard one of the guests died on Tuesday?" Bernie said.

"Yeah. The TV chef. Everyone's talking about it in town. They all want to know if I met him, but I never did.

All I can tell them is that he kept his room as neat and tidy as I've ever seen."

"I should have asked you this earlier," Bernie said. "I don't suppose you came across anything in his room that might point to his killer. Like a letter saying, *My name is Inigo Montoya. You killed my father. Prepare to die?*"

Jean chuckled. "'Fraid not. The police asked me that, too, without quoting from *The Princess Bride*. They had me look around his room to see if anything had been disturbed before they took away his stuff. I couldn't help them." She began to walk past us, and then she stopped. "I shouldn't gossip about the guests, and I never do. Well, almost never, but . . ."

"But?" Bernie and I chorused.

Her face crinkled in thought. Jean was in her early sixties and had spent most of her working life cleaning rooms in hotels and B & Bs like this one. She'd probably, I thought, seen everything there was to see. "Never mind," she said. "It likely doesn't have anything to do with his death."

"What?" Bernie said. "You can't keep us in suspense after that."

"Four TV people were staying here, right? The dead guy and the three others, who are still here."

"Yes?" I said.

"Meaning they took four rooms, right?"

"Yes," Bernie said.

"They could have saved their money and taken three. If you know what I mean." Jean winked.

"Do I?" I asked.

"At first, anyway. The younger woman, the one with all the makeup and the clothes, who is, by the way, a complete and total slob and has enough prescription pills in her toiletry bag to supply a veterinary clinic—"

"Good thing you never gossip about the guests," Bernie muttered under her breath.

"Did not spend the first two nights in solitary slumber."

"Huh?" I said.

"You mean she had company," Bernie said. "In her room. At night. In her bed."

"Oh, yeah. The signs were unmistakable."

Bernie and I glanced at each other.

"What do you mean, the first two nights?" Bernie said. "They arrived here on Sunday. So someone was with her Sunday and Monday but not again?"

"Yup."

"Tommy Greene died Tuesday night or early Wednesday morning, right?" Bernie asked me.

"The police said his bed wasn't slept in on Tuesday night," I told her, "so they assumed he didn't go to bed. Is it possible he visited another bed? What about his room on the mornings after Scarlet had . . . uh, company? Was his bed slept in?"

"It appeared to be," Jean said. "But that doesn't necessarily mean anything. It's not unusual when people are sneaking around between rooms and don't want anyone to know to spend part of the night in their own room. His bed hadn't been used after I made it on Tuesday. On Wednesday I hadn't been up to clean the rooms when the police arrived, and they told me not to touch anything. The bed was still made when I eventually came in."

"Did you tell the police this? About Scarlet and . . . whomever," I asked.

"No," Jean said. "They didn't ask. I don't gossip about the guests."

"Much," Bernie muttered, and Jean winked at her.

"Exactly." She hefted her laundry basket onto one ample hip and carried on her way.

"That is worth knowing," I said. "So Scarlet was sleeping with Tommy."

"Not necessarily him. Don't jump to conclusions. Jean said his bed had been slept in the first two nights they were here."

"Who else could it have been? He's married, as we know, and supposedly it's a close, loving marriage. He wouldn't want word to get out if he was fooling around. I can't see Scarlet sneaking a boyfriend in by the back door when everyone else was in bed."

"I can," Bernie said. "People have all sorts of reasons for keeping relationships secret. I'll admit Tommy's the most likely suspect, but there are other possibilities. Josh. Maybe even the notorious Gary Powers."

I thought over the sequence of events. "Highly unlikely to be Gary. Scarlet and the rest arrived here on Sunday. Jean said Scarlet had company Sunday night, but the first day of filming was Monday, and by all appearances, Gary hadn't met Scarlet yet."

"It might not have been a man, you know."

"There is that. Interesting that the police never asked Jean the right sort of questions."

"I'll bet you anything she was questioned by Williams, not Amy Redmond. He seems to me like the sort who assumes the rooms are cleaned by the cleaning fairy. And cleaning fairies, as we all know, don't notice things like who slept where or with whom."

"Have you discovered anything interesting about Scarlet?" I asked.

"Nothing other than that she's a former Miss Louisiana, a former mid-level model, and now a reality-TV star with a reputation for being quite the prima donna. She was married at one time, to a strictly bit-part actor, but that ended a couple of years ago. No children. She now lives in California. I'll speak to my accountant friend and ask him to widen the focus of his search to include her. What room's Scarlet in?"

"Why do you want to know?"

"No reason."

I shook my head firmly. "No. You are not breaking into her room and searching for clues. That would be illegal, and the reputation of Victoria-on-Sea can't risk it."

She gave me a bright smile and fluttered her eyelashes. "Pretty please?"

"Bernie. No."

She deflated. "Oh, all right. I'll find another way of uncovering Miss Scarlet's secrets."

Guests came down the stairs, ready for a day on the water, and Bernie and I said no more.

Speak of the devil and she will appear.

But first, Bernie found me a short time later relaxing on my porch, having my coffee and watching the bay come to life before I went up to the tearoom to start that part of my day.

"That was quick," I said.

Bernie leaned on the fence. "Rose didn't have much to report. We decided last night what she'd do today, but she wanted to talk it over again. She's meeting her friends for lunch and will dig for more dirt about Cheryl, Allegra, and Chuck Williams. I must say, the idea of Detective Williams being a young man with . . . romantic inclinations gives me a shiver up my spine."

I laughed.

"Are you going to tell Redmond what we learned from Jean?" Bernie asked.

"I've been thinking it over, and yes, I have to. It's not up to us to decide what's significant in a police investigation and what's not. I'll give her a call when I get to the tearoom. She'll be annoyed that we're interfering in her case, but I'll inform her that I'm simply passing on local gossip that might be of interest." I stood up and called to Éclair. "Are you leaving?" I asked Bernie.

"Yup. I have some calls to make and some . . . other things to do . . . once business opens in the city."

"Do I want to know what other things those might be?"

"No. You do not. But I'm going to tell you, anyway. Gary Powers. He was, if you remember, mighty angry at Tommy Greene on Monday. Angry enough to kill? Who knows? I don't know enough about the man to say. Rose will dig for the local gossip, but I want to see what I can find out about his business affairs. As for his wife, Mayor Powers, I wonder if she has any financial interest in North Augusta Bakery."

"I can't see the mayor being involved in the murder. She might have a shaky marriage, and everyone in town knows it, but she's a popular mayor, and she's considered to be fiercely loyal to the town. Tommy's death brought all his groupies flocking to the area, but the long-term reputation of North Augusta as a family-friendly holiday destination won't be helped by an unsolved murder."

"You never know," Bernie said sagely. "Until you do."

I called to Éclair, put her in the cottage, told her to have a nice day, and walked around the house with Bernie.

Who did we see sitting on the veranda but Scarlet McIntosh. She was alone, her head bent over her phone as her thumbs flew. I made to slip past, but Bernie changed direction and bounded up the steps, calling a cheerful "Good morning, Scarlet."

Scarlet started and put her hand to her chest. "Goodness, you frightened me." She was fully made up, and her hair fell in sleek waves around her shoulders. She wore capri-length white jeans, fashionably shredded, and a white T-shirt under a cropped blue linen jacket. I glanced at her phone as she put it on the table. The screen showed a photograph of Scarlet herself standing on a beach at sunset.

"So sorry," Bernie said. "Lovely day, isn't it?"

"It is. I guess." Her eyes wandered to her phone.

Bernie dropped into the chair on the other side of the small table. "I realize it must be so difficult for you hanging around, waiting to see what happens. On top of the shock of Tommy's death, of course. Were you two close?"

"We were colleagues rather than friends. But . . . I admired him a great deal. He did so much for the welfare of the average low-paid restaurant worker in America. He worked tirelessly on their behalf." The words rolled out of her lipsticked mouth, stilted, rehearsed. Was she grieving the death of a lover? I couldn't tell. If the woman had an ounce of warmth, she'd never shown it to me.

"Lily and I were thinking it would do you good to see the sights of the area," Bernie said.

"We were? I mean, yes, we were thinking just that." I threw Bernie a questioning look. She ignored me.

"Have you been to Cape Cod before?"

"No," Scarlet said.

"Lily, why don't you take Scarlet inside and show her the tourist brochures you keep at the reception desk. Perhaps you can help her organize a whale-watching expedition or a fishing trip or something."

"I don't want—" Scarlet began.

"It's no bother. Is it, Lily?"

"Uh . . . right," I said. "No bother at all."

"Off you go, quickly now. Lily's happy to help, but she has to get to the tearoom soon." Bernie made fluttering gestures with her hands. "Won't take but a couple of minutes. So many wonderful things to see and do."

Scarlet slowly, reluctantly, got to her feet. She reached for the purse on the floor beneath her chair, but Bernie lifted a hand. "I'll wait here and watch your things. Not that there's ever any danger of anything going missing. Not at Victoria-on-Sea. Hurry up, Lily. Don't keep Scarlet waiting."

"I don't want to go whale watching," Scarlet said. "And I certainly don't want to go fishing. I didn't much like the spa I was at the other day. Maybe there's a better one?"

"Let's see what we can find." I ushered her inside.

We soon returned to the veranda, Scarlet's arms laden with tourist brochures she'd shown not the slightest interest in. I hadn't been able to find any for spas.

Bernie leaned back in her chair, eyes closed, the picture of comfortable relaxation. Her eyes fluttered open when she heard the door, and she gave us a bright smile as she leapt to her feet. "All settled? How nice. Have a pleasant day, Scarlet."

Scarlet dropped into her chair, tossed the brochures to one side, and picked up her phone.

Bernie bolted for her car, and I followed. "What on earth was that about? Scarlet's not going to book herself a whale-watching trip or a fishing charter, of all things."

"Not Tommy," Bernie said. "Josh."

"Josh what? Oh, you think she's sleeping with Josh?"

"Yup."

"How do you . . . ? You read her phone."

"Yup. That's why you had to get her out of the way and fast, before the screen locked me out."

"Is that legal?"

"If people don't want other people to read their text messages, they shouldn't leave their phones in a public place, unlocked."

"I don't think it works that way."

"Regardless, it works my way. I had time to quickly scan a string of text messages between her and Josh. Last night he said he'd missed her the night before and would be coming to her room when, and I quote, the coast was clear. She replied she had a headache. The oldest excuse in the book. Various messages of a personal nature, which I won't burden your innocent ears with, all from him to her. Her replies aren't exactly enthusiastic praise of his manly charms, but she isn't telling him to get lost, either. Sunday, shortly after they arrived here, he said he'd missed her and couldn't wait to see her again. Followed by a bunch of pink hearts and other silly emojis. The guy probably thinks using emojis makes him look young. Instead, as I could tell him but won't—"

"I shouldn't ask, plausible deniability and all that, but was there anything between her and Tommy?"

"A week ago Tommy sent her directions to where they were meeting for lunch. Reilly and Claudia were included in the distribution list. I found nothing private between Tommy and Scarlet. Some texts to her from Reilly, but they were updates about where to go and when to be there. One told her to . . . and I paraphrase . . . wipe that scowl off your face before it freezes in place. I didn't have time to read them all. Reilly's most recent message was sent to a long list of people, who are probably the crew, telling them to sit tight until further notice."

"So Scarlet's having an affair with Josh. He's not married, is he? She's not. What's the problem? Why all the secrecy?"

We stood by Bernie's car, keeping our voices low. I could see Simon in the rose garden, bending and straightening as he nurtured the plants. At Tea by the Sea, Cheryl raised the big, colorful umbrellas above the tables, while Marybeth wiped dust and sand and dew away. Two seagulls, arguing by the sounds of it, flew overhead.

"Maybe Scarlet's not a very expressive person," Bernie said. "She's cold enough to me, but then again, I'm not her lover. The tone of her messages to Josh is basically tolerating him and not much more."

"It's the time of #MeToo," I said. "If he's coercing her into a relationship, or even if she's going along with it to further her career, if word got out, the fallout would be heavy."

"It could put an end to the show," Bernie said.

"What a fool. Josh, I mean." I glanced across the yard toward the veranda. Scarlet had returned her attention to her phone. A sudden gust of wind lifted the topmost brochure and blew it over the railing. Scarlet watched it go but made no attempt to catch it. Simon, I thought, would not be pleased at the litter. I was not pleased at the litter.

"Do you think this has anything to do with the death of Tommy Greene?" I asked.

"It might. Josh would have a great deal to lose if word of what he's been up to gets out. Did Tommy threaten to expose him?"

"My take on Tommy, which admittedly isn't worth much, is that he wasn't the threatening type. If he'd wanted to expose Josh, he would have. He would've been fully aware of the potential impact of the story getting in the papers, meaning the cancellation of the show. I wonder . . ."

"What do you wonder?"

"I'm not sure how committed Tommy was to *America Bakes!*" I thought back to the night he and I walked in the gardens and along the bluffs. He'd talked about leaving TV and returning to his cooking roots. If he'd wanted to quit, he could have. He hadn't needed to threaten blackmail. "Detective Redmond needs to hear about this."

"Whatever you do, do not tell her how you know," Bernie said firmly.

It was half past ten when I got to Tea by the Sea. I put my earbuds in and tucked my phone into the pocket of my

shorts while I gathered equipment and ingredients necessary for a day of baking. "This is a private phone call," I
said to Marybeth, who was starting on the sandwiches,
using the fillings Simon had prepared last night, while
Cheryl finished laying the patio tables.

Marybeth rolled her eyes. "I promise I won't listen, seeing as to how we're so far apart. Excuse me, can I get to
the fridge?"

I sucked in my stomach and wiggled a couple of inches
to one side to give Marybeth room, and then I called Detective Redmond.

She answered right away. I could hear the sounds of a
busy office, or maybe a busy coffee shop, in the background. "Good morning, Lily."

"Detective. I've learned one or two things about the . . .
situation surrounding the TV people I thought you might
like to know. If you don't know them already, I mean."

Marybeth leaned so far toward me she was in danger of
toppling over. I turned my back to her and decided to
begin the day's work with a batch of orange scones. Made
with a touch of orange zest and cream rather than the
usual milk, served with marmalade instead of the usual
jam, they were a popular accompaniment to our more expensive royal tea.

"Where are you now?" Redmond asked me.

"At Tea by the Sea."

"Put the kettle on. The coffee in this place is beyond
dreadful." She hung up.

I was putting the orange scones in the oven when the detective arrived. We couldn't talk in the kitchen, not with
Marybeth and Cheryl constantly coming and going, so I
led the way to a small table on the patio. We opened at
eleven, and so far, only a handful of customers were knocking down the gates, trying to get in.

I'd had Redmond to tea before, and I had a pot of tea

steeped and ready, along with a plate of scones (not the special orange ones) and an assortment of sandwiches left over from yesterday. Today I used my second-best china. I'd enjoyed teaching the detective about the traditions around a proper afternoon tea, as well as watching her appreciate my offerings.

"No tarts?" She eyed today's spread.

I started to stand, but she waved me back down. "Just kidding, Lily. This will do. More than do."

I poured the tea, and she added a splash of milk and half a teaspoon of sugar to hers and took a sip. "I like this one. What's it called?"

"English breakfast. One of the most popular teas. As I pulled you away from your morning coffee, I thought you'd appreciate something full bodied."

"Thanks. Okay, what's up?"

"We've learned two things that might be of interest."

"By *we* I assume you mean you and Bernadette Murphy and your grandmother." She sipped her tea. "The very people who were instructed not to get involved but somehow always manage to do so, anyway."

"Uh . . . yes."

"Only because you've helped us in the past did I come out here, Lily. That and for tea and scones, of course. I can't believe what I've been missing all my life." She sliced a scone in half and spread butter and strawberry jam on it and added a dab of clotted cream.

Detective Redmond had automatically taken the seat with her back to the garden wall, so she faced the outdoor room. Behind me I could hear Cheryl welcoming the first of the guests and showing them to their tables. I realized Redmond was watching Cheryl. Then she focused her attention back onto me and said, "What do you have to tell me?"

"First, Josh Henshaw, the director, is sleeping with Scarlet McIntosh, and they are most definitely trying to keep that relationship secret."

Her face didn't react. I couldn't tell if my bombshell came as news to her or not. "How do you know, if it's such a secret?"

"We run a hotel. Like downstairs staff of historical dramas, no secrets are safe from us. Whoever interviewed our housekeeper should have asked better questions. Staff notice things. Lots of things."

"Fair enough." Her face tightened in a flash of anger. "I might mention that to . . . certain of my colleagues. What else?"

"Gary Powers, husband of the mayor, is a half owner of North Augusta Bakery."

"I understand you wanting to tell me the first piece of info, but not the second. Why does it matter?"

"First, Gary got into an argument with Tommy Greene on Monday. He was being difficult, Gary was, and Tommy put him in his place. Did he want to get back at Tommy for the humiliation? We also considered he might have another reason to kill Tommy Greene—to help out the bakery. In the competition, I mean."

"When I last spoke to Josh Henshaw about an hour ago, he was whining about not knowing if there would even be a competition. I'm afraid you're off base there, Lily. No one at the bakery would have wanted *America Bakes!* to cease production."

"Still," I said, "it's a connection."

She finished her scone and reached for an herbed cucumber sandwich.

"Otherwise," I said, "how's the investigation going?"

She lifted one eyebrow.

"Just wondering," I said.

"Early days yet. The autopsy report will be public soon enough. Mr. Greene died somewhere between eleven p.m.

and one a.m., the result of a cerebral hemorrhage caused by a blow to the back of his head."

I thought of my marble rolling pin and regretted taking a big bite of a chicken sandwich.

"You told me you spoke to him around eleven o'clock that night. Is that correct?"

I nodded.

"No one has come forward to say they'd seen him or spoken to him after he left you. His phone records show that he did not make or receive any calls or texts since much earlier that evening. He died almost instantly, where he was found. Meaning in your kitchen. What he was doing in your kitchen at that time of night, and with whom, is the question. It's highly unlikely he would have gone there with a stranger. You still maintain that you can't remember if you locked the door or not?"

"I've been trying to remember, but I simply can't. Sorry."

"We have feelers out to the authorities in Los Angeles, where Greene's been living for the past five years. By all accounts, he was a successful and honest businessman. I've learned to be skeptical. We're also interested in the dynamics of the TV production company and the people who work there."

"Josh and Scarlet were apparently not together on Tuesday night."

"Hotel people really do know things about their guests, don't they?"

"*Apparently* is the important word. We don't know everything that goes on." Jean had said Scarlet hadn't had company that night. She'd also said Scarlet was a slob, but it wasn't entirely beyond the bounds of possibility that she'd tidied up in the morning. "If they were together, then I might have just provided both of them with an alibi."

"I'll speak to them again. They said they hadn't gone

out after returning from dinner. I don't like it when people lie to me, but I have to admit I never actually came out and asked them if they were together at the time in question."

"You think someone involved in the show lured Tommy into Tea by the Sea under the pretext of wanting to talk over a detail of the filming?"

"I think nothing. Not yet." She popped the last of her sandwich into her mouth. "Thank you for this, Lily. The tea as well as the information. I'd like to ask you once again to stay out of it and not discuss what I told you with your grandmother and Bernie, but I fear I'd be wasting my breath."

I gave her a weak smile.

She stood up. Something behind me caught her attention, and her face tightened as her eyes moved across the patio. "Other avenues of investigation are still open, and of particular interest to Detective Williams." She walked away.

I turned in my seat to see Cheryl taking the orders of a table for six behind me. I could tell by the set of Cheryl's shoulders that she was well aware the police officer was walking past her.

The rest of the day passed uneventfully. I fell into my routine of baking, preparing sandwiches, and arranging the food. Cheryl and Marybeth ran in and out of the kitchen, shouting orders, making tea, filling their trays with fine china and attractively displayed treats, returning used dishes, and loading and unloading the dishwasher. They told me every seat was taken and we had a line waiting for tables.

I received no urgent phone calls from either Bernie or Rose with breaking developments, for which I was grateful. I work well in my routine, and I didn't need any "breaking developments" to interrupt the flow.

"Good one." Marybeth put down her load of dishes and pressed her hands into the small of her back and groaned. "I'm dead beat."

I glanced up from the cupcake papers I was filling with vanilla batter and said, "What time is it?"

"Five thirty. We've been closed for half an hour, Lily. The dining room's empty, but a few people are lingering outside over the last of their tea."

"I completely lost track of the time."

Scones and pastry shells for strawberry tarts were cooling on wire racks, as were chocolate chip cookies for the children's tea. Macaron shells had been baked, and the creamy pistachio filling prepared.

Cheryl brought in another load of dishes and started filling the dishwasher.

"What's the reservations book look like for tomorrow?" I asked.

"Overwhelming," she said. "In a good way. We had some weeping Tommy Greene fans and some morbidly curious scene-of-the-crime groupies, but less of them than yesterday. Word of the excellence of this place is spreading by word of mouth, Lily."

"It is," Marybeth said. "One group of women told me they were staying in Chatham, but a friend suggested they come here for afternoon tea. They were glad they did."

I let that sink in for a moment. It felt good—all my hopes and dreams and hard work and the gamble of starting my own restaurant were paying off.

I didn't get to enjoy the feeling for long.

The three of us started at the sound of sirens coming closer. I put down my spoon and the bowl of cupcake batter and went to the window, hoping the sirens were not heading for us.

They were. Two police cruisers, lights flashing, sirens screaming, turned into the driveway and came to a screeching halt outside Tea by the Sea. Doors flew open, and men and women poured out.

"What's happening?" Marybeth said.

A knock at the back door was followed a moment later by the sound of boots moving rapidly through the dining rooms.

Marybeth, Cheryl, and I stared at each other.

Before we could move, the kitchen door flew open, and Detective Chuck Williams burst in, red-faced, tie askew, coffee stain on his shirt, all puffed up with his own importance. A uniformed officer stood behind him, eyes darting around the room, hands resting on her utility belt. Two more officers came into the kitchen from the public area.

Williams stared at us. We stared back. His face was set into serious lines, and the cop behind him wasn't looking at all friendly. The dancing spark in Chuck Williams's dark eyes gave me a very bad feeling.

"Cheryl Dowd Wainwright," he said, "I am arresting you for the murder of Thomas Greene."

Chapter 14

"You've no idea why?" Rose said.

"None. Marybeth went after them, and she said she'd call me when she found out what's happening, but I've heard nothing yet."

"You don't think—"

"I do not," I said firmly. "Cheryl didn't kill Tommy. Notably, Amy Redmond wasn't part of the arresting party. That might be significant. Chuck Williams is impulsive, not to mention lazy. Let's hope it's nothing more than him trying to look as though he's being decisive, and after shouting at her for a while, he'll let Cheryl go."

Rose and I were sitting on the veranda of Victoria-on-Sea. A gin and tonic rested on the table next to her. I'd declined a drink, thinking I might be needed either at the police station or at Cheryl's or Marybeth's house. Éclair peered through the slats of the veranda railing, on guard for squirrels or rabbits daring to invade her territory, and Robert the Bruce snoozed on Rose's lap with one eye open.

Unfortunately, the police had timed their arrival to coincide with B & B guests returning to their rooms after the day's outing to get ready for dinner, and more than a few had lined the veranda to watch what was happening.

Fortunately, it hadn't happened for long. Cheryl was cuffed, bundled out the door, stuffed into the back of the police car, and taken away with a scream of sirens and the squeal of wheels taking the corner too fast, while Marybeth and I were still trying to gather our wits about us.

Rose had attempted to assure her guests there was nothing to be concerned about. "A minor irregularity," she said. No one looked all that assured, but they'd hesitantly continued with their plans.

Bernie's car pulled up, going almost as fast as the police vehicles had earlier, and she leapt out as though she also was taking down a murder suspect. She climbed the steps and dropped into a chair. "Any news?" Éclair wandered over to give her a sniff, and she absentmindedly rubbed the dog's ears. Robbie closed one eye and opened the other.

"No," I said.

"You don't think—"

"No. I do not think."

"Okay."

"Drink, love?" Rose said.

"Sure."

"You know where it is."

Bernie pushed herself to her feet and raised one eyebrow at me. I shook my head, and she went into the house. As she came back, carrying a glass of white wine, Simon's motorcycle turned into the driveway. Instead of heading toward us, it veered off onto Matt Goodwill's property, and I remembered that Simon and Matt had made plans to work together on Matt's house.

"The police didn't say anything about why they were taking Cheryl in?" Bernie asked.

"Not to me. I considered going to the police station to be with Marybeth, but it's up to her to ask for my help, if she wants it."

"Perhaps you should go, anyway," Rose said. "Marybeth has young children. She can't hang around the police station all night."

"Are Josh, Scarlet, and Claudia still in residence?" Bernie asked.

"They are," Rose said. "Josh went into town some time ago, supposedly to meet with Reilly and the crew and talk things over. Scarlet didn't go with him. She called a cab shortly before noon and hasn't returned. As for Claudia . . ." Rose's voice trailed off.

"What about Claudia?" I asked.

"She spends what seems to me to be an inordinate amount of time in her room." Rose dropped her voice to a near whisper, and Bernie and I leaned forward to hear. "It's not my place to tell her she needs to get some fresh air, but it is summer in Cape Cod, and the weather has been perfect these past few days. If she doesn't feel like venturing far, I'd think she'd at least sit outside to catch a breath of air, or go for a short walk."

"Might she be ill?" I asked.

"As you know, love, I don't like to interfere in my guests' stay here, but I was concerned enough to knock on her door earlier. I asked if she needed anything, and she said she was fine."

"Did it sound like she'd been crying?" I asked. "Maybe she's grieving more for Tommy than anyone realizes?"

"Not crying, no, but she was sharp with me. Prior to knocking, I just happened to overhear her talking on the phone." Rose touched her hair with one hand, stroked a purring Robbie with the other, and then picked up her drink and sipped at it.

"Feel like going into town for a burger?" I asked Bernie. "We could go for ice cream after."

"I'm always up for ice cream. Now that you mention it, I'm always up for a burger, too."

"Do you not want to hear what I overheard?" Rose sniffed.

"I'm sure you'll get around to telling us eventually," I said. "No point in dragging it out."

Rose harrumphed. "Claudia's voice is normally in the softer range. She's generally gently spoken and scrupulously polite. I was able to hear clearly through the door because she was almost shouting. I'd say *agitated* is the word."

"What was she agitated about?"

"I don't know who she might have been speaking to, but she was wanting him . . . or her . . . to lend her money."

"Really?"

"*More money* is the phrase she used. She told this person she needs more money and she needs it now. She did not say please."

"That is interesting," I said. "She has to be fairly well off, wouldn't you think, Bernie? With her bestselling cookbooks and her restaurants and *America Bakes!*"

"*Well off* means different things to different people," Bernie said. "Maybe she needs more money so she can buy herself a second yacht."

"She has a yacht?" Rose asked.

"I'm speaking rhetorically. What else did you just happen to overhear her saying?"

"Nothing. It went quiet, and I assumed she'd hung up on this person without saying good-bye. In the old days she would have slammed down the receiver."

"You didn't get the name of the person she was talking to?"

"No. I waited a suitable interval, allowing enough time to pass that it wouldn't seem as though I'd been listening at keyholes—"

"Although you had been doing precisely that," I said.

Rose waggled a bushy gray eyebrow at me. "I knocked and asked if she needed anything. She didn't even open the door, just shouted, 'No.' "

"Perhaps," Bernie said, "we need to expand our inquiries to include Claudia."

"I can ask my Manhattan contacts how her restaurants are doing," I said. "Did you manage to learn anything about Gary Powers today?"

"Nothing of significance. He and the mayor seem to be under the surface exactly what they are on the surface. They own their house outright, they have no major debts, they went on a nice European vacation last year, but nothing out of the ordinary for the financial situation of a dual-income couple with no children. He's an insurance broker, as I told you earlier, and the company appears to be totally on the up-and-up." Bernie frowned, clearly disappointed at not having found ties to organized crime or international terrorist outfits.

"I have not much more to report," Rose said. "I had lunch with my bridge friends, during which I appeared to be trolling for gossip—"

"Nothing *appearing* about it. You were trolling for gossip," I said.

"In the pursuit of the greater good," Rose replied haughtily. "That's different. My friends, however, were keen to dish the common gossip, but nothing new was revealed. The marriage of Susan and Gary is a topic of conversation in all the best card clubs for miles around, but he has never, as far as anyone knows, been in legal trouble. Either for harassing women or financial misdealing. It's believed he bought a share in the bakery in order to help Allegra out. Not that he particularly cares much about her, but Susan insisted. The sisters are, so I've been told, close. They say Susan's the only person in the world Allegra actually likes. And that includes their mother."

"In that case, is there any chance Susan might have killed Tommy if she thought she was helping Allegra and the bakery?" Bernie asked.

"I can't see it," I said. "But I suppose it's possible."

"Anything's possible," Bernie said, "given the right conditions. However, I consider it unlikely. She's the mayor. She's under constant local observation. If she had any, shall we say, psychotic conditions, it would have come out."

"Susan was here on Monday, but not Tuesday," I said. "When Tommy got angry at Marybeth."

"She might have heard about it," Rose said.

"Okay, I'm moving Susan to the bottom of my suspect list," Bernie said. "She's on it, but at the bottom."

"You have a list?" Rose said.

"Of course I do. Don't you?"

"Of course I do."

Bernie put her empty glass on the table. "If that's all, let's go."

"Would you like to come with us, Rose?" I asked. Robbie's ears perked up.

"You two run along," my grandmother said. "I'm rather tired, and I had a late lunch today."

My phone rang, and we all jumped. Marybeth's name appeared on the screen, and I answered quickly. "Marybeth, what's happening? Are you okay?"

"I'm fine." Her voice was thick from crying. "As for what's happening, I don't know. You asked me to check in, so I am. I'm waiting at the police station. I haven't seen Mom yet."

"Do you need me to come down? I can call you if anything happens, if you need to get home to your family."

"Thanks, Lily, but no. My husband's with the kids, and my dad's here with me. I called a lawyer. The only lawyer I know is the guy who handled the buying of our house, but he recommended someone we could use. She's on her way, so I want to be here."

"You will call me right away if you need anything?"

"Thanks. It's not likely Mom will be at work tomorrow. I'll try but—"

"Never mind that." I looked at Bernie. "I have plans for backup."

Bernie pointed to herself and mouthed, "Me?"

"You," I said after I'd hung up, "have a new job starting tomorrow."

"I don't need a job."

"Maybe not, but I need a waitress. Do you think Edna would help out?" I asked Rose.

"If you asked her nicely."

"Give me a sec," I said. I called Edna and explained the situation. Word had traveled, as it does, and she knew Cheryl had been arrested. She said she'd be willing to help me out tomorrow. But, she added, she couldn't promise more than that.

Bernie and I ate cheeseburgers and fries and then joined the line at the candy store on the boardwalk for ice cream. Cones in hand, we walked along the busy pier, watching the sun dip into the bay, boats returning to harbor, and seals playing in the cool waters under the pier. While we'd driven into town and then enjoyed our burgers and fries, we'd managed not to talk about the subject uppermost on our minds, but I couldn't hold back any longer.

"Amy Redmond," I said, "told me she's working with the police in LA investigating Tommy's life and his contacts there. She hinted broadly that Williams's focus lies closer to North Augusta. Meaning, we now know, Cheryl."

"Do you think there's something personal about it?" Bernie asked. "Between Williams and Cheryl, that is, in light of what Rose learned."

"Possibly. I don't think he's a very good cop, and that's no secret, but I don't think he's corrupt, either. He must have some reason for arresting her. Beyond her verbally threatening Tommy in the presence of not only a good number of people but television cameras, too." I remembered Redmond's face when she saw Cheryl earlier in the day. Amy Redmond wasn't ready to count Cheryl out, either.

We reached the end of the pier and stood together, looking over the darkening water.

"Ready to go?" I asked.

"Yeah. I'll drop you off, and then I'll try to find any reason Claudia D'Angelo might be in desperate need of money. *More money* is an interesting way of putting it, don't you agree?"

"I do. Although I can't possibly see what benefit Tommy's death would be to her. Not if *America Bakes!* ends up being canceled because of it."

"People don't always think logically, Lily."

"That's why I like baking. Everything happens as it should. Mix air with eggs, flour, and butter, and cake batter rises. Add yeast to salt, flour, and water and the result is a lovely crusty loaf of good bread. Bake a pie at the right temperature for the right amount of time, and you get a crispy golden crust. Outcomes, if the baker is competent and conditions are right, are guaranteed."

"You lead a boring life, Lily Roberts. Good thing I'm around to provide the occasional jolt of excitement."

"For real excitement, you'll be working in the tearoom tomorrow. Ten o'clock. Don't be late."

"Simon would be glad to help out."

"I know he would, but he's busy enough in the garden. I can't impose."

"He'd do it in a heartbeat, Lily. If you ask him nicely."

I didn't reply.

Bernie increased her pace. "If I'm private detecting tonight and waitressing tomorrow, we'd better get a move on."

We arrived back at Victoria-on-Sea to find two police cars in the driveway. Detectives Williams and Redmond stood on the veranda, facing down a diminutive yet irate Rose, firmly gripping her cane, dressed in her tattered pink dressing gown and fuzzy green slippers, hair sticking out in all directions to resemble a crazed halo. Simon and Matt stood on either side of my grandmother like a couple of bodyguards. Both men were in work clothes of dark T-shirts streaked with sweat and sawdust, well-worn pants, and thick-soled boots.

"What on earth?" Bernie said.

I was out of the car before it had come to a complete halt and took the steps two at a time. "What's going on?"

"I don't need your permission, Mrs. Campbell," Williams said.

"I insist you wait until tomorrow."

"I don't much care what you insist," he said.

Redmond turned to me. "Good. You're here. We need to speak to your guests, and Mrs. Campbell doesn't want them disturbed."

"Speak to them about what?" I asked.

She simply looked at me.

"Are Scarlet and Josh back?" I asked Rose.

"All your guests," Redmond said, "who were here on Tuesday night. Plus, you two," she said to Simon and Matt.

"Us?"

"Were you here after dark on Tuesday night?"

"I don't live on the premises," Simon said.

"That's not what I asked."

He shook his head.

"Me neither," said Matt.

"Ms. Murphy?" Redmond asked Bernie.

"No," Bernie said.

"You three can go, then."

"I'll stay," Bernie said.

"No," Detective Redmond said, "you will not."

"It's okay," I said. "Simon, Matt, thanks for coming over."

"I was leaving Matt's," Simon said, "when I saw this lot drive up. Thought Rose might need some company."

Williams growled. He might have muttered something about arrests for interfering with a police investigation.

The door behind Rose opened, and Josh Henshaw's head popped out. "Everything all right here?"

"Perfectly all right," I said. "The police have a few minor questions about the events of earlier in the week, isn't that right, Detectives? Rose, can you show our guests to the drawing room?"

"If I must," she said.

"You must," I replied.

Matt and Simon stepped aside, and slowly, very, very slowly, they left the veranda to stand with Bernie. I gave Bernie a nod, and then I took Rose's arm and led her into the house.

If the police were here with more questions about Tuesday night, it had to do with the arrest of Cheryl. And I wanted—I needed—to know what that might be.

The two detectives and a uniformed officer followed us. The latter, whose name I knew from previous interactions was LeBlanc, firmly shut the door behind him.

"I need to speak," Williams said, "to all the people who were here on Tuesday night."

Scarlet, dressed in a casual summer dress, stood at the

top of the stairs, watching. One hand rested on the banis-
ter, and her eyes were wide with interest. Josh glanced up
at her, and then he turned back to the police. "Shall I assume this has something to do with the death of Tommy?"

"You may," Williams said. "Everyone gave statements
to us on Wednesday, but in light of recent further developments, I have to speak to you again."

"What sort of developments?" Josh asked. "Have you
arrested someone?"

"We have."

"Who?"

"We'll speak to Mrs. Campbell and Ms. Roberts first."
Redmond glanced up the staircase. "Everyone else, please
wait in the dining room. We won't be long. Mrs. Campbell, if you tell Officer LeBlanc what rooms the guests are
in who were here earlier in the week, he'll ask them to
come down."

"I'd prefer Lily do that," Rose said. "I won't have police
knocking on my bedroom doors."

Redmond looked as though she might argue, but she decided to save her battles with Rose for another day, and
she nodded. Moving about as slowly as she was able, in
some sort of power play with the police, Rose went to the
registration desk and carefully sat down. She fumbled in
her pockets for a few moments and then produced her key
chain. She found the correct key, unlocked the drawer,
took out the registration ledger, and slowly, ever so slowly,
flipped the pages. She peered through her bifocals, took
the glasses off, wiped the lens on the sleeve of her nightgown, and then she readjusted the glasses on her nose.

Redmond cleared her throat, and I said, "We haven't
got all day here, Rose."

"You don't?" my grandmother said. "I do. Here we are.
Mr. and Mrs. Grant in one-oh-two arrived on Friday, and
Ms. and Ms. Sullivan in two-oh-one on Sunday. They are

mother and daughter, I believe. So nice to be able to vacation with your mother, wouldn't you agree, love?"

I didn't bother to answer.

"Ms. D'Angelo is in two-oh-four," Rose said.

I headed down the hall while Redmond said, "Mrs. Campbell, drawing room, please."

Mr. and Mrs. Grant opened their door so quickly, it was obvious they'd been listening to the activity in the hallway. They were both dressed and gave me broad, expectant smiles.

"I am so sorry," I said. "But the police are here with some questions about the events of Tuesday night into Wednesday morning, and they'd like to speak to you. They ask that you wait in the dining room, please."

"Happy to be of help," Mr. Grant said. "Can't say I've ever seen that TV program myself. Not much interested in cooking, you know. I like the end results, though." He chuckled heartily and rubbed his round belly. His wife tittered. They were in their late sixties, with plump, cheerful faces, sparkling eyes, and noses peeling from an excessive amount of sun.

"Thank you," I said.

In the short time I'd been talking to the Grants, the police detectives and Rose had gone into the drawing room, and LeBlanc had followed Josh and Scarlet into the dining room. I ran up the stairs. The TV was blaring from room 201, and I knocked loudly.

"Just a minute," a voice called. The sound died, and the door opened. Two faces, identical but for a difference of about twenty years, peered out at me. Both women were ready for bed. I explained what I needed, and they said they'd be right down.

I knocked at the door of room 204, waited, and knocked again. Finally, the door opened. Claudia D'Angelo wore a baggy T-shirt and equally baggy Bermuda shorts. Her face was clear of makeup, and her hair tied roughly at the back of her head. Her eyes were tinged red, and I thought how much older she looked than she did on TV, or even how she had at breakfast this morning.

"What do you want?" she snapped at me.

Startled at the tone, I took a step back. "I'm sorry to bother you, but the police are downstairs."

"So?"

"They have more questions about Tuesday night."

"I'm busy." She half turned and glanced back into her room. Room 204 was our nicest one, with a king-sized bed and a small, comfortable seating area. It had a view over the bay and a private balcony with a lounge chair and low table. The bed was made, and the pillows untouched. Her iPad sat on the desk, and a chair was pulled up to it. A sleeveless, puffy pink shell was draped over the back of the chair. The screen flickered, and I assumed she'd been watching a video. *An uncomfortable way*, I thought, *to watch a program.*

"I don't think the police will care if you're busy," I said.

"Ten minutes." The doyenne of American baking shut the door in my face.

When I got downstairs, I went into the drawing room. Rose had taken her favorite wingback chair, and Robbie was curled on her lap, staring malevolently at the police. "Here you are, love," Rose said to me. "I was explaining to Inspector Williams—"

"Detective," he mumbled under his breath.

"That it is my custom to turn out my light around ten o'clock. I can't account precisely for my movements last Tuesday, as unlike in days of old, I hadn't been watching a regularly scheduled program on the telly, so I couldn't confirm precisely what time it ended. I was watching *Death in Paradise*, season five, not one of the best, in my opinion. I switched off the telly when it was over and read in bed for about half an hour. I must have turned out the light around ten thirty, but I cannot be positive about the time. I did not go out again, and I didn't so much as glance out the window."

"Lily?" Redmond said. "Do you have anything more to add to your original statement about Tuesday night?"

Redmond had told me the autopsy reported that Tommy had died between eleven p.m. on Tuesday and one a.m. Wednesday. I assumed these questions were a further attempt to place his movements, and anyone who might have been with him, around that time. "No. I told you I spoke to him around eleven, but I didn't see him after that."

"Did you see anyone, anyone at all, on the property around that time?" she asked.

"No. I said good night to him and went to my own cottage and then to bed."

"Neither of you saw anyone other than Greene on the property after, say, ten o'clock?"

"No," I said.

"No," Rose said.

"Thank you," Williams said. "That'll be all."

I hadn't taken a seat. I held out my hand and helped Rose to stand. Robbie jumped onto the floor and hissed at Detective Williams.

"Do pardon my cat, Inspector," Rose said as she made her way out of the room. "He likes most people."

The prospective witnesses were gathered in the dining room, watched over by the keen eye of Officer LeBlanc when we entered.

Death in Paradise, I thought, might be an appropriate comparison. Outside, darkness had settled. The French doors thrown open to the hot night air and the sound of the sea crashing against the rocks on the shore; the warm room; the ever-alert uniformed officer standing next to, but not leaning against, the wall, feet apart, shoulders straight, as though on guard in case one of them would make a break for it any minute now. Josh and Scarlet, going to great lengths to ignore each other from their separate tables, both trying hard to appear so dreadfully bored. The Grants and the Sullivans, by contrast, perched eagerly on the edge of their seats, wanting their chance to be of help to the police.

And the missing suspect.

"Where's Claudia D'Angelo?" Redmond said.

Josh shrugged.

Scarlet shook her head. "Haven't seen her for hours. Come to think of it, I haven't seen her for days. Has anyone checked that she's still alive?" Scarlet must have seen our faces, because she added quickly, "Sorry. Bad joke."

"I told her you were waiting for her," I said. "She . . . uh . . . said she was busy."

Redmond turned to LeBlanc. "Room two-oh-four. Tell her to get down here now."

He left. Scarlet's mouth formed a small O, and her eyes danced with amusement. No love lost between the two female judges of *America Bakes!*, I guessed.

"Ms. McIntosh, Mr. Henshaw, come with me, if you please," Redmond said.

"When do you want to talk to us?" the elder Ms. Sullivan asked. "It's getting late, and we have to be up early to go whale watching tomorrow."

"I appreciate you waiting patiently down here, ma'am. We won't be long."

"We don't mind," the younger Ms. Sullivan said. "It's okay, Mom. We have to wait our turn."

"I suppose you're right, dear," her mother said.

Redmond gestured to Josh and Scarlet to precede her. As they left, I heard two sets of footsteps descending the stairs, one treading in heavy boots, the other moving lightly in slippers.

"How nice of you to join us, Ms. D'Angelo. Finally," Redmond said.

"I'll have you know I was on an extremely important business call," Claudia sniffed. "I can't drop everything to come running when summoned. I told you all I know about Tommy and his movements that day, and I have nothing to add."

"Why don't I be the judge of that?" Redmond said as their voices drifted away.

I'd have loved to listen in from the secret room, but Redmond had not shut the door behind her, and Officer LeBlanc had taken a new position next to the door. If he happened to glance out when I was slipping into the linen closet, he'd see me.

"You can go to your room, Rose," I said. "I'll stay here until the police are finished, and lock up after them."

"Thank you, love. I will. I'm feeling quite tired all of a sudden."

I walked with her into the hallway. "Why do you wind him up like that?" I said in a low voice.

"Wind whom up?"

"Don't play the innocent. Detective Williams."

"Whyever not? He's a pompous fool, and it amuses me."

"The death of Tommy Greene is not a laughing matter, Rose. I might not like Detective Williams, either, but I respect the job he has to do and the authority he represents."

"You're right, love. As you usually are. I apologize. It's just that poor Detective Williams is such an easy target, one can't resist."

"You've been watching too much *Death in Paradise*."

She smiled at me and said good night. Robbie ran down the hallway ahead of her as she and her pink cane tapped their way to her rooms. I love my grandmother so very much, but I have to admit she isn't always the most sensible of women. Or the easiest to live with. I gave my head a shake and returned to the dining room.

The younger Ms. Sullivan was chatting to Officer LeBlanc. She was in her late twenties, tall and slightly plump, pretty in a well-scrubbed, corn-fed way, long hair streaked by the sun, and a light tan on her face. He was about the same age, he did not wear a wedding ring, and he was smiling back at her.

"Great place to live," he said. "Although we sure get busy in the summertime with all you fun-loving tourists."

She cocked her head to one side. "Fun loving, that's me. Although"—she jerked one shoulder to indicate the woman across the room—"I am on vacation with my mom."

"That's nice. That you and your mom are close, I mean."

They smiled at each other some more. He broke away first and nodded at me. "Everything okay, Ms. Roberts?"

"Fine, thank you." I should be serving my guests coffee and whatever was left of the breakfast baking, but I was reluctant to leave the room in case someone said something significant. Deep in my pocket, my phone was vibrating with enough energy to cause a small tsunami. I'd glanced at it earlier, to see desperate pleas from Bernie, wanting to know what was going on.

Ms. Sullivan the younger said, "This week's my birthday present from my mom."

"Happy birthday," Officer LeBlanc said. "That's a nice present. This place is one of the best around."

"One of the most expensive, anyway," she said. "Mom wanted to come here because of the gardens. She's a keen gardener. I don't do much myself—I don't have the time—but I like walking in a garden."

I'd decided to see if I could find some cookies or leftover muffins to offer when Ms. Sullivan gasped and her face

froze as she remembered something. "Goodness. I'd totally forgotten. Do you think your boss will want to know
about the walk I had in the garden Tuesday night?"

LeBlanc, I decided, was no fool. The casual flirtation
was wiped from his face in a flash, and he was all business.
"Walk? Tuesday? When?"

"Around eleven." She dropped her voice. "I had way
too much wine at dinner, so I fell asleep as soon as we got
to our room. My mom snores like a freight train, and it
woke me up. You know what it's like when you get to
sleep really fast and then wake up. It's hard to get back to
sleep. So I got up and went for a walk to enjoy the air and
hoped Mom would stop snoring. It was a clear night, and
the moon was really bright. I went around to the front to
see the flowers in the moonlight, and I saw . . . someone.
In the yard, I mean."

"You saw someone? A man? A woman? Had you earlier
seen the man who died? Might it have been him?"

"Not a man. It was a woman. I am so sorry. Is that important? I went to bed right after and totally forgot until
now. I didn't see her face, but she was short and sort of . . .
chubby." She turned to me. "Mom and I'd gone to your
tearoom on Sunday for tea. It was super nice. I can't be
positive, but the woman I saw that night might have been
one of your waitresses. The one who's about my mom's age."

Chapter 15

"And what does Cheryl have to say about that?" Bernie asked.

"She insists it wasn't her. She admits she couldn't sleep, so she went for a drive, but she didn't come anywhere near here."

"So no alibi and no real reason to explain why she was out that late."

"No."

We were in the kitchen of Tea by the Sea, getting ready for another day of feeding the famished hordes of the Outer Cape. My mind was, to say the least, not on food. Officer LeBlanc had called Redmond and Williams out of their interview with Josh, Scarlet, and Claudia and had huddled in a corner with them, whispering. Whereupon Ms. Sullivan the younger, who I'd finally learned was named Robyn, had been bundled into the drawing room. She emerged several minutes later, wide-eyed, looking very pleased with herself, practically bubbling with her own importance. Officer LeBlanc had given her a huge smile and a thumbs-up, and she'd blushed. I wondered if he'd also given her his phone number.

Muttering darkly about suing the police for harassment, Claudia went upstairs, followed by Josh and Scarlet. I couldn't help but notice the jerk of Josh's head toward the younger woman and the firm shake of hers in return. The detectives didn't even bother to take the Grants into the drawing room for a private interview, just asked if they had anything to add to their original statements. On being told no, the police left in a great hurry, without telling me where they were going. I assumed they were heading for a confrontation with Cheryl, and I was right. Marybeth called to tell me she and her mother wouldn't be in to work today. Cheryl was being held over, and Marybeth was in no fit state to be handling hot liquids and being polite to customers. Marybeth told me what I already knew, but added that her mother firmly denied being anywhere in the vicinity of Victoria-on-Sea late Tuesday night.

"I'm sorry," Edna said, "but Frank can't hold the story back. Front page of today's paper will say that Cheryl's been arrested for the murder of Tommy Greene."

"Do you think . . . ?" I began.

"No," Edna replied. "I do not. I don't know Cheryl well, but I do know her. She might have been angry enough to bash Tommy over the head when he insulted Marybeth, but not hours later. I admit, it looks mighty bad for her. She told the police originally that she hadn't gone out again after getting home from work. Lying to the police is always a mistake. They canvassed her neighborhood and found someone who claims to have seen Cheryl tear out of her driveway, as though she was in a big hurry, around ten thirty. He, the neighbor, is confident of the time as it was his usual time to walk his dog. He also says he wouldn't have paid any attention except Cheryl was going far too fast for their quiet residential street, so fast she almost took out the garbage can on the curb waiting for pickup. The police then began looking for evidence that she'd come here that night. They found it—a witness who says she saw Cheryl at Victoria-on-Sea not long before Tommy Greene died."

Edna had come in from setting the patio tables, and Bernie was making sandwiches, while I mixed the dough for the day's first batch of scones. I'd given Bernie the binder containing my recipes, complete with pictures illustrating the appearance of the final product.

"Circumstantial evidence," Bernie said as she sliced the delicate salmon sandwiches into pinwheels.

"Circumstantial evidence can be enough for a conviction," Edna said. "If you want my opinion—"

"And we do," I said.

"Chuck Williams will focus all his attention on Cheryl because that's the easiest route to a trial and conviction. Amy will want to keep digging, but she won't be able to. Chuck's her superior, and he's the one who has the chief's ear. Not her. She'll be told to drop it, while Chuck works on building their case."

"You mean it's up to us to keep digging, if Amy Redmond can't," Bernie said.

Edna said nothing. She loaded her tray with another set of linens and cutlery and left the kitchen.

"My friend in LA sent me two pieces of information last night." Bernie popped a freshly made sandwich into her mouth.

"Don't eat up all my profits," I said.

"We haven't yet discussed the important matter of my wages for a hard day's work."

"Help yourself to another sandwich." It was nice, beyond nice, of Bernie and Edna to help out in the tearoom today, but neither of them was a full-time waitress, nor did they want to be. One day's work, maybe two at the most, would be the best I could fairly ask of them. Meaning if Cheryl never came back to work and Marybeth had to take time off, I'd be frantic to hire more staff. As the season had already begun, that wasn't going to be easy.

"What did he have to say?" I folded the thick square of dough several times prior to slicing the circles with my cutter.

"CookingTV's in serious financial trouble. Their latest show, which was going to be the next big thing, involved cooks cooking under pressure. Not only time pressure, as most shows have, but things like equipment deliberately sabotaged, ingredients being spoiled, the hosts interfering with the cooking process. Even an exploding oven."

I froze in the act of laying the scones on the prewarmed baking sheet and stared at Bernie. "That sounds horrible!"

"It does. So horrible, the network got cold feet and pulled the plug on the show. They wouldn't even agree to toning it down a fraction. Outright cancellation. The cooks had been organized, the sets created, the hosts and judges hired. The judges were big names, too, so they didn't come cheap. They're suing CookingTV."

"How much financial interest does Josh have in CookingTV?"

"That I can't find out. More than zero is all I know."

"So he might be in financial difficulties. Meaning he needs *America Bakes!* to continue being a success."

"Right. Unless we can find out for sure, and I have absolutely no idea how we can do that, that he feared Tommy was going to reveal details of his affair with Scarlet, I suggest we move Josh down to the bottom of our list of suspects."

"The famous list."

"I discovered something else," Bernie said, "but once again, I can't see this person rubbing out Tommy."

"Who? What?"

"Claudia's latest cookbook was a flop. A huge flop. A spectacular flop. I didn't even have to use my contacts to find that out. I checked the stats on Amazon and other booksellers and the bestseller lists. It was supposed to be a big book—I found tons of promo for it leading up to its release date. Tons of promo, meaning the publisher splashed out the big bucks. And . . . flop. Such a flop it seems to have dragged sales of her older books down with it, when a new book should increase sales of the backlist."

"Why? Claudia's a big thing in the world of American baking. I have some of her books myself."

"Did you buy the newest one?"

"No."

"The words used in the reviews were *stodgy food, old-fashioned, out-of-date, repetitive,* and *unimaginative.* The review I liked best said the reviewer was surprised not to find a recipe for Jell-O salad made with canned pineapple."

"Ouch."

"Ouch indeed. Some of the reviews were down and out nasty, suggesting that certain people need to know when it's time to retire."

"We know Claudia needs money. *More money.* I guess we know why. Again, no reason to kill Tommy Greene."

"No reason we know of," Bernie said.

Edna came into the kitchen. "Eleven o'clock. Showtime. The first table has arrived, and cars are pulling up. You going to be okay, Bernie?"

"Probably not," Bernie said.

"Now, remember," I said, "if you think you can't manage, don't fill all the tables. If you're getting behind, explain there's a slight delay. People don't mind waiting, as long as they're told what's going on. I hope Frank's story's not going to mention where Cheryl works, is it?"

"Unlikely," Edna said. "It's not relevant. Not yet, anyway."

Bernie took off her hairnet, retied her hair, smoothed

her apron over her hips, said, " 'Once more unto the breach, dear friends,' " and sailed out of the kitchen.

Edna rolled her eyes, gave me a wink, and followed.

We worked steadily all afternoon. Edna was smoothly efficient, and if Bernie stumbled or made the odd mistake, they were cheerful and apologetic, and I heard no complaints. I was taking a short, very short, break to make myself a cup of Creamy Earl Grey while the shells for the latest batch of pistachio macarons dried when my phone dinged to tell me I had a text message. As I was having a break, I checked it. It was Alicia, one of my restaurant friends in New York City. I read quickly:

You were asking about Tommy G. The great Claudia D'A's involved in that show. Did you know she doesn't own her restaurants anymore? Sold them all about a year ago. Rock-bottom prices. Text if you want more.

I did want more.

Me: **Rock bottom? Why?**

Alicia: **Needed money ASAP. Bad time to sell. Rumor says she didn't have time to wait.**

Me: **Do we know why she needed money?**

Alicia: **Gambling habit, rumor says. Too much time overseeing Las Vegas restaurant.** *[Money emoji]*

Me: **Thx.**

Alicia: **Next time you're in NYC, drinks on you.**

Me: *[Smiley face emoji]*

I sipped my tea and thought. If Claudia had lost her money gambling, to the extent she'd had to sell her restaurants, and she was still in need of money—*more money*—that might mean she had debts she couldn't pay. Organized crime, or so I've been told, has a presence in Las Vegas. It certainly has a presence in the world of gambling. Did Claudia owe so much money to the mob, she had to kill to pay it off?

Why would the mob want to kill Tommy Greene?

I thought back to last night when I'd knocked on Claudia's door. She'd been sitting in front of her iPad. She'd been blurry eyed and red faced and "too busy" to come downstairs and talk to the police. I hadn't deliberately looked at the screen, but I'd seen bright colors and symbols. Rose had previously commented that Claudia spent all day in her room.

Claudia was engaging in online gambling, and I'd be willing to bet she had an out-of-control habit. She'd sold her restaurants, her latest book was a flop, she was begging people for money, and yet she was still gambling.

Had Tommy known about it? Had he threatened to expose her? Had she killed him to keep her secret, secret?

I put down my teacup and took a step toward the door to the restaurant, intending to tell Bernie what I'd learned. Then I remembered Bernie was working. Yes, she was working for me, but I needed her to keep working.

It would keep until the end of the day.

The end of the day didn't arrive fast enough. At quarter to five, Edna came into the kitchen. "You have a customer."

"I hope I have lots of customers. I did have lots of customers. It's been a good day, and you and Bernie have been outstanding."

"This one you might not want. Allegra Griffin's here. She's on her own. She's taken a seat at a table for four and ordered a cream tea. She asked if she could have coffee instead of tea."

"You said no, I hope."

"I said yes, Lily, as per your instructions."

Hard as it is for me to believe, some people don't care for tea. Why they'd come to a tearoom is beyond me, but we do get the occasional reluctant guest tagging along with their friends, so we keep coffee, as well as iced tea and lemonade, on hand.

"All right," I grumbled. "If we must."

"She's asked to speak with you. If you're free, she said. 'Not very busy in here, is it?' she added."

"Like her place is busy at five. Come to think of it, they close at four."

"Irrelevant, Lily."

Bernie carried in a tray laden with used china and crumpled napkins and one single miniature coconut cupcake. She put down the tray and popped the cupcake into her mouth. "I thought I saw Allegra from the bakery sitting outside. Surely my eyes have deceived me?"

"Sadly, no."

"Chin up." Edna put a small pot of coffee on and began laying out the cream tea: two scones served with butter, jam, and clotted cream. "She might have seen the light and is here to compliment you on the quality of your food."

I harrumphed.

"She threw us out of her place," Bernie said. "Are you going to return the favor and show her the door, Lily?"

"The thought did cross my mind," I admitted. "But no. I can be friendly." I bared my teeth in the same manner Éclair does when Robert the Bruce swipes at her tail.

Bernie and Edna raised their eyebrows at each other. I ignored them, took off my apron and my hairnet, retied my hair, and sailed into the garden to greet my guest.

The tearoom closes at five, and only a scattering of tables in the restaurant and on the patio were occupied. Allegra sat in the center of the patio, under the shade of the old oak, the chipped, cracked, and faded teacups clinking cheerfully overhead in the light breeze. Allegra herself looked almost cheerful when she saw me approaching.

"Good afternoon," I said. "Welcome. Edna said you wanted to speak with me."

Edna arrived with the platter of scones and accompaniments, and Bernie brought a mug of coffee. They put the things on the table, but Allegra didn't say thank you. Instead, she said, "Surprised to see you here, Edna. Although perhaps I shouldn't be. Times are hard for the newspaper business, I hear, and I guess you're happy to get the extra income. I don't suppose serving breakfast in a B & B pays much."

"I'm always happy to help out when needed," Edna replied with a smile. "Everyone in North Augusta benefits when a locally owned business does well, don't you agree?"

"Edna's working here today," I said, "as a favor to me, because I'm temporarily short of staff."

"Excuse me, miss," a woman called. "Could we have more hot water in our teapot, please?"

Edna slipped away, but Bernie remained standing beside and slightly behind me. Allegra eyed her.

"Another temporary replacement?"

"I'm researching a book," Bernie said. "I'm getting into the mood of being one of the working classes. This place isn't quite right, though. In my book the boss is a mean-tempered tyrant cheating her employees and threatening her competition. How about I put in a day's work at your place? I won't charge more than double minimum wage."

Allegra's eyes narrowed. I shifted my foot and bumped Bernie's, telling her to behave.

Bernie edged her foot away, telling me she had no intention of behaving.

"I'm not surprised you're short of staff," Allegra said. "Don't make the mistake of thinking this is a temporary situation. I doubt Cheryl will be coming back, and her daughter, poor Marybeth, won't be good for much, not with the stress of the trial and then prison time for her mother. Lawyers are dreadfully expensive, aren't they?"

Her eyes glimmered with malice. She paid no attention to her coffee and scones.

"What are you saying?" I asked. "Not that it's any of your business, but I'm confident the police will soon realize their mistake." I was confident of nothing of the sort, but I felt compelled to offer a retort.

"I'm saying you're the one who made a mistake, a bad one, by hiring that Cheryl Dowd and her stupid daughter. You came here and set up your silly little tearoom." She waved her right hand in the air, taking in the patio, the tinkling teacups, the old stone building, the happy customers. "Without so much as bothering to do due diligence into the community."

Four laughing women came out of the restaurant. They called to us, "That was great! Thanks so much!" as they let themselves through the gate.

"Lily did plenty of due diligence." Bernie was getting angry. I could tell by the way she bit off every word, but she kept her voice low, so as not to disturb the people lingering over the last of their tea. "I know because I helped her. Which makes me wonder why you care. I checked out what might be the nearest competition and found none. Your place isn't directly competitive with this tearoom and, as Lily and I believe, successful businesses are good for everyone in the community."

"Successful businesses, sure, but how long is this place going to be successful? That's what I'd like to know. You don't have the staff to keep going for the rest of the summer."

"Lily has me," Bernie said.

Allegra's expression showed what she thought of that.

"You've made your point," I said. "If you're not going to enjoy my baking, please leave. We're closing soon."

Allegra stood up, scones and coffee forgotten. "That Cheryl Dowd is poison. I could have warned you about her."

Allegra's considerably shorter than I am, not much more than five feet four, and I was glad of it as I tried to stare her down. I felt the blood rushing to my face and my fists clenching. I was conscious of the Warrior Princess standing next to me, powerful and steadfast, like a bodyguard. "I want to live and work in this community and get on with everyone, and my grandmother does also. We're not here to make enemies, but if you want to make yourself one, so be it."

"Enemies? I said nothing about enemies. I came here today to express my sympathy for your situation. Not your fault, but you should have taken more care in the hiring of employees." She started to walk away.

"Twenty dollars, please," Bernie said.

"What?"

"The cream tea with coffee is twenty dollars. Nineteen ninety-five, plus tax, but I'll let that go. You didn't eat your food, but that's not our problem. Twenty dollars." Bernie held out her hand.

Allegra stared at her. Bernie's hand remained perfectly steady.

Allegra's nerve broke first; she fumbled in her purse, found two ten-dollar bills, and slapped them onto the table. "Outrageous price for a couple of dry biscuits and bad coffee." She walked away, her back and shoulders stiff with anger.

A gust of wind lifted the money off the table, and Bernie snatched the bills before they could escape. She stuffed them into the little bag tied around her waist. "What a perfectly horrid woman. Why do you suppose she came here? Not for scones, that's for sure."

"To gloat," I answered. "She can't go down to the police station and taunt Cheryl through the bars, as though in some old-time western movie, so she had to find the next best place. I'm thinking that when Cheryl does get out of jail, Allegra's hoping she's poisoned me against her and I won't have her back."

"Instead, she did the opposite."

"As that sort of maliciousness often does. Her visit might have accomplished something else, though."

"What?"

"Tell me quickly, how would you describe Cheryl physically? Don't stop to think about it."

"Middle aged. Dyed hair. Short and overweight."

"And how would you describe Allegra? Again, quickly."

"Middle aged. Dyed hair. Short and overweight. You're thinking Allegra might have been in the garden on Tuesday night and the guest mistook her for Cheryl."

Allegra looked nothing at all like Cheryl, but in the dark, at night, from a distance? Might it have been Allegra wandering in our garden on Tuesday, not Cheryl?

"Robyn Sullivan had met Cheryl, but probably not Allegra," I said. "She'd met Cheryl here on the property, so the connection would be in her subconscious. Yes, it's possible."

"Why would Allegra be poking around at night?"

"Who knows, but we can't dismiss the possibility. Did she come to talk to Tommy Greene? Had she seen Cheryl driving around and decided to make mischief at Tea by the Sea, and instead she encountered Tommy out for a late-night walk?"

"Murdering a man is more than mischief."

"Who knows how far her anger at Cheryl might take her."

"What are you going to do?"

Only two tables on the patio were still occupied, and the last of the customers were leaving the dining rooms. "I have to call Marybeth. She needs to know that Allegra's intent on stirring the pot. And then I'll bake."

"Because," Bernie said, "it's what you do best."

* * *

"I'm so sorry that happened," Marybeth said over the phone.

"Not your fault. I wanted you to know, that's all."

"Thanks." Her voice sounded tired. "I'm glad you called. I intend to come into work tomorrow."

"If you need more time . . ."

"There's not a lot I can do. Dad and I had a meeting earlier with Mom's lawyer, and she seems confident that the testimony of the woman who says she saw Mom in the garden on Tuesday night is too nebulous. She couldn't really describe Mom, more like a general impression of a woman, and she named Mom because she'd seen her earlier. On further questioning, she admitted she might have been mistaken. Victoria-on-Sea is private property, but it is open to paying guests, and any one of those guests might have gone for a nightly stroll. The lawyer pointed out, quite forcefully, that Robyn Sullivan herself was enjoying a walk. The lawyer's going to move for Mom to be released tonight."

"That's great." I let out a sigh of relief. Not only at the prospect of Cheryl getting out of jail, but also because it took a burden off me. I'd been wondering if I should call Detective Redmond with my suspicions about Allegra. I had not the slightest proof that Allegra had been lurking about the garden and then murdered Tommy Greene. Redmond was, I thought perhaps optimistically, becoming less wary of me and my ideas, but I didn't want to push her patience, particularly if all I had was speculation and a feeling about a woman I didn't like.

"In the meantime," Marybeth said, "I can try to find a replacement."

"A replacement for what?"

"A replacement for Mom. Temporary, of course. One of my cousins is in law school in Boston, and she's come here to be with Dad and offer any advice she can. Law school's not exactly cheap, so she might be willing to help out at the tearoom. She's waitressed before."

I glanced across the kitchen at Bernie, unloading the dishwasher. Her face was flushed, her hairnet askew, her apron dotted with chocolate fingerprints. One of my big wooden spoons slipped between her fingers and hit the floor with a clatter.

"I need her," I said.

Chapter 16

Simon popped into the kitchen to say he'd give me a hand with tonight's baking, if I needed it, although he'd earlier arranged to help with the work at Matt's house.

"I'm fine," I said, meaning it. "My two makeshift waitresses turned out to be surprisingly competent, and I wasn't needed out front."

"Surprisingly?" Bernie said.

"I had no doubts about Edna."

Bernie muttered under her breath. Simon left, chuckling. Edna had hung up her apron, told me she enjoyed the day—although her old bones were glad she wouldn't be needed again tomorrow—and waved a cheery good-bye, saying she'd see me in the B & B in the morning.

Bernie helped herself to one of the scones rejected by Allegra, spread it lavishly with butter and strawberry jam (made by Edna herself), added a dollop of clotted cream, and took a huge bite. "I feel that we should be doing more, but at this point, I don't know what else we can do."

"Maybe nothing. If the police let Cheryl go, that's good enough for me."

"If the police don't have enough evidence to take her to court, the stigma will hang over her all her life. In a small town like this one . . ."

"Chances are good someone followed Tommy here to North Augusta. If so, that someone went back to wherever they came from long ago."

"I hate not knowing what happened," she said.

"As do I, but not all questions in life get answered. I wonder when the TV bosses are going to decide whether or not to continue with the show. Surely, the indecision itself is costing them money."

"Money we know they can't afford to waste. If you don't need me anymore . . ."

"I don't. You've been a marvel. Thanks. I'm going to put a few more hours of baking in, get ready for tomorrow."

"I'll try to find out more about Allegra, particularly if she's ever been in legal trouble. I'll also try to dig a bit deeper into the affairs of CookingTV and their backers, as well as Tommy himself. I haven't spent a lot of time trawling the celebrity gossip forums, but maybe I should. Everyone says he was a happily married family man, but that might not be true."

"I got that impression talking to him."

"You never know."

We exchanged a giant hug, and then Bernie left.

I finished around nine, pleased with the results of my labors. I had plenty of baking in the freezer and fridge to get us through most of the day tomorrow as well as premade sandwiches and sandwich fillings. I hung up my apron and switched off the lights. Last of all, I confirmed more than once that the doors were locked before I left.

The Lexus SUV drove past me as I walked up the driveway. It parked in the guest lot. Reilly was driving, and he got out, along with Josh, Claudia, and Scarlet.

Scarlet wore a white summer dress with yellow trim on the hem, a yellow jacket, and sandals with killer heels and yellow ribbons that wound their way up her calves. Claudia's outfit was plainer but far more sophisticated: black pants and a gray sweater worn under a puffy pink vest as protection against the night chill.

"I am so tired of this," Scarlet said. "If we're not going to be filming, I want to go home."

"This must be the first time ever I've agreed with Scarlet," Claudia said. "This place is a total bore." She saw me join them and added, "Although some people seem to like it."

Scarlet headed for the stairs. "Good night," she called, her voice sharp and pitched to carry. "I'll see you in the morning, Josh."

His face tightened as he got the message. I got it also: Scarlet was finished with Josh.

Claudia followed the younger and much taller woman into the house. I stared after them, frozen in my tracks.

Claudia was substantially shorter than Scarlet and me, about five feet four at a guess. The same height as Cheryl and Allegra. Those women were plump, and Claudia was not, but the puffy vest added bulk to her thin frame. If she'd been out at night, she might well have been wearing that vest, or something similar, against the cool night breezes. Might it have been Claudia, not Cheryl or Allegra, whom Robyn Sullivan saw in the garden the night Tommy Greene died?

"Can I help you with something, Lily?" Reilly asked me.

I shook the thought out of my head. "No, nothing. I'm assuming you have no news."

Reilly's face twisted, and Josh said, "Not yet. I hear the

police have released that woman they arrested, your waitress."

"I'm glad to hear it," I said.

"It might be good news for you," Reilly said, "but it's not for us. The uncertainty's making the network nervous."

"It's good for Cheryl," I said.

"Whatever," Reilly said. Josh had started to climb the steps, but Reilly called after him, "Hold up. We haven't finished what we were talking about."

"I'm finished with it. I'm tired."

"Well, I'm not. Not finished, and not tired. Let's go inside and talk." He glanced at me. "Is that okay, Lily?"

"Of course," I said. "Josh is a guest here. You can use our drawing room, if you like."

"Thanks." He caught up with Josh and marched into the house. Josh reluctantly followed. The lights in the hall had been turned down, and all was quiet. I waited at least thirty seconds after Reilly shut the door to the drawing room before I slipped into the linen closet.

It's a tricky situation, opening your home to paying guests. They are paying and thus have the expectation of privacy, but it's still your home, and thus what goes on in it is your concern. If Reilly wanted to talk to Josh about family matters or *America Bakes!*, that wasn't any of my business. But Tommy Greene had been murdered on my grandmother's property and one of my employees had been arrested, and as far as I was concerned, that made it my business. Because of that I felt no guilt at listening into their conversation.

"We've gone over this enough," Josh was saying as I settled myself into the chair.

"I intend to go over it again," Reilly said. "But before we do, I couldn't help but notice a frosty air between you and Scarlet. Frosty as in she's freezing you out."

"So? She's a spoiled brat. She changes her mood with the wind. Tonight she decided to make nice with Claudia. That won't last."

"You assured me there'd be no more, Dad."

I didn't catch Josh's reply.

"Do I have to be your babysitter? I shoulda known better than to allow you to stay in this place with her."

"Mind your own business, Reilly."

"The show's my business, and thus the talent's my business, too."

"If there still is a show."

"There will be. I'll make sure of that. Just keep out of it, okay? I've made some recommendations on how we can continue, and the network seems to like them. We'll finish this segment, make it a tribute to Tommy. His fans'll love that."

"That's in exceptionally bad taste, Reilly. Not only that, but a dumb move. People aren't fools. They know when their emotions are being manipulated."

"Good thing neither I nor the network cares what you think anymore."

I sat up straighter in my chair. Wasn't Josh the director of the show?

Reilly paced the room as he talked. "You think our audience won't believe what they want to believe? They want to believe we're honoring Tommy because he was such a nice guy. We'll finish filming the segment with the pretty blonde and her fancy sandwiches."

I assumed that meant me.

"We'll show the scenes where Tommy talks to the guests who were critical of the place, and then Tommy himself saying the icing on the cupcakes is far too sweet, too American, for his taste. And then the clumsy waitress and Tommy giving her what for."

"He tripped her," Josh said. "I told you not to have him do that, but—"

"But nothing. His fans love that he doesn't take any nonsense from anyone. They'll love it even more now that he's dead. And then we'll shoot Scarlet and Claudia at the bakery in town. We'll go through the usual routine, but all the time they can blather on about how much Tommy would have preferred that place to the fancy tearoom, and then they'll choose the fat woman at the bakery to go on to the next round."

"No." Josh's voice was sharp with anger. "I told you and I told Tommy I didn't want him deliberately upsetting the waitress, but you two went ahead with it, anyway."

I was momentarily confused. The day of filming, I'd seen Reilly and Josh arguing. Josh had appeared to come out the winner, and Reilly'd gone away angry. After Tommy tripped Marybeth, I'd assumed Josh had wanted that to happen and Reilly hadn't. Now I began to understand that it had been the opposite. Josh had thought he'd gotten his own way, but Reilly had gone behind his back and told Tommy to humiliate Marybeth.

Reilly, not Josh, was the person in charge of *America Bakes!*

"Then we'll be done with this segment and move on," Reilly said. "We should be able to replace Tommy fast enough. I'm thinking that Scottish guy everyone loves to hate. While we're at it, we'll dump Claudia."

"Claudia? You can't be serious. Claudia brings legions of her own fans to the show."

"Claudia's finished. Washed up. I don't know what her problem is, but word's out that she's in desperate need of money, and fast."

"Isn't that a reason not to fire her?"

"What are you saying, Josh? Coming over all soft in your old age? You never hesitated to dump the talent in the past, not the second they ceased to be of use to you."

"Maybe—"

"I don't want a clean sweep. We've lost Tommy. That can't be helped. I'd rather ditch Scarlet than Claudia, but I can't do that now, can I? Thanks to you."

"What does that mean?"

"It means, *Dad*, if you've been fooling around with Scarlet and you fire her, because it won't be me pulling the plug, she'll have reason to hit social media with all the sordid details. Public opinion's not on the side of old men coercing their employees."

"I don't have to coerce anyone."

"You think the likes of Scarlet McIntosh would give you the time of day if you weren't the director of the country's top reality show?" Reilly snorted. "Get real."

Josh said nothing.

The floorboards creaked as Reilly continued to pace. "Losing Tommy was bad, but not unsalvageable. We can save this segment by using lots of shots of him. Then we move on. Two new judges will freshen the show up, give it a jolt of adrenaline."

"I'd say Tommy's death did that."

"I've already got feelers out to the Scottish chef, and he seems to be interested. We find an up-and-coming man to replace Claudia. That'll provide better balance. Experienced older guy, hungry young guy, empty-headed but pretty woman."

"You're getting ahead of yourself, Reilly. The network hasn't agreed to this."

"They will. If I present it to them."

"What's that supposed to mean?"

"It's time for you to step aside, Dad. Your last idea was a bust, and the network won't forget."

"My last idea? Seems to me all that about making things challenging for the cooks was your idea."

"Maybe it was. But we didn't present it that way, did we? You were happy enough to be the face of the new show when everyone thought it was a good idea. Not so happy now."

"Reilly . . . son . . ."

I felt sorry for Josh. He sounded lost. He was accustomed to being in charge, the one calling the shots, and now his son was taking over, pushing him aside. Dethroning the king.

"I'm off," Reilly said. "It's early enough to call LA. I'll tell them I . . . that is, you . . . want a decision now, tonight, or we're leaving. They'll fold. I'm going to tell the crew to be ready to start shooting tomorrow."

The sound of the door opening, footsteps crossing the hall, the front door opening and slamming shut. I held my breath, listening. It sounded as though only Reilly had left, and I couldn't slip out of the secret room if I was taking the chance Josh would suddenly appear and catch me. Although, I reasoned, men like Josh were unlikely to wonder why the linens would need sorting at ten p.m.

"Scarlet." Josh's voice came through the walls. "Listen to me." He was on his phone. "Reilly's calling the network tonight. He has this idea that as long as we have to replace Tommy, we should get another new judge. Shake things up. He thinks we need Claudia, because she's got gravitas in the baking world, but you're expendable."

Scarlet's screech was so loud, I could hear it pouring down the virtual phone line, crossing the room, and charging through the walls.

"Yeah," Josh said. "I told him you've got the looks and the perky charm the show needs, but I'm not sure I convinced him. How about I come up to your room and we can talk over a plan of attack? Great. See you in a couple of minutes."

He chuckled.

I no longer felt sorry for Josh Henshaw.

Chapter 17

When I got home, I called Amy Redmond.

"What is it now, Lily?" Her tone was sharp.

"I'm sorry to bother you, Detective, but I had an idea."

"Another idea? What now?"

I cringed at the implied rebuke. I was only trying to help. "I'm wondering if you asked Claudia D'Angelo where she was around eleven the night Tommy Greene died."

"Lily, are you suggesting you don't trust me to do my job? Of course I asked her that. I asked them all."

"It occurred to me that she might be the person Robyn Sullivan saw in the garden around that time. She's short, same height as Cheryl. Claudia is thinner than the woman Robyn described, but she sometimes wears a puffy vest of the sort that makes a person look larger than they are."

"That's hardly conclusive proof of anything, Lily."

"I thought it worth mentioning, that's all. I'm sorry."

She let out a long sigh. "And I'm sorry I snapped at you. It's natural for you to be interested in the progress of this case, and you have a sharp, inquisitive mind."

"I do? I mean, yes, I do."

"I'll speak to Ms. D'Angelo again, suggest she might have neglected to mention something."

"If she was up late, wandering in the garden, she has a reason to have trouble sleeping. Are you aware she's in financial difficulties?"

"I won't ask how you know that, Lily, as I assume the woman didn't tell you."

I said nothing.

"In a case such as this one, a murder with no obvious suspects, we are interested, very interested, in the financial situation of the people involved with the deceased, particularly if they are having trouble maintaining their accustomed lifestyle. So yes, Lily, Claudia D'Angelo is on my radar. As are other people." She hung up without telling me who those other people might be.

The following morning I was overjoyed to see Cheryl, rather than Marybeth's law school cousin, arrive for work with Marybeth. And not only because I needed my best waitress. I wrapped Cheryl in a fierce hug. I then hugged Marybeth, and Bernie eagerly leapt into the hugging circle.

"Thank heavens you're here," my friend said as she took off her apron. "I never want to do this again."

I'd told Edna I wouldn't need her help, as Marybeth would be back today. Cheryl had been released from jail, but she might not be feeling up to putting in a day's work, and the cousin was an unknown factor, so I'd asked—more like begged—Bernie to come again.

"Not so fast, Bernie," I said now. "Cheryl, are you sure you want to work today? You must be exhausted."

"Not a whole lot to do in jail," she said. "I'm mentally worn out from worrying, that's all. A day at the beck and call of you and your customers will take my mind off my troubles."

I smiled at her and touched her arm. "I'm glad you're here."

"I'm not in the clear yet, Lily. Chuck Williams is still hunting for proof of my guilt."

Marybeth made a sound that indicated what she thought about that.

"Still, one step forward," I said. "You're wearing your good luck earrings again today."

She touched her right earlobe. "I need all the luck I can get if Chuck Williams is out to get me."

"What's the story?" Bernie said. "Between you and him? If you don't mind my asking."

"No story," Cheryl said. "We dated for a while in high school. Believe it or not, he was a mighty good-looking guy back in the day. He played football."

"That is hard to believe," Marybeth said.

Cheryl laughed. "About as hard to believe as that I was also quite the looker in those long-ago days. Or so the boys, and my parents, told me. Chuck went out with Allegra for a while. They broke up, and he and I started dating. Allegra blamed me for the breakup, although I had nothing to do with it. It was high school in a small town. Everyone dated just about everyone at some time or other. Allegra didn't need an excuse to not like me. Allegra didn't like many people, and not many liked her in return. It's sad really. All these years later and she's still not liking people."

"Did you break it off with Williams?" Bernie asked. "Do you think he holds a grudge?"

"A grudge? No. We didn't last long. We married other people, and we carried on with our lives. I never thought there was anything personal about him arresting me, and I still don't. You can't police the small town you grew up in without arresting people you knew when you were younger."

She checked her watch. "Eleven o'clock. I'll unlock the door."

Marybeth went with her.

"If you don't need me . . . ," Bernie said.

"Thanks for coming, but it looks as though we're back on track."

She wiggled her fingers and skipped out the back door.

Bernie'd arrived shortly after nine, in time to enjoy a cup of coffee and a muffin on my small porch with me after I finished the B & B breakfast shift. She had no new information, she reported. No rumors of Tommy Greene, involving marital fidelity, financial difficulties, or anything else, and nothing more on CookingTV or Josh Henshaw. I told her what I'd overheard between Josh and Reilly last night, while not telling her about the secret room, and I'd suggested she check into Reilly's background.

I was putting the finishing touches on vanilla cupcakes when a loud rap sounded at the door, and it opened to admit none other than Josh and Reilly.

"Great news!" Reilly pumped his fists. "We're good to go."

Josh didn't look quite so pleased. His smile was tight, and it failed to reach his eyes.

"You mean the filming's going to continue?" I asked.

"Yup. We got the green light last night." Reilly turned to Josh. "Sometimes you have to force people into making a decision. That's what my dad taught me, right, Dad?"

Josh made a noncommittal grunt.

"That's good," I said. "I suppose. But I have a schedule to keep. I have reservations for the rest of the day and continuing through the weekend. I can't close my restaurant without notice."

"Not necessary," Reilly said. "We have pretty much all we need from you."

I knew that. I also knew they'd decided I wouldn't win.

I didn't mind. All I wanted was to see the back of them. "Are you going to continue with only Claudia and Scarlet as judges?"

"We have lots of footage of Tommy at this place. Instead of filming the final day's meeting with you as planned, Claudia and Scarlet are going to sit together over one of your teas and reminisce about Tommy. We'll shoot that this afternoon, out in the garden. Don't worry about moving your reservations around. People love to be in the background on TV."

"But—"

"We won't need you for that. A nice friendly chat between good friends, talking about their favorite memories of an old pal. Then when we air the piece, we'll intersperse it with shots of Tommy being Tommy. There won't be a dry eye in a living room in America. Right, Dad?"

"Whatever you say," Josh said.

"Hey! Look who's here!" Reilly proclaimed as Cheryl came into the kitchen. "Glad to see you're out of the slammer."

She eyed him warily as she read off her notepad, "Traditional tea for four. Two children's teas. One order of light tea for two. Can you excuse me, please?"

"What?" Reilly said.

"I need to make the tea, and you're in my way."

"Oh, sorry." He stepped aside, and she got down the appropriate canisters of loose tea.

Josh looked at me and jerked his head to indicate Cheryl. "Maybe don't use that one this afternoon."

"What does that mean?" I asked.

"It would look odd, don't you think, if she gets rearrested for killing Tommy?"

Cheryl's back was to us as she spooned loose tea leaves into pots, added water at the correct temperature for the appropriate blend of tea, and set the timers. She didn't react, but her shoulders tightened, and the back of her neck flushed with enough color to match the stones in her earrings.

"That might not be a bad idea," Reilly said. "Talk about adding extra drama to the scene."

"I . . . ," I said.

"Okay, maybe not," Reilly said. "We'll use the younger one."

I continued arranging the trays of food as per Cheryl's orders. Reilly snatched a chocolate chip cookie off the children's tea tray.

"Hey," I said.

He grinned at me. "That's settled, then. Great. The crew will be here at three. Josh, make sure you send that waitress to Melanie to get some make up on and her hair fixed." He popped the cookie into his mouth as he left the kitchen.

"He seems in a good mood today," I said to Josh.

"Reilly's always in a good mood. When he gets what he wants."

As Reilly had mentioned, my customers didn't mind in the least when the TV crew arrived and began setting up. The only complaints I overheard were that people wished they'd known in advance so they could have dressed better/had their hair done/fixed their makeup/brought their friends/told all their friends/told all their enemies.

Word had spread, and I was not happy to see Allegra, in the company of Susan and Gary Powers, being shown to a patio table. My fellow baker hadn't bothered to change out of her work jeans and stained T-shirt, but our mayor was dressed as though she were on the campaign trail, in a powder-blue power suit with four-inch heels. Gary, ever the supportive political spouse, had slicked his gray hair back and dressed in khaki slacks ironed to a knifepoint and an equally well-laundered blue shirt. Italian loafers were on his feet.

"You couldn't have told them we were full?" I said to Cheryl.

"Susan called and asked for a table for three. She didn't say who'd be joining her. We were full, but I figured I should squeeze her in. It never hurts to play nice with the political powers. Hey, that's a pun! I didn't know she'd be bringing the dratted Allegra."

"Stuff and nonsense," Rose said. My grandmother wore a brilliantly colored concoction of baggy purple pants, a yellow blouse so blindingly bright it was like looking directly into the sun, and a long red silk scarf that trailed behind her. She leaned on her pink cane.

"It also never hurts to play nice with the people who pay the bills," Cheryl said. "Rose, the table in the far corner is for you and Bernie."

"You're staying?" I asked.

Rose beamed at me. "More than staying, love. I'm putting in a cameo appearance."

"A what?"

"It's been arranged for Rose and me to stop by Claudia and Scarlet's table and extend our condolences on their loss," Bernie said. "Josh called Rose earlier and asked if she'd do that, and she extended the invitation to me. She can't sit all by herself at teatime."

"Okay," I said, trying not to be offended that Bernie and Rose were needed in front of the camera, but I, the actual owner and head chef at this establishment, was not. I didn't want to be on the stupid TV show, but that was beside the point.

"The gang's all here." Bernie nodded toward the parking area, where Detectives Redmond and Williams were getting out of a car. At least they hadn't come in a marked cruiser, and no uniformed officers were with them. No mistaking the two of them for anything but cops, though. They glanced our way, but they didn't come over to chat and took positions next to an equipment truck.

"Afternoon ladies." Melanie, the makeup woman, came up to my small group. "Bet you'll be glad to see the last of us."

"Something like that," I said.

She laughed. "I don't blame you. As for me, I'm just glad we're back at work. Your town's lovely and all that, but we were all getting mighty restless at the not knowing. This gig's hard enough as it is."

"I do hope there's shortbread on offer today," Rose said. "Come along, Bernadette. That young man is trying to get everyone to take their seats."

I watched Bernie and Rose walk across the patio, Rose tapping the way with her cane, Bernie's arm linked through hers. Rose said something to Susan Powers as they passed the mayoral table, and Susan smiled in return. Gary Powers, on the other hand, ignored my grandmother and pointedly checked Bernie out. She pretended not to notice, as did his wife.

The patio was full, more than full, as we'd moved chairs from the dining room to squeeze additional people in. Cheryl went about her duties apparently unfazed, arranging place settings, jotting orders on her notepad, serving tea and food, and accepting payment with a bright smile. Marybeth fluttered about, trying to do her job but clearly nervous at the prospect of her turn in front of the cameras. I'd briefly wondered if Reilly was intending to set Marybeth up to fail again, the way he and Tommy had done, but I'd decided I had nothing to worry about. Today's segment was intended to feature the two women reminiscing fondly about a good friend. No high drama needed.

"Okay, everyone!" Josh shouted. "We're about to begin. Enjoy your tea and talk amongst yourselves. Pay no attention to the camera."

Easier said than done, I thought.

"Ms. D'Angelo and Ms. McIntosh will be available for photographs and autographs after the filming."

A couple of women squealed, and one clapped her hands.

"You!" Josh pointed to Marybeth, and she jumped. "Think you can do this?"

"Yes." The word came out in a croak. She cleared her throat and said, "I'm ready, sir."

"Any chance of a cup of tea?" Melanie, the makeup artist, asked me. "I can provide all the latest gossip in payment."

"I don't need payment, but I do have tea. Come with me. As long as people are out here eating, I have to be in there baking."

I poured a cup of English breakfast for Melanie and one for myself, and then I got pastry dough out of the fridge and prepared to roll it out for tarts. "What did you mean," I asked her, "about this gig being a hard one? Is it worse than most?"

Melanie leaned against a wall and cradled her tea. "Not as bad as some. Harder than a lot. Any TV or movie set is a titanic battle of egos, and frankly, the smaller the stars, the more the ego. Scarlet McIntosh isn't exactly Meryl Streep, who, by the way, is an absolutely delightful woman, but she would like to be. She doesn't want anything to do with reality TV. She wants to act with a capital *A*, but she's not getting any roles, and that's making her angrier and meaner toward the crew. Most of whom, including me, couldn't care one hoot for her and her dreams of stardom. As for Claudia, I've been with this show from the beginning. At first, Claudia was nice. Not overly friendly, but simply polite enough to everyone. Something's been bugging her badly these past couple of weeks. It's become a regular job for me, getting the redness out of her eyes and nose in the morning. She's putting in a lot of late nights, and no, I don't know what she's up to, but whatever it is, it's not making her happy. This tea's good. And these cookies are to die for." I'd served her some of my shortbread to accompany the tea.

"What about Tommy?" I rolled the dough to an eighth of an inch thickness.

"Tommy was a doll. Toward me and most of the crew, anyway, although he and Josh and Reilly could really get into it. He couldn't stand Scarlet, and even though I think he genuinely liked Claudia, he thought she should have retired long ago. Even the nicest of men think a woman over fifty has no place in front of the cameras."

I cut circles of dough and folded them into the tart pans. "You're being very frank with me."

"Why not? Nothing's a secret on a TV set. Besides, I like you. I like your cookies, anyway."

"Try a macaron," I said, indicating the delicate pale green treats laid out, ready to be served.

She reached around me. "Don't mind if I do. Yummy. This is not a happy set, Lily. Josh is losing control, as he's being pushed out by Reilly. A power play among the higher-ups is never good for morale."

I nodded as I thought of some of the restaurants I'd worked in. Talk about power plays and titanic egos.

"Scarlet and Claudia hated each other from the get-go. Fair enough on Claudia's part, I thought. She has solid cooking creds, whereas Scarlet serves no purpose but to look good for the cameras. Reilly's long wanted to dump Scarlet, but Josh won't hear of it." She sipped her tea, and her eyes sparkled.

"Why might that be?" I asked innocently.

"Everyone knows they're up to something. Josh and Scarlet, I mean. Everyone always knows, although the parties concerned think they're being *sooo* discreet. Scarlet originally made a play for Tommy. He wasn't interested, didn't even pretend to be polite about it. The air between them was mighty chilly for a while. She pretended not to care that Tommy had rejected her, but believe me, honey, your hairdresser knows for sure. And I'm talking about more than hair color. She was absolutely furious. After a while, she turned her attentions to Josh, and it went from there. Whether that was because she was hoping Tommy'd get jealous, I don't know. I could have told her not to bother, but why would I? Tommy was a straight arrow. I liked him. Most of the time."

"Scarlet came on to Josh?"

"Oh, yeah. I can't say she found it hard to convince him. It's obvious she's gotten tired of him, but he's not ready to let go. More ego stuff, you know."

I mulled that over for a few minutes as I poured lemon filling into the tart shells. "Do you have any idea who might have killed Tommy?"

Melanie shook her head. "If someone had murdered Reilly or Josh, I wouldn't have been at all surprised. If Scarlet or Claudia had been killed, I'd assume the other had finally snapped and done her in. The police have spoken to me and the rest of the crew several times, asking about everyone's relationships with Tommy, where we'd been that night, if we'd seen anyone suspicious hanging around the set. As though I'd know what suspicious looks like, if it's not some teenage girl thinking this is her big chance and trying to get herself into a shot. Who killed him? Haven't got a clue." She put down her cup and dusted crumbs off her shirt. "Thanks for this."

"My pleasure."

Melanie passed Cheryl on her way out. "Traditional tea for four and royal tea for two," Cheryl called.

"How's it going out there?" I asked as I slipped the baking sheet into the oven.

"Marybeth hasn't dropped a tray, and she didn't spill hot tea all over Claudia D'Angelo, so I'd say it's going okay. I'll be so glad when this is over."

"As will I."

"They're wrapping up now. Claudia and Scarlet are chatting to the guests, most of whom seem thrilled to be chatted to. A couple of tables have left, so we've seated some new arrivals." She fiddled with tea canisters and airpots while I arranged food on the three-tiered stands.

Marybeth came in, her tray piled high with used cups and plates. I was pleased to see she was smiling broadly. "It's finished, and I think it went okay. Gary Powers kept his big mouth shut, and no one on camera spoke to Allegra. They're starting to pack up."

"Glad that's over." I washed my hands and took off my hairnet. "I'm going to say good-bye. I won't say I hope never to see any of them again, but I'll be thinking it."

Marybeth began loading the dishwasher, and I went out front. The dining rooms were largely empty; most people had wanted to be seated outside. I spotted a discarded napkin on the floor in one of the alcoves and veered to pick it up. At that moment Bernie came out of the hallway leading to the ladies' room, and Gary Powers stepped out of the vestibule. It looked to me as though he'd been waiting for her.

"Hi," he said.

"Hi."

I picked up the napkin but remained where I was.

"You're Bernadette Murphy," Gary said. "The writer?"

She blinked in surprise. "I'm writing, yes. I've written a couple of things. I guess that makes me a writer."

He put out his hand, and she took it. He might have held her hand a fraction longer than was polite before letting go. He stood close to her and looked deeply into her eyes. "I'm Gary. I've been wanting to meet you, Bernadette. I've always been interested in the creative process. I have no talent myself, so it's fascinating to me how highly skilled people such as yourself can create something beautiful and meaningful out of next to nothing. Paint in a tube becomes a magnificent painting. A bunch of letters formed in the right way make words and then a novel that speaks to the soul."

She blinked. "Uh. Yeah. I do that. I guess."

"I've had a great idea. When I said I don't write, I meant fiction. I contribute the occasional article on the arts scene to local rags, and sometimes my stuff gets into papers like the *New York Times,* the *Washington Post.* When it's a slow news day." He chuckled modestly. "I'd love to do a write-up on you."

"You would?"

"I would. How about we get together one night, have a drink, talk it over? I'm free tonight, as it happens."

"That," Bernie said, "would be so great! My chance at fame at last. Thank you so very much, Gary."

I couldn't believe what I was hearing. Surely Bernie, practical, no-nonsense Bernie, wasn't falling for this line? I remained in the shadows.

"Let's do it this way," she continued. "I'll check up on what you've had published in the *Times,* see if it's the sort of thing I like, and if it is, I'll meet with you. Evenings are no good for me, as that's my prime writing time. We creative people have to stick to our strict schedule, you know, otherwise the muse gets confused. Evenings are out, and afternoons aren't all that good, either, so how about I meet you and your wife over breakfast at the bakery in town for the interview? Will that work?"

"I'm . . . I'm not sure if my wife will want to get involved."

"Oh, Gary," Bernie said, "I'm so glad to hear that, but now you'll never get to hear how I intend to be the next big thing in American historical fiction. Too bad. Rose will be wondering where I've gotten to. Nice talking to you. Love to the mayor." Bernie skipped away.

I stepped out of the alcove. Gary's round face was puce with what I hoped was humiliation.

"Good afternoon," I said cheerfully, making sure he knew I'd been listening. "I hope you're enjoying your tea."

He glared at me and stalked away. Presumably to join his wife and sister-in-law.

I gave him a minute and then followed. Outside, the crew was rolling up thick cables and dismantling equipment on the patio and loading it into the trucks. Amy Redmond was still there, watching everyone, but Williams had wandered off. Bored probably.

Claudia was seated in the shade of a blue umbrella, smiling and laughing with the women gathered around her. Scarlet stood near the gate, also smiling and laughing, or at least pretending to do so. Bernie had joined Rose at their table, and Rose beckoned to me.

"Nice one," I said to Bernie.

"I thought I saw you lurking in the shadows." She glanced over at the mayor's table, where Gary was pretending to be engrossed in what his wife was saying. "Guy's a sleazeball of the highest order."

"Who is?" Rose asked.

"We'll tell you later," I said. "How'd it go out here?"

"An agent will be calling soon, I'm sure, with offers from Hollywood. I'm hoping for a part in the next *Downton Abbey* movie. I hear Maggie Smith isn't interested."

"You keep hoping, Rose," Bernie said, and I laughed.

"It went fine, love. We stopped at Claudia and Scarlet's

table, as asked, and taking great care to have our faces pointed toward the camera, as also asked, and looking suitably somber, we offered our heartfelt condolences on the untimely death of their friend."

"I'm going to wave good-bye. Talk to you later." I took my position at the gate as Josh joined Claudia and her admirers.

"I'm sorry to interrupt, ladies, but I'm afraid it's time we're on our way," he said.

"Already?" Claudia said. "I'm having such a lovely time. Oh, well, can't be helped." She stood up and said her good-byes. The women tittered in excitement.

Josh then beckoned to Scarlet, and she joined them. They, followed by a man with a camera propped on his shoulder, approached the gate, where I was standing. I was prepared to say good-bye and thank them for coming, but I didn't expect to be filmed. I'd been told I wouldn't be on camera today, so I hadn't done my hair or had Melanie fuss with my makeup or even put on a nicer T-shirt. I felt my smile freeze in place. It froze even further when I saw Reilly indicate to Allegra to join us.

Claudia took both my hands in hers; she gazed deeply into my eyes. Melanie, I thought, was a very good makeup artist indeed. "So lovely to get to know you, Lily. You've done a wonderful job with this delightful place. Our next competitor will have to pull out all the stops if she's going to beat you."

Reilly gave Allegra a nudge, and she stepped forward. The cameraman took a step back to get her in the shot. "I'm more than capable of doing that, Claudia," she said in a loud, firm voice. "North Augusta Bakery was started by my mother, and I've been proud to build on her legacy."

"That's what I like to hear," Claudia said. "Baking is all about tradition, isn't it?"

"It is, Claudia." Scarlet's teeth flashed white. "But it's also about not being afraid to try new and original things. That's what we're looking for on *America Bakes!* Do you think North Augusta Bakery is up to it, Ms. Griffin?"

"Most certainly," Allegra said. "Not only is my baking top notch, as I'm thrilled to have the opportunity to show you, but"—she lifted her right arm and pointed one chubby finger directly to where Marybeth and Cheryl were standing together under the oak tree, watching—"I don't hire murderers to wait tables."

"Cut!" Josh yelled.

"Keep it moving," Reilly ordered. The camera swung around and got a great shot of Cheryl's shocked face.

Chapter 18

Josh leapt forward and put his hand in front of the camera lens. "Turn it off."

The cameraman glanced at Reilly.

"You don't ask him," Josh shouted. "You do what I tell you."

The camera was switched off.

Allegra smirked, and Scarlet's eyes danced with amusement. Claudia looked as shocked as Cheryl. Marybeth burst into tears. I thought Bernie was going to hit someone, and Rose would serve as her wingman. Alerted by the abrupt increase in tension, Detective Redmond came to join us.

"Are you trying to get us sued?" Josh yelled at Reilly. "I don't want footage of that."

"No one can sue us," Reilly casually replied. "I didn't tell the lady what to say. She has every right to speak her mind."

"Yes, I do," Allegra said. "It's a free country."

"Why don't you take your mother inside for a bit of a sit-down, dear?" Rose said to Marybeth. "Lily and I can see our guests out."

More a matter of Cheryl taking Marybeth inside, but no one argued, and the women walked away. Cheryl paused in the entranceway, and the look she threw over her shoulder at Allegra would have curdled my clotted cream. Allegra merely smirked.

"If I were you, Ms. Griffin," Amy Redmond said, "I wouldn't be throwing around accusations."

"It's a free country," Allegra repeated.

"It might be, but responding to a lawsuit isn't free. Looks like you people are finished here," she said to Reilly. "Unless you have more stunts to pull?"

He grinned at her. "All done."

She did not smile in return. "Glad to hear it."

"We'll be at your place at seven tomorrow," Reilly said to Allegra. "Be ready."

"I'm looking forward to it. Susan, Gary, are you finished here? Let's go." She started to walk away, and then she turned and threw what she probably thought a clever bon mot at me. "Your salmon sandwiches didn't have enough mayonnaise. And that chocolate tart? Did you use real chocolate or brown food coloring?"

"Bye!" I gave her a cheerful wave.

"Don't hurry back," Bernie called.

Susan Powers, looking genuinely embarrassed, followed Allegra. Gary tried to slip past Bernie unnoticed, but she called, "Bye, Gary. Let me know when you next have a feature in the *New York Times*."

"What feature in the *New York Times*?" Susan asked her husband.

"I'm sorry about that," Josh said once Allegra and her companions had gone and Reilly had left to supervise the dismantling of the last of the equipment. "Reilly's getting too far ahead of himself. I'm the director here. I promise you that last footage won't see the light of day." He stalked off.

"What happens next?" Rose asked me. "With the competition, I mean. Do you and Allegra go at it armed with
rolling pins and cream pies?"

"I really, really do not care," I said. "I am so tired of
this."

A local woman stepped up to say a word to Rose, and I
pulled Bernie aside and told her briefly what I'd heard
from Melanie.

"Basically, you're telling me no one involved in this
show liked anyone else, and that probably includes Josh
and his son. About the only one everyone did like is the
dead guy. That's not much help, Lily."

"We've done all we can do," I said. "Cheryl's out of jail,
and there's not going to be any more evidence that will
lead to her being rearrested and charged. Meaning it's
none of our concern anymore."

"Except for having Allegra accuse Cheryl of murder.
Cheap stunt," Bernie said. "You should have evicted Allegra from the premises."

"While the cameras got good footage of me wresting
her out the door? Maybe not such a good idea."

"Maybe not. I could have done it, though. How long is
the merry gang staying at the B and B?"

"Doesn't matter. All I have to do is stay out of their way."

"I'll walk Rose to the house. Call me if you need anything more."

I watched Bernie join my grandmother and her group,
and then I went inside to help Marybeth and Cheryl
clean up.

I found them in the kitchen, taking a break over cups of
tea. "You okay?" I asked Marybeth.

"Yeah. I'm fine." She didn't look fine. Her hands shook
so much, I feared for the delicate china teacup she was
holding, a vintage Windsor pattern of pink flowers and

gray leaves on a white background, part of a set I'd found at an estate sale.

"Don't let her get to you," Cheryl said. "You know that's what Allegra wants."

"Hard not to when she out and out accused you." Marybeth turned to me. "You and Bernie and Rose have been investigating Tommy's death . . . ?"

"I wouldn't say investigating, exactly."

"That's what Rose and Bernie call it. Is there any chance you can find some way of framing Allegra?"

I blinked.

"Never mind her," Cheryl said. "I mean, never mind Allegra or Marybeth. I know you'd like to win, Lily, and so would we, but when it comes down to it, the best thing that could happen would be Allegra winning the grand prize, selling the bakery, and moving away from North Augusta, as she's always wanted."

"I'd hate to lose to her," Marybeth said.

Cheryl leaned over and patted her daughter's hand. "Regardless, we've managed to stay out of her way for a lot of years, and we can continue to do so."

"Do you know you're wearing only one earring?" I asked.

Cheryl's eyes widened in shock, and her hands shot to her ears. "Oh. No. It must have come loose."

"When did you see it last?" I asked.

"I didn't even notice until now," Marybeth said.

Cheryl rubbed at her clothes and shook out her apron. "I don't know. I checked my face and tidied my hair in the mirror before the TV crew arrived, wanting to look okay if they got a shot of me in the background. I would have noticed if one was missing. I've been busy ever since." Her face twisted. "Maybe I can check the footage of when Allegra called me a murderer."

"I'll help you look outside," Marybeth said.

"I'll sweep up in here." I kept my eyes on the floor as I went for the broom.

The three of us searched high and low, including Marybeth going through the copious amount of trash, but we didn't find the missing earring.

"It'll turn up," I said, trying to sound positive.

Cheryl had tried to keep her spirits up in the face of Allegra's insults and then the accusation of murder, but the missing earring seemed to be the last straw, and her face showed the strain she'd been under. She rubbed at her eyes and said, "I'm sure it will," in a voice without any confidence at all.

"A regular day tomorrow," I said. "Thank goodness."

I put in a few more hours after my assistants left, and then dragged myself home. Guests lingered on the veranda, and the clink of glasses and the ripples of their laughter drifted on the wind. I greeted Éclair and was enthusiastically greeted in return, and I took her out for her nightly walk. I was in no hurry, and we walked along the bluffs, accompanied by the sound of the sea crashing to shore below us. The moon and stars were hidden behind a thick bank of clouds, and a strong wind was blowing off the ocean, bringing the threat of rain. We rounded the house for a turn around the rose garden to enjoy the scent of the flowers on the night air. Simon's motorbike was parked by the garden shed, but lights were on at Matt's house, and the sound of steady hammering broke the peace of the evening.

I was woken by Éclair's frantic barking and a pounding at the door. I threw off the covers and leapt out of bed. Éclair stood at the door, ears up, still barking. I switched on the hall light and threw open the front door, perhaps unwisely, not first checking to see who was there.

A man fell in, and I yelped in shock. Instinctively, I grabbed his arm to keep him from hitting the floor. "Simon? What on earth?"

His clothes were wet, his face streaked with mud. I guided him to a chair.

"Are you okay? No, you're not okay. I'm calling an ambulance."

He groaned. "I'll be fine. Give me a minute." He touched the back of his head, and his fingers came away dotted with blood. I gasped.

Éclair whined and rubbed her muzzle against his leg. "It's okay, girl. All okay," Simon said.

I crouched next to him. "Why are you so wet?"

"It's raining out. What time is it?"

I scrambled to my feet and ran for my phone. "Quarter after twelve."

He sighed with relief.

"What?"

"I must've been lying in the rain for no more than a couple of minutes. Can I have a glass of water?"

I ran to get it and handed it to him. "What happened? Wait, don't tell me yet. I'll be right back."

I found a clean washcloth and soaked it under running water from the kitchen tap. I stood behind Simon, and he bent his head forward so I could gently probe the injury. "It's been bleeding but looks as though it's stopped." I pressed the damp cloth to the wound, and he groaned again. "Any other injuries?" I asked.

"No. Don't think so. As for what happened, I don't know. I left Matt's place not long after midnight. We finished the work we'd planned for tonight, had a quick beer, just one, and I left. I was crossing the lawn, going for me bike when . . ."

"When what?"

"I think I was attacked, Lily."

"It certainly looks like it." I lifted the cloth and studied it. I felt a great shudder of relief go through me when I saw it was stained a watery pink, not bright red.

"I had my phone in my hand, using it as a flashlight, but I dropped it when I was hit, and the light went out. I couldn't find it. It's pitch dark out there, away from the lights of the house. I didn't want to disturb Rose. I hope you don't mind that I came here."

"Mind? Don't be silly. We need to call the police."

"Yes, I'm afraid we do." He reached up behind him and put his hand on mine. "That feels nice." He caressed my fingers.

My heart stopped.

Simon stood up and turned around. His eyes were dark and serious as he looked down at me. He took the wet washcloth out of my hands and laid it on the table.

"Police?" I squeaked.

"You call them. Tell them we need a detective. This was no random attack."

"You think this has something to do with the death of Tommy Greene?"

"It has to."

"I agree." The idea of some stranger lurking around outside Victoria-on-Sea, waiting for a chance to pounce on an innocent passerby, was too ridiculous to contemplate. "You didn't see who did this?"

"No. I didn't. I sensed someone behind me, started to turn, and next thing I knew, I was lying on the ground and trying to clear my head."

"I'll call Detective Redmond. I have her number on speed dial."

She answered surprisingly quickly, sounding not at all as though I'd woken her in the middle of the night. I suppose she's used to being called out at all hours.

"Detective, Lily Roberts here. Simon McCracken, my

gardener, has been attacked by . . . uh, person or persons unknown."

"Where are you now, Lily, and is he in need of medical attention?"

"We're at my cottage, and he says no. A bash on the head bad enough to knock him out for a few moments, but no more."

"I'm on my way."

"Thank you. Oh, can you please, please, if possible, not have lights and sirens? I don't want to disturb the B and B guests. Thanks." I pushed the button to hang up and went to slip the phone into the small breast pocket of my pajama top. I was suddenly aware that I was dressed in my pajamas, cute little shorty yellow things with a pattern of cartoon characters. My cheeks burned.

Simon put his hand on mine. He took the phone out of my fingers. "Can I borrow this? Unless you have a flashlight? I'll meet Redmond up by the road."

"I'm coming with you."

"I'd rather you didn't. Whoever it was might still be out there."

"They'll be long gone," I said with more confidence than I felt. "Besides, if they're not, you're the one who had a blow on the head. Not me. You need me to protect you."

He smiled at me, and then he said, "Let's go, then."

Not wanting the dog to disturb what there might be of a crime scene, I told Éclair to be on guard and left with Simon. I'd found a flashlight in a kitchen drawer and handed it to him. He took my hand in his, and I did not pull it away. I held my phone in my free hand and used it to help light our way. The rain had slowed to a drizzle, and the grass was sodden underfoot. Raindrops dripped from the trees and the roof. The grand old house was shrouded in darkness, except for the soft yellow glow cast by the lamp over the front door and one in the hallway. I put my finger to my lips as we rounded the corner next to Rose's rooms. My grandmother, so she'd told me, didn't sleep very well these days. "Old bones," she'd said.

We didn't have long to wait before headlights lit up the night and turned into our driveway. Simon dropped my hand and lifted his in greeting. The car pulled to a stop next to us, and Amy Redmond got out, bathed in a circle of light from our flashlights. She lifted one hand to block the light from her eyes and said, "What happened?"

Simon told her what he'd told me.

"You didn't see this person?"

"No. Not a glimpse. Sorry. They got me." He pointed. "There."

She switched on her own heavy Maglite and studied the back of his head. "Yeah, that's gonna be sore. Nice bump starting. Sure you don't want to go to the hospital?"

"I'm good."

"You don't have to play tough guy, you know," I said.

"I know."

"Where did this happen?" Redmond asked.

Simon shone his light over the grass. "Right around there. I'd gone straight from work to Matt's to give him a hand installing his new kitchen cabinets, so I hadn't taken the bike. I was coming from his house, walking in a more or less straight line to the garden shed to get the bike. I used the flashlight on my phone to light my way. I didn't see anyone around, but I wasn't looking, and it was pitch dark. Like now. I'd crossed the driveway, taken a few steps, and then I felt as much as heard something behind me and . . . *wham*." He started to walk.

I made to follow, but Redmond put one arm out to stop me. "You stay here." She fell into step behind Simon. I shifted and glanced nervously around me as they walked away. The shadows were very deep. I tiptoed after them.

"There." Simon focused his beam of light on the ground,

and Redmond's joined it. "The grass is disturbed, and there's my phone over there. I dropped it when I fell."

Redmond cast her light in a circle. It caught the sparkle of wet grass, the edge of a flower bed, the glow of white daisies, the shiny metal of Simon's phone. And glittering red stones hanging from a silver earring.

Chapter 19

"She told you she lost it," Amy Redmond said. "Doesn't mean she did."

"But I saw for myself," I protested. "She had only one of the earrings on. That happened before Simon was attacked, not after. She couldn't have predicted she'd lose it."

"It might have been caught in her clothes," Redmond said. "And fell out later. That's happened to me more than once, and I'm sure it's happened to you." She lifted one hand to stop my protests. "I'm not saying that's what happened here, Lily, but I am saying I need to talk to Cheryl Wainwright tonight. I have to tell Detective Williams I'm bringing her in."

We were standing at the side of her car. Simon had thrown his arm around my shoulders as I tried to argue with the detective.

"I saw Cheryl this afternoon," Redmond said as she dropped the earring into an evidence bag, "but I can't say if she was wearing one of these or two or none at all."

I wished I'd kept my mouth shut. The moment I'd seen the earring in the grass, I said, "There it is. Cheryl was looking for that." I moved to pick it up, but Redmond had stopped me.

"Cheryl has no reason whatsoever to attack me, Detective," Simon said.

"Do you know of people who do have reason to attack you?"

"Well, no."

"Then that doesn't help, does it?"

He said nothing.

"I'll have people here first thing in the morning to go over the area in the daylight." She'd taken a length of yellow police tape out of the trunk of her car and looped it around the trunk of a stately maple, through a boxwood hedge, and tied it off on a fence post. "In the meantime, keep people out of there."

She got into her car and drove away. Simon and I watched until her lights had disappeared in the distance.

"Perhaps we shouldn't have called her," Simon said.

"We had to. It was the right thing to do. Someone hit you over the head, and whoever that person was has to be found."

"You don't think—"

"No. I do not. Cheryl wasn't creeping around tonight, ready to pounce on the first person who wandered by. I can only hope she stayed in all night and her husband was with her." I had a moment of doubt. Had I put too much faith in Cheryl? How well did I know her, really, and did it matter if I did? How well can we know anyone? Maybe she had killed Tommy Greene because he was rude to her daughter. Maybe she thought Simon was a threat to her in some way only she understood.

"If not Cheryl," Simon said, "then who? And why? I promise you, Lily. I don't have any enemies. No debts to the mob. No enraged former girlfriends. No jealous husbands or boyfriends of former girlfriends." He tried to laugh. "Not in America, anyway."

"A distraction maybe, to take the police's focus off Tommy Greene's death?"

"Funny way to go about it. I'd say the police focus is back on."

"Back on Tea by the Sea. Maybe off someone else." I groaned. "What an awful, awful mess. I wish that TV program had never called me. I didn't want to do the show, but Rose and Bernie talked me into it. See if I ever listen to them again."

"Come on. I'll walk you back." He took my hand, and we crossed the yard. No lights had come on in Victoria-on-Sea, not even in Rose's suite. The lights were all off at Matt's place.

"How's the work on the house coming?" I asked.

"Slowly but steadily. Matt's pleased. He got a big foreign language rights deal for his last book, which means he has some more money coming in, so he can afford to gut the main bathroom sooner than he'd planned."

We climbed the steps to my cottage. I opened the door, and Éclair rushed out. She sniffed at Simon's feet and then went on to investigate what scents the short rainstorm had deposited.

"I'm not happy at that blow to your head," I said. "And you did black out for a while."

"I'm okay."

"Yes. Yes. Famous last words. You're sleeping here tonight."

His eyebrows lifted, and his eyes widened. Something sparkled inside them.

Blood rushed to my face. "On the couch, so I can check on you every two hours. Like they say to do in case of a possible concussion."

"If you insist," he said.

"I insist." I led him into my house, called to Éclair, and shut the door. Then I pulled out my phone.

"Who are you calling at this time of night?" Simon asked.

"A text to Bernie. I have a bad feeling I'm going to need her in the tearoom tomorrow."

I made up the couch for Simon, brought out a clean bath towel, and told him to help himself to anything he might need in the kitchen. Éclair danced happily around our feet, delighted to have an overnight guest. When I was finished, I said, "Good night. For now. I'll be checking on you soon. You'd better get out of those damp clothes." My face burned as I realized he had nothing to change into.

"As should you. Your pajamas are wet." He took a step toward me. He ran his fingers lightly across my right cheek. I looked into his eyes, and I liked what I saw there. I liked it very much.

"Good night, Lily." He dropped his hand and took a step backward.

I managed to stammer, "Good night," before running for my bedroom. Éclair didn't follow.

Chapter 20

I set my alarm to wake me every two hours, but I needn't have bothered. I didn't get a wink of sleep that night between the need to get up and check on my guest, burning awareness of Simon lying only a few feet from me (wearing what?), and tumbled thoughts of what had happened.

Every time I checked on Simon, I found him sleeping peacefully. The blanket was pulled up to his chin, so I couldn't tell what he was wearing, if anything. I shook him gently and said, "It's Lily. Tell me you're still alive."

"Alive," he grunted and fell back to sleep. Éclair spent the night on the floor next to the couch.

I lay on my back in the dark, looking up at the ceiling, and thought.

How had Cheryl's earring come to be found at the spot where Simon had been attacked? She could have gone for a walk earlier to admire the daisies, and it had fallen out then, but she hadn't told us she'd been in the garden when we were searching everywhere for the lost earring. That left two possibilities.

That Cheryl, for some deranged reason, had attacked Simon. If so, the police would get the proof, and they would charge her. I'd be minus a waitress, probably two, as it would be unlikely Marybeth would keep working for me, but so be it.

If, however, someone else had attacked Simon in an attempt to frame Cheryl, that was another matter entirely. The chance that this was unconnected to the murder of Tommy Greene was infinitesimal. Cheryl had been arrested and then released. Was the real killer wanting to apply pressure on her, keep the police's focus on her? If so, it could be for only one reason: to keep police attention away from the actual killer.

I'd told Bernie I was no longer interested in doing what I could to find the killer of Tommy Greene.

As I stared up into the darkness, I changed my mind.

We'd speculated that Tommy's killer might have come from outside of North Augusta, a personal or business enemy who had no connection to the filming at my tearoom. That this person had known where Tommy was staying and had somehow lured him out of his room and into meeting them. But if this same person had deliberately attempted to frame Cheryl by dropping her lost earring at the scene of the attack on Simon, then they had to have been at my tearoom today. I imagined Cheryl's earring slipping unnoticed out of her earlobe, falling to the ground or the floor. Someone silently scooping it up and slipping it unnoticed into a pocket or bag in case they got the chance to use it.

I mentally drew up my version of what Bernie had called a suspect list. The list was long—the entire film crew, including the two remaining judges, Claudia and Scarlet; Josh, the director; and Reilly, the assistant director. "Not a happy set," Melanie, the makeup artist, had told me. Everyone bickering with everyone else. Power plays, rivalries.

Allegra Griffin and Gary and Susan Powers had been at the tearoom today. Gary had been angry at Tommy for mocking him on that first day of filming. Angry enough to kill? Who knows what might make some people angry enough to kill? That Gary had attempted to set up an assignation with Bernie, a woman twenty years younger than him, in a public place, with his wife sitting only a few yards away, told me the man was arrogant beyond belief.

As for Allegra . . . I underlined her name on my mental list. Did she hate Cheryl enough to frame her for murder? Seems a heck of a stretch to still be carrying that much anger all these decades later over high school humiliations.

Did Allegra try to frame Cheryl because she hated her? Or because if Cheryl was charged, the police would focus their attention on building their case against her? Not on trying to find a new suspect.

Robyn Sullivan had hesitantly identified Cheryl as being in our garden the night Tommy died. But, as was pointed out, it was dark, she was at a distance, she didn't get a good look, and Allegra and Cheryl had similar body shapes.

Allegra had been in the tearoom when Tommy yelled at Marybeth. Allegra had been on the patio today when Cheryl lost her earring. Any motive Allegra might have to kill Tommy seemed dubious to me, but I was aware that the police don't always need a motive. People can act in strange ways and do things that seem beyond all common sense. Had she been so worried that I'd win the competition, she decided to fix the judging by "fixing" one of the judges?

I became aware of movement in the outer room, Éclair shuffling about, and the opening of a door.

I glanced at my bedside clock. Twenty to six. I turned off the unneeded alarm, climbed out of bed, and peeked into the living room. Simon was dressed in yesterday's clothes and folding the blankets. Éclair was nowhere to be seen, so I assumed Simon had let her out.

He turned and saw me watching him. He gave me a grin. His sandy hair was tousled from sleep, his clothes damp and badly wrinkled, his feet bare. "Morning, Lily."

"How are you feeling?"

He touched the back of his head. "As though I've been hit on the noggin and someone woke me up every two hours. Do you have any paracetamol?"

"Any what?"

"Headache pills."

"Oh, sure. In the bathroom vanity. Help yourself. I'll get dressed and be right out."

I scurried to do that. When I emerged, Simon was sitting at the kitchen table, nursing a glass of water and talking to Éclair.

"Did you sleep okay?" he asked me.

"As though I had to get up every two hours and had something on my mind. I have to get to the house and start breakfast. You don't have to work today, if you're not feeling up to it."

"I'd like to go home. Have a shower and change. Give those tablets a chance to kick in. Then I'll decide how I feel, if that's okay."

"Sure."

"Before I go, why don't you call Amy? Ask if she found out anything more about what happened to me."

"Amy is it?" I said.

"Why not?"

I made the call. It wasn't yet six a.m., and Amy Redmond had been here after midnight, but she answered, sounding bright and perky.

"Good morning, Detective," I said, wondering if it was time I started calling her Amy. Maybe not. "I'm calling to see if there've been any developments regarding last night's incident."

"How's Simon? Have you spoken to him yet today?"

"He's right here," I said. "He has a headache."

"Is that so?" she said, and I flushed at the touch of amusement in her voice.

"He couldn't go home alone, not after a blow to the head."

"I'd like to speak to him again, see if he remembers anything. Have him give me a call when he's up to it."

Simon indicated to me to turn on the speaker, and I did so.

"I'm here, Detective. I don't remember anything new. I scarcely remember what happened yesterday. You'll be pleased to hear Lily paid close attention to my welfare last night."

"Glad to hear it. If you do remember anything, anything at all, let me know."

"Will do."

"In the meantime, a couple of forensics officers are on their way to check out the ground I marked off, see if anything got dropped that we didn't see in the dark. Lily, will you tell your grandmother what's happening?"

"Sure. Did you, uh . . . speak to Cheryl?"

"I did. Detective Williams and I went to her house. She appeared to be unaware of why we were there, so I decided it wouldn't be necessary to bring her down to the station. Her husband was at home, and he told us they went to see friends for dinner and to watch a movie last night. He and Cheryl left together around ten thirty. I'll be confirming that with the friends this morning. Cheryl insists she didn't leave the house again, and her husband says he was restless in the night, the result of too many beers consumed during the movie, and he would have noticed if Cheryl wasn't in bed. That may or may not be true, but I don't intend to arrest a woman because we found a piece of her jewelry in a public garden not more than a few dozen yards from her place of employment. Despite," she added in a low voice, "what other officers may suggest."

By which I assumed Williams wanted to rearrest Cheryl, and Redmond had managed to talk him out of it.

We hung up, and Simon prepared to leave. "I could use a cup of coffee before I go home."

"Then you've come to the right place." I called to Éclair, and we left the cottage. As we walked along the edge of the bluffs, I texted Rose: **Minor incident in the night. No harm done. Nothing taken. But police will be poking around outside this a.m.**

I took the three steps down to the kitchen door, but Simon lingered on the path. "Don't you usually leave that light on all night?"

"Yes, I do. It's often still dark when I get here."

"You'd better check. It's not on now."

I opened the door and flicked the light switch several times.

"Nothing," Simon said. "You've probably got a blown bulb. I'll replace it later."

"No hurry." I put the coffeepot on. My phone beeped with an incoming message in response to my text to Bernie telling her she was on standby to work at the tearoom this morning.

Bernie: **Just getting up. Major writing day planned. My brain is alive with ideas! What's up?**

Me: **All okay. Happy writing.**

Bernie: *[Thumbs-up emoji]*

"Are you okay on your bike?" I asked Simon. "I can give you a lift, if you think not."

"I'm fine, Lily. It's not far to go, and the headache's fading already." He gave me a smile that lit up his handsome face. "I appreciate your concern."

I blushed and set about assembling baking ingredients.

A cinnamon coffee cake today and muffins out of the freezer if the cake proved popular and went quickly. When the coffee was ready, I poured us both a mug. "As your employer, your health and safety is my primary concern."

He lifted his mug in a salute. "Got it."

I blushed some more.

As he drank his coffee, he washed and sliced the fruit that would make up the breakfast salad.

Edna came in, calling good morning as she reached for her apron. That she didn't ask us about last night's incident meant the paper hadn't picked up the story yet. Hopefully, they never would. We didn't need B & B guests thinking their lives were in danger.

"I'm off." Simon rinsed his mug in the sink. "I'll check in later, Lily."

"Bye," I called.

"What's he got to check in about?" Edna asked.

"Nothing."

She gave me a look but said no more.

"Have the TV people come in?" I asked Edna later, as she prepared to carry the first of the breakfast plates into the dining room.

"Yes."

"How do they look?"

"Look? What does that mean?"

I'd meant, do any of them look as though they'd been creeping around in the night and attacking a man. But I didn't say so.

"The usual cheerful bunch," Edna said. "They're seated at separate tables, ignoring each other. Reilly's here, talking to Josh."

"I'll go out and make friendly," I said.

Edna gave me a sideways look. I took the plates from her. "Flip those sausages, will you? And check on the bacon. Who are these for?"

"Fully loaded's for Josh. The poached eggs and toast are for Claudia. Scarlet's having yogurt and fruit."

I took Claudia her breakfast first. "Good morning."

Her iPad was propped on the table in front of her, next to her coffee cup. She moved it so I could put the plate down, and I caught a glimpse of an online gambling page. She gave me a smile and said, "Good morning, Lily." The smile on her face and the sparkle in her eyes told me she was on a winning streak. That wouldn't last. It never lasted.

I studied her face as I said, "Off to North Augusta Bakery this morning?"

"Yes, we are. I don't mind saying, they'll have to do an excellent job to beat you." She wiggled her finger at me and gave me a wink. "Don't get overconfident. I'm sure they're up to the challenge."

Yup. She was winning, and it had put her in a good mood. Her eyes were clear, and her skin was fresh. She did not look like a woman who'd been creeping around a dark garden in the rain at midnight.

Next Josh. He and Reilly were talking in low voices, but I didn't have to hear the words to know they were arguing. Josh broke off when I put his plate in front of him.

"Good morning, gentlemen."

Josh growled, and Reilly said, "Morning, Lily. Another lovely day." Josh picked up his fork and attacked his sausage with such force, I wondered if he was wishing it were his son's face. I wanted to linger, find out what they were arguing about, but I didn't see any way of doing that without being totally obvious, so I left them to it.

"Sorry, Josh," I heard Reilly say, "but that's the way it's going to be." He pushed his chair back and stood up. "Be at the car in twenty minutes, or I'm leaving without you. Claudia, Scarlet. Twenty minutes."

Claudia waved her fork in acknowledgment, but Scarlet

scowled into her bowl of yogurt and muttered under her breath.

"Everything okay?" I asked.

"I don't know who died and made Reilly god," she snarled. "Too big for his britches, that one."

"Have a nice day," I said.

As the morning routine continued its regular rhythm, I finally made up my mind and decided on a course of action. Cheryl or Marybeth had not called to say they wouldn't be in today. I'd gotten a good amount of baking done last night, enough to allow them to manage for a few hours without me.

Shortly before nine, Robert the Bruce ran into the kitchen. Éclair, who'd been lying under the table, alert for any scraps that might fall, rose to her feet and gave her nemesis a half-hearted bark. The cat ignored the dog, as he always did, and leapt onto the table. I lifted him off the table and put him on the floor. He ignored me, as he always did, and jumped back up as Rose came in.

"Good morning, love. Good morning, Edna. I'll have my tea in here this morning."

"That's nice," Edna said as she took a batch of muffins into the dining room. I put the kettle on.

"What's this about police activity?" my grandmother asked me. "I peeked out and saw two people crawling through the shrubbery and a section of the garden marked off with yellow tape."

I jerked my head toward the door and mouthed, "Later."

One shaggy eyebrow rose. Robbie crawled onto her lap and gave me a supercilious smirk.

"I've decided to watch the filming at the bakery today," I said.

"Good heavens, why? Surely you're not hoping to throw Allegra off her game?"

"Nothing of the sort. Even if I wanted to, I won't get into the kitchen. I'm going to enjoy a nice lunch out." I poured boiling water over two tea bags in the sturdy old brown teapot. "Want to come?"

"Need you ask? Are we inviting Bernadette to this nice lunch outing?"

"Not today. She told me she's wanting to get writing done." I poured my grandmother a cup of tea and put it in front of her, along with the sugar bowl and milk jug.

"Best not disturb her, then." Rose added a splash of milk and a heaping spoonful of sugar and stirred. "Heaven knows if this book will ever be finished, the way that girl can get distracted."

I didn't bother to mention that much of that distraction was caused by Rose herself summoning Bernie on some mad scheme or another. My phone rang, and I pulled it out of my pocket. Bernie. "Looks like she's been distracted," I said to Rose as I answered.

"Someone attacked Simon!" A screech came down the line.

"How do you know?"

"Matt just called me. The cops were around at his place first thing, asking if he'd seen anything shortly after Simon left him last night."

"Had he?"

"No. He called Simon before calling me, to check up. Simon says he's okay, nothing but a sore head, and that he spent the night at your place." Her voice dropped. "Does that mean he *spent the night*?"

"It means he needed supervision in case of a concussion, so we thought it prudent that he sleep on my couch."

My grandmother choked on her tea. Edna stared at me from the doorway, her arms full of used dishes. I shrugged.

"Wow! You don't know who did it?" Bernie asked.

"The police are investigating."

"I bet. It obviously has something to do with the death of Tommy Greene. Unless you have two random killers running around your property, which you probably don't want to consider."

"No. I do not."

"Okay. What's our plan of attack?"

"Aren't you writing this morning?"

"Writing can wait. I'll be there in a few minutes, and we can put our heads together and come up with a plan."

"I'm ahead of you for once. I have a plan. It's almost nine now. I need to open the tearoom, and you can get some writing done. Then I'll pick you up at one o'clock. Don't have lunch."

Edna and Rose were staring at me. "I guess you want to know what that was about," I said.

They nodded, and I filled them in, emphasizing that Simon had emerged unscathed but for a headache and a sizable lump on the back of his head.

I phoned Cheryl on my way home from the B & B, watching as Éclair chased a squirrel up a tree.

"I assume you're calling because you know I had a visit from the police last night," Cheryl said.

"Yes. I also know they didn't arrest you, and that's good."

"Detective Redmond said she'll have someone check that we were at the Reynolds' house last night. We were, and they'll say so."

"Yesterday you didn't by chance take a break and go for a walk in the garden?"

She laughed without humor. "Redmond asked me that, and I told her I didn't go into the garden, because I didn't get a break all day, what with the fuss over the stupid TV show. Is Simon okay, Lily? Redmond was noncommittal about that."

"He's fine. Sore head, but nothing more."

"Good. I like him. He's always so cheerful. I can't imagine who would attack him or why they'd have my earring on them. Marybeth and I'll be at work at the regular time."

"Glad to hear it," I said. "I have some errands to run this afternoon, but I'm pretty well set, so you should be able to manage for a couple of hours without me."

"We always can."

"Which is why I pay you the big bucks."

When we'd hung up, I wondered if it was time to give Cheryl and Marybeth a raise.

I decided to forego my half hour of relaxation on the porch this morning and start work early if I was going to be skipping out of the tearoom in the afternoon. I took Éclair home as soon as everyone had been served their breakfast, and apologized to her for no yard time this morning. Judging by the look on her little face, I'd announced that the end of the world was at hand. "Don't give me that," I said. "Jean will be around later to take you for your walk."

She wagged her tail.

Chapter 21

Sandwiches were made and resting in the fridge, covered in plastic wrap; scones in the freezer; and a fresh batch on the cooling rack, next to an Earl Grey chocolate tart and almond macarons. Mini cupcakes had been iced and decorated, lemon tarts baked, strawberry tarts assembled, and shortbread and chocolate chip cookies were thawing in the pantry.

Last night's rain had ended before dawn, and the rising sun soon dried everything out. We had a full reservations book for today.

Confident I was leaving my business in good hands, at quarter to one I trotted up to the big house to collect Rose and her car. My grandmother was waiting for me on the veranda, cavernous purse on her lap, cane gripped in both hands. Robbie had been confined to the house. I regretted mentioning the outing to Rose. I'd invited her to come with me before I knew Bernie would be joining us. Three can sometimes be a crowd. Oh, well. Couldn't be helped now. Once Rose decided she was doing something, she did it.

As I've lived my entire life in Manhattan, I've never owned a car. Here in Cape Cod Rose and I share her Ford

Focus. I got it out of the garage and drove it to the foot of the stairs. Rose regally descended the steps and got in.

"I shall assume this visit to the bakery is part of your master plan."

"It is."

"Are you going to tell me what this master plan is?" She fastened her seat belt.

"No. I have a suspicion as to who killed Tommy Greene and thus is the person who attacked Simon last night."

"Are you planning to accuse him or her? I don't think that would be wise, love."

"Fear not. I want to watch what happens this afternoon and then think about it some more. I won't do anything. I'll tell the detectives and let them handle it."

Bernie was waiting for us in front of the dilapidated old cottage she'd rented for the summer. The only reason she could afford it was because no one else wanted it. Dealing with last night's rain would have involved the use of a copious number of buckets.

She hopped into the back seat.

"How are you today, love?" Rose asked.

"Tired. I was up most of the night lugging buckets full of rainwater and dumping them out the back. I swear there's a new leak in that roof every time it rains. Where are we going, Lily, and why are we going there?"

"To the bakery. I want to catch some of today's filming."

"Why?"

"She has a master plan," Rose said.

"I have a vague suspicion," I said.

I couldn't get anywhere near the bakery to park, so I had to let Rose and Bernie out and then drive in ever-increasing circles through the back streets of North Augusta until I finally happened upon a vehicle about to vacate its space, and I pulled in behind it. I locked my car and jogged to the bakery.

Unlike at Tea by the Sea, which is nestled on its own spacious property, the TV trailers and equipment vans had to park along Main Street. That, of course, attracted passersby, and a substantial crowd had gathered on the sidewalk outside the bakery.

"We're not going to get in," Bernie said when I'd tracked them down to a bench outside a clothing store.

"Follow me," I said. "Rose, keep that cane handy."

She hefted it in her hands and gave me a wicked grin.

We pushed our way through the crowd in front of the North Augusta Bakery. Rose's cane wasn't needed: this was a mellow bunch, people on vacation straining to see what all the fuss was about and maybe catching a glimpse of a TV personality.

"Closed to the public," the security guard at the door said to us.

"You know me," I said. "From Tea by the Sea?"

"Oh, yeah. Sorry, Ms. Roberts. I don't have you on my list, but I guess you can go on in. Hi, Mrs. Campbell. Nice day, isn't it?"

"Following a most welcome bit of rain," Rose replied.

The scene inside the North Augusta Bakery was much as it had been at Tea by the Sea. Every seat was taken, with customers enjoying a light lunch or a baked treat with their coffee or tea. Scarlet and Claudia sat at a center table for two, finishing their sandwiches and about to get stuck into dessert. Apple pie for Claudia and a slice of chocolate cake stuffed with buttercream and covered in a thick layer of ganache for Scarlet. Men with gigantic cameras mounted on their shoulders moved through the crowded space, filming people trying to enjoy their lunch while pretending they weren't being filmed, Susan and Gary Powers among them. Gary Powers was seated facing the door. He flushed when he saw us, meaning Bernie, and turned away. Other members of the crew stood at the edges of the room, watching the activity and fiddling with their equipment. Melanie was at the ready with her portable makeup kit and brushes in case a last-minute touch-up to one of the stars would be needed. Reilly supervised the shoot. I didn't see Josh. He might be in the kitchen with Allegra, filming her at work.

As I watched, Scarlet said something to Claudia, who laughed delightfully. Scarlet patted her lips with her napkin, stood up, and began moving through the room, stopping at tables to chat to guests and presumably ask if they enjoyed the food. Or, more likely, to ask them to criticize it. At one point Reilly stepped up to her and whispered in her ear. She shook her head vehemently. He repeated it. She threw him a vicious look but then replastered the smile on her face and sailed to the next table. Claudia, once the camera was off her, shoved the barely touched slice of pie to one side, leaned back in her chair, sighed, and closed her eyes.

Reilly turned and caught sight of me watching him. His face tightened for an instant; then he wiped the expression away and came over to greet us. "I wasn't expecting to see you three here today."

"This is all just *so* interesting," Rose said. "I've had a wonderful idea, and I couldn't wait to tell you about it. A show featuring grandmothers making their favorite family recipes. Do you think your company would be interested?"

"You don't cook, Rose," Bernie said. "So you couldn't be on it."

"I can cook. I simply choose not to. No matter, I'll be a judge. I do eat." Her blue eyes twinkled, and Reilly gave her a fond, but slightly patronizing smile.

"Not my department. You'll have to speak to Josh about that," he said.

"Where is Josh?" I asked.

"In the kitchen, with the cook."

"Running the show from back there?"

"Even Josh can't be two places at once. Nor can you. No work at your tearoom today?"

"I'm all caught up. Like my grandmother, I can't get enough of watching TV being made."

He gave me a suspicious look. I shrugged. That was a lie, and he knew it.

At the table next to the one Scarlet was visiting, a woman let out a shout of near-hysterical laughter. The cameraman was so startled, his camera jerked. Reilly spun around. The woman clapped her hands to her mouth in horror, but he bellowed, "Cut! You do that again, and you'll be out of here. Do you understand?"

She nodded.

"Never mind. No second chances. You're out of here now." He jerked his thumb toward the door. "Get lost."

The miscreant slowly got to her feet. She lifted her bag off the back of her chair; her lower lip trembled as she fought back tears. "I'm sorry," she mumbled. She crossed the room, head down, and hurried out the door. Notably, her three tablemates didn't bother to join her.

"You." Reilly pointed a finger at Bernie. "Take her place."

"What?"

"I don't want an empty chair. She hasn't touched her pie yet. Order a cup of coffee and have the pie."

"I don't want pie."

"Sure you do, sweetie. You'll look good on camera." He took her arm and just about dragged her across the room. Bernie threw a glance at me over her shoulder as she dropped into the recently vacated chair. Reilly had a word with the cameraman, and the camera was turned toward Bernie.

"Claudia," Reilly yelled.

Claudia's head was thrown back, and her eyes were still closed.

"Claudia!"

She jerked awake, gave her head a shake, and straightened up. "I'm here. What do you want?"

"Talk to this table. First, your makeup's smeared." He snapped his fingers, and Melanie appeared at the older woman's side, as if in a puff of smoke. While Melanie dabbed powder on Claudia's cheeks and added a touch of fresh lipstick, Reilly said to Bernie, "Eat that pie and tell Claudia what you think of it. What you think of it is something along the lines of the best blueberry pie you've ever had."

"It's blackberry," one of Bernie's tablemates said.

"What?"

"It's not blueberry pie. It's blackberry."

"If I say it's blueberry, it's blueberry," Reilly said. "Or would you like to join your friend on the street?"

"Blueberry," she chirped.

On her way back to her corner, Melanie found a chair on the sidelines for Rose, and my grandmother gratefully sat down. I stood next to her, watching the filming. Reilly didn't seem to be in a good mood today, and he snarled at pretty much everyone.

Josh and a cameraman came out of the back, and Reilly called a temporary halt to the filming. Claudia and Scarlet returned to their table. Scarlet pulled out her phone, while Melanie made more adjustments to Claudia's lips and hair. The servers, the same ones who'd been here when I'd visited last week, cleared away the dirty dishes and began laying the tables with fresh cutlery. The guests didn't turn over but got themselves ready to dig into another round of lunch. Bernie, I noticed, had eaten all her pie and was chatting happily with the two women and one man at her table. At a different table, a woman left, and one of the crew asked Rose if she'd like to take the vacant seat, and she accepted.

"Hi," Josh said to me.

"Hi."

"Surprised to see you and your friend here. And your grandmother."

"We're interested in watching how my competition's doing. How's it going in the kitchen?"

"Well. Your competitor's a highly competent baker. She's mighty temperamental, and she must be a nightmare of a boss, but she can cook. I got some good footage of her berating her poor waiter."

"He's her nephew," I said.

"I thought he seemed used to her."

As if hearing her name, Allegra appeared at the entrance to the kitchen. She wore a long apron over jeans and a T-shirt. Her hair was pulled back into a too-tight bun. If Melanie had worked any of her magic on Allegra, the effect was long gone. Allegra studied the room with an expression I knew well: she was making sure everything was to her satisfaction. She nodded at Gary and Susan Powers, and her gaze passed on. She started when she saw Bernie and then Rose, and her eyes flew to me. The look she gave me was not friendly. I wiggled my fingers in greeting, and she turned and stomped off into her kitchen.

"Are you going to use the footage," I asked Josh, "of her berating her nephew? It will be embarrassing for him."

"Not sure yet. We'll see what we have." He sighed. "I could have counted on Tommy to give me the drama and the temperament I need to keep the show interesting." He shook his head. "But Tommy's not here, is he?"

"Do you need drama and temperament? That British baking show where everyone's so nice to everyone else is hugely popular. Canadians are doing a version of the same program, I've heard."

"That's *that* show. I've got my show." He glanced across the room to where Reilly was instructing Claudia and Scarlet. "I thought I had my show."

Reilly turned and saw Josh talking to me. He lifted his hand in a wave to his father before addressing the room. "Everyone ready? Great. Let's do it one more time. Now, remember, if Claudia or Scarlet stops at your table, be natural and friendly, but don't fuss. Josh and Eddie, can you two get some more shots in the kitchen? Thanks, Allegra."

Allegra had come back out to find out what was going on. She gave me another one of her hostile stares and then retreated, followed by the director and his cameraman.

I'd seen enough. I was ready to leave, but Rose and Bernie were filling seats as orders were being taken and a second round of lunch was being served. I was too timid to face Reilly's wrath by dragging them away, so I slipped outside to make a phone call.

I got no answer from Amy Redmond and left a message, asking her to call me back. By the time I was able to get Rose and Bernie away, both of them stating that they could never eat another thing, the detective still hadn't returned my call. As I went to get the car, I tried again. I left another message.

"How was it?" I asked when we were heading back to Victoria-on-Sea.

"The lunch?" Bernie answered. "I have to say, Lily, it was good. Seriously yummy. Her pastry isn't as good as yours, not by a long shot, but her cake's up there. She does hearty soups and thick sandwiches of the sort you don't, so if that's what the judges are looking for . . ."

"You had pie *and* cake?"

"And an oatmeal cookie. I like your shortbread better."

"Good to hear. Rose?"

"Too much salt in my soup. I told Claudia that. I think Claudia was surprised to see me there."

"Considering you're not exactly an impartial diner," I said.

"There is that. I get the feeling impartiality isn't of concern to them. Claudia said something interesting to me during the break."

"What?" Bernie asked.

"She thanked me for my hospitality and mentioned she'd like to come for a proper vacation later in the summer, when she has a gap in her schedule. She wants to reserve two rooms, including the one she's in now, for a week. The other room's for her daughter, who also, according to Claudia, needs a vacation by the sea."

"A week for two at Victoria-on-Sea at the height of the season in the best rooms isn't cheap," I said.

"It is not."

Bernie rested her arms on the back of our seats and leaned between us. "Maybe Claudia's not as badly off financially as we assumed."

"Or she's expecting a change in her fortunes," I said, thinking of how cheerful she'd seemed at breakfast this morning.

"More likely the expectation of a change in her fortunes," Rose said. "Every gambler in the world is the same. Their luck's about to change. Any minute now. My childhood friend Roz was a maid at the home of Sir Reginald Mathers and Lady Mathers. Sir Reg, as everyone called him, gambled away the entirety of the extensive fortune his ancestors made in coal mining. Roz said the screaming fights, night after night, between Sir Reg and Lady Mathers were something to behold. All he needed, he kept telling her, was one big break. When he did get the big break, he gambled the lot again, and the cycle continued. The estate wasn't entailed, and eventually they had to sell it and creep off into the night ahead of the bailiff. No one had much sympathy for him or his family. Dirty money, coal, particularly in Yorkshire."

"Do you think Tommy Greene's death had anything to do with this expected change of Claudia's fortunes?" Bernie asked. "Maybe she bumped him off in a contract killing and is about to get paid."

"No," I said. "Rose's story, excessively longwinded though it might be, has a point. Claudia had one good night at the virtual tables and is now confident her luck will continue."

"I suspect you're not telling me something," Bernie said.

I turned into the driveway and didn't reply. I checked my phone as Rose and Bernie got out of the car. Still nothing from Amy Redmond. I considered trying Chuck Williams, but I decided not to. He was as likely to smile condescendingly at me and tell me not to worry my pretty little head about men's business as listen to what I had to say.

I knew, I thought I knew, who killed Tommy Greene. And why. But that person wasn't going anywhere, not immediately, and I'd wait until I could speak to Redmond.

As my grandmother climbed the steps to the veranda I signalled to Bernie to wait. I put the car in the garage and then joined her. Redmond wasn't answering my calls, but I needed to tell someone what I was thinking.

"I have no proof," I said, "but I've been thinking it over and—"

Her phone rang. She looked at me, and I gave her a wave, telling her to answer if she wanted.

"Hi, Matt. What's up?" Her eyes widened as she listened. She turned her back on me, but I could still hear. "Nothing much. Yes, that would work. Yes, I'd like that. Thanks. See you then."

She put her phone away and turned back to me. The

color was high in her cheeks, her green eyes sparkled, and her face was one big grin. "That was Matt."

"Was it now? What did he want?"

"He thought that if I wasn't doing anything tonight, maybe we could go out. There's a new band playing at this place he likes in town, and he wants to hear them. Maybe we can grab some dinner first. That's if you don't have anything you need from me. Do you?"

I almost said I'd been counting on her helping me work tonight just to see the expression on her face, but I decided not to be mean. "Nothing. I'm going to bake for a while. Not too long."

"Great! I mean, okay. I mean, it's a casual outing with a friend to hear some music. Nothing important, right?"

"Right. Super casual."

"I wonder what I should wear. He said a band, but he didn't say what kind of band. Heavy metal? Classical ensemble?" She spun on her heels and took two steps toward her car. Then she stopped and turned back. "Sorry. You had something you wanted to say?"

"It'll keep. Have a nice evening."

I arrived at Tea by the Sea just in time. They were running out of scones and getting low on fruit tarts and cupcakes. I put my apron on, my head down, and got stuck into it.

Marybeth and Cheryl cleaned up after closing and prepared the dining room for another day tomorrow. When they were taking off their aprons and gathering their purses, I asked, "Did you hear anything more from the police?"

"I saw Chuck Williams in the garden, poking around that area they'd cordoned off," Marybeth said. "Looking as though he was Sherlock Holmes searching for patterns in the turn of a leaf or a bent blade of grass or something.

All he needed was the deerstalker cap and magnifying glass. He looked like a fool."

"He is a fool," Cheryl said, "always has been, always will be, but he's also our town's lead detective. He saw me watching him when I was serving on the patio and gave me the death stare." She wrapped her arms around herself against a sudden shiver.

"He didn't come in?" I asked. "He didn't try to talk to you?"

"No."

They left, and I continued baking. I'd been wanting to try a new recipe for a coconut and lime drizzle cake, and tonight seemed as good a night as any.

The ringing of my phone dragged me out of a comfortable baking reverie. When I looked up from the dough in the bowl in front of me and glanced out the window, I was surprised to see that the trees on the far side of the road were dark shapes outlined against the eastern sky. I can get lost sometimes, lose all track of time, when I'm working. My hands were sticky with cookie dough, but when I saw the name on the phone's display, I stabbed the button with a finger and yelled, "Detective Redmond. Hold on a minute. I have to wash my hands."

I ran for the sink, scrubbed and then dried my hands. I scooped the phone off the counter. "So sorry. Are you still there?"

"I am. What's up?"

"Did you get my messages?"

"I've been tied up. I'm in Boston."

"Has some evidence regarding the Tommy Greene case arisen in Boston?"

"Believe it or not, Lily, the police often have to work on more than one case at a time. Never mind. I'm here on a personal matter."

"Oh, sorry." I never stopped to consider that Amy Redmond had a personal life. I knew she'd come from Boston to join the NAPD.

"It's okay, Lily. My grandmother's caregiver took ill suddenly, and my parents are out of town. I flew in a short while ago to check on Grandma and stay with her tonight. The agency that provides the caregivers will have someone here tomorrow morning. I expect to be in North Augusta by lunchtime. Do you have some new information? Something about the attack on Simon last night? If so, you can speak to Chuck Williams."

"No new information, but I've been thinking it over, and I—"

I heard a low, shaking voice in the background, and Redmond said, "Hold on, Grandma. I'll be off in a minute."

"It'll keep," I said.

"Okay. Talk to you tomorrow. If anything happens, call Detective Williams." She hung up.

I studied the phone in my hand. I could call Williams, tell him what I suspected. Instead, I decided it could wait until Redmond got back tomorrow. The TV crew wasn't going anywhere—they had several more days of filming before they were due to leave North Augusta.

It was fully dark by the time I decided I'd done enough baking for tonight. I was pleased with the new cake recipe, and I hoped my customers would be, too. I put the ingredients away, washed up the baking equipment, wiped down the countertops, and threw my apron and dishcloths into the laundry basket.

I checked that the back door was locked, and the light over the door was on, and left through the dining room. I paused for a moment to admire the empty restaurant in the dim glow coming from the vestibule. My place. The jams and jellies, chutneys and teas we sold were neatly lined up on their shelf, next to teacups and side plates, teapots, and assorted teatime accessories. The tables were laid with crisp white tablecloths and colorful linen napkins. The cutlery was silver; fresh flowers were tucked into slim glass vases. The center table featured a wide silver bowl overflowing with short-stemmed red roses grown in our own gardens. The light was dim, the room quiet, the air full of the lingering scents of tea and fresh baking.

I smiled to myself, feeling genuinely happy. I might not be chosen as the winner of *America Bakes!* but I was a winner in my own mind, and that's all that mattered.

I left through the vestibule, leaving the light on and ensuring the door was locked behind me, and walked slowly home.

Cloud cover was thick, and only a scattering of individual stars broke the velvet blackness of the night sky. Lights shone from some of the upstairs guest rooms at Victoria-on-Sea. I walked slowly, enjoying the night and the scents of freshly cut grass and a myriad of flowers, mingling with salt from the sea. Simon had texted me earlier to say he'd come to work, and I'd been vaguely aware of the buzz of the Weedwacker late this afternoon, but he hadn't come into the tearoom.

Other than the dim light over his porch, Matt Goodwill's house was wrapped in darkness. I wondered if he was still out with Bernie, and how their date was going. She might have tried to downplay it, tell me it was nothing other than a casual night out with a friend, but the excitement on her face told me otherwise. I liked Matt. He was good for her, and I was happy they'd finally realized it. I should say, she'd finally realized it. He'd liked her from the moment he first laid eyes on her. She'd suspected him of being a murderer.

I should have been on alert. I should have remembered

what had happened to Simon only last night, but I was in a place I loved, and the peace of the night put me off guard.

I rounded the big house, heading for my cottage and my dog, and the lights faded away. A figure stepped out of the shadows.

"Good evening, Lily. I figured you'd be passing this way before much longer."

Chapter 22

I should have told Bernie what I knew, even if she'd then decided to skip her date with Matt. I should have told Amy Redmond what I knew, regardless of whether her grandmother was calling her. I should have called Detective Williams and ignored his scorn.

But I hadn't. I'd foolishly not told anyone.

I instinctively took a step backward as I swallowed heavily. I slipped my hand into my pocket and gripped the comforting weight of my phone. I fumbled at it, trying to find the tiny indentation that was the ON button. "Goodness. You startled me," I said, trying to keep the fear out of my voice. "You're out late. What brings you here?"

"You do, Lily," Reilly Miller said. "Let's take a walk."

"Thanks, but no. It's late, and I've had a long day. We can talk tomorrow." I started to walk away, ready to break into a run. I could see my little cottage up ahead, wrapped in darkness.

Reilly grabbed my arm. "I said, let's walk."

Reilly had killed Tommy Greene and attacked Simon. Reilly was ambitious. Reilly didn't want to be assistant director under a father he didn't like or respect. He wanted control of *America Bakes!*, and he wanted everyone who mattered to know he had control. Make that show an even bigger hit, and he'd be invited to go on to bigger and better things. Tommy Greene had decided to quit. He didn't like being on TV, he didn't like being away from his family, and he missed cooking and running his own restaurant. He'd made up his mind as he walked with me through the garden, as he realized that a job that involved upsetting innocent people like Marybeth wasn't something he was prepared to do any longer.

I'd left Tommy standing at the bluffs. His phone records showed he hadn't made any calls in the hours before he died, so he hadn't told Reilly he needed to talk, but I believed Reilly had been lurking around the property all week. He seemed to like to keep an eye on what was going on. He'd been watching Simon last night; he was waiting for me tonight. Had Tommy run into Reilly and told him then and there what he'd decided? Why they'd gone into Tea by the Sea, through the door accidentally left unlocked, I didn't know. It didn't really matter, not now. Maybe Tommy needed to talk his feelings over, to explain, and he wanted to show Reilly what restaurants meant to him.

Tommy's death was a huge blow to the program, and for that reason, I hadn't at first considered either Reilly or Josh to be serious suspects in his death. But Tommy leaving voluntarily would have also been a huge blow to the show, and it might not have been able to survive. Tommy Greene was the star; he was the reason people watched *America Bakes!* Another chef of his caliber and reputation might not have wanted to follow him, to be nothing but the replacement, the second choice.

Tommy's death changed everything. Mega publicity for the show. A highly publicized hunt for his replacement. Big-name chefs, like "that Scottish guy," would be happy to take the place of their fallen comrade and garner all the attention that would receive.

And so Reilly made his move and got rid of Tommy before Tommy could announce his intention to quit. Emboldened, he began pushing his father aside, making the decisions himself. Turning *America Bakes!* into his show. Earlier, he'd argued with Josh about having Tommy humiliate a waitress. Reilly was finished with arguing.

Did Josh know his son had killed Tommy? He might, although if he did, he kept that knowledge somewhere deep inside where he didn't have to face it.

Reilly tugged at my arm. "Let's go."

I lost my grip on my phone, and it fell to the bottom of my pocket. I dug my heels in and tried to pull myself free. "I'm not going anywhere with you. I don't know what you want with me."

"I think you do. You're not as stupid as you look, are you? Not quite the little blond piece of baking fluff I'd taken you for."

I was so insulted I almost forgot that this man likely intended to kill me.

"I saw the way you looked at me this afternoon. You figured it out, didn't you, with all your nosing around and the questions about things that have nothing to do with you?" He began dragging me toward the cliff edge.

I screamed.

He yanked on my arm, throwing me off balance, swung me around, and clapped his hand over my mouth. I struggled to free myself, but he was stronger than me and powered by rage.

It wasn't yet eleven o'clock. Surely someone in the house would be up? Someone would come to the window to have a last look at the night sea before turning in?

Reilly shoved me toward the edge of the bluffs. In the distance I could hear Éclair barking, trying to raise the alarm. Would someone come to see what she was barking at?

Not until it was too late.

My feet scrambled for purchase on the damp grass, but the thin ballet flats on my feet couldn't find a hold. I struggled to breathe. Colorful circles danced in front of my eyes, and through them I could see the edge of the bluffs getting closer, the thin wooden railing, which wouldn't stop anything crashing through it, the drop into empty darkness beyond.

"Hey! What's going on down there?" A light came on above, and a woman's voice called out.

Reilly startled, and his grip on my arm relaxed just a fraction, but it was enough that I could jerk forward and put a couple of inches between us. I brought my heel up sharply and got him hard at a tender point. He grunted and staggered away from me, and his grip relaxed further.

I broke free and ran, yelling, "Police! Call the police. Help. Help!"

Reilly was between me and my cottage, so I sprinted along the edge of the bluffs behind the house, heading for the safety of the kitchen. I fumbled in my pocket for my key ring and found it. The light over the door was off, and I remembered that it had burned out. Simon hadn't yet replaced the bulb. I keep a lot of keys on my ring. Keys to both doors of the tearoom, to two entrances to the B & B, to Rose's suite, to my cottage. Each key was marked by a colored plastic cover to help me keep track of which was which, but I wouldn't be able to distinguish the individual colors in the dark. If I went down the three steps to the kitchen door and couldn't find the needed key fast enough, I'd be trapped. I kept running. Reilly was behind me, so close I imagined I could feel his hot breath on the back of my neck.

The alarm had been sounded. I hoped it had been

sounded, and that whoever had called out hadn't decided to go back to bed. If I could get to the veranda, to the front door, into the light, I could get into the house. If the police had been called, if people had been alerted, Reilly wouldn't dare step into the light and kill me.

At the far end of the house, past the French doors to the dining room, past the steps to the kitchen, a wooden staircase leads down to the rocky beach at the bottom of the bluffs. A few steps beyond the stairs, the house ends at the kitchen garden, where Simon grows herbs and vegetables for use in the B & B and the tearoom.

Reilly must have realized where I was heading. He veered to his left, intending to intercept me as I rounded the house. Without thinking or hesitating, I went right. I hit the stairs leading down to the rocky beach and the incoming sea.

It was tricky running in the dark on the narrow, steep staircase, but I'd been this way many times before. My hands slid over the railing as I flew down. Above me, the steps shook as Reilly's greater weight landed on them. To my infinite relief, lights in the house were coming on and people were shouting.

"The police have been called," I yelled over my shoulder.

He didn't reply, and the pounding of his footsteps didn't let up.

I hit the beach. My right foot skidded on the wet rocks, but I grabbed at the railing and managed to keep myself upright. In the shelter of the looming cliffs, all was dark. The tide was coming in, and white water crashed over rocks, and waves washed the shoreline almost to the edge of the cliff. I'd been raised in Manhattan, so I'm not much of a swimmer, but that didn't matter. No one could survive for long in the dark in those waves, being thrown against those rocks. Moving as quickly as I dared, I picked my way across the wet boulders and slippery stones. Cold water rushed over my feet. I pulled my phone out of my pocket, but I hesitated to turn the flashlight on. I needed the light, but the light would show Reilly exactly where I was.

"You can't get far," said a calm voice close, too close, behind me. "Tide's coming in, looks like. I see some rough shoreline up ahead."

I said nothing. No point in telling him the police were coming and if he didn't leave, they'd find him down here, whether I was dead or not. He had a single-minded focus on his mission, and nothing would stop him now.

I could only hope whoever'd been looking out an upper window had seen us taking the stairs, otherwise my rescuers would arrive too late to do me any good.

I was heading for a cluster of boulders ahead. I intended to scramble up them and crouch in the shelter of them to hide, and that would also keep me out of the reach of the rising tide.

So far, the dark night was working to my advantage. I know something of my way around down here, and Reilly didn't. He hadn't turned a light on, and I wondered why. Perhaps he'd dropped his phone as he struggled with me. Perhaps he was also aware that a light down here would attract attention he didn't want.

"You can't get far," he said, his voice so calm he might have been ordering a pot of oolong and the cream tea at Tea by the Sea.

I didn't bother to reply. It was slow going, as I carefully felt my way across the wet sand and slippery rocks and loose stones and shells, around the rapidly filling tidal pools. I'd gained my night vision, but that meant Reilly had, as well. High overhead, an airplane passed. A speck of light on the bay marked the passage of a boat. A particularly large wave crashed against the rocks and threw cold, salty spray onto me.

When I reached the boulders I'd hoped to find shelter in, I realized I'd been far too optimistic. Not much of a decent hiding place here at all. If Reilly walked past me and turned around, he'd see me. Still, it was the only hope I had. If he did pass me, I could slip out and try to make my way back to the stairs.

I lifted one foot and felt for a place to put it, so I could begin scrambling up. I found a crack in the boulder, fitted my right foot in, braced myself, and pushed off with my left leg. My thin, wet shoe slipped on the damp surface, and I fell, emitting an unwanted cry. I hit the ground hard and lay on my back, looking up into the dark sky.

"There you are," Reilly said.

Praying I hadn't broken anything, I flipped myself over and leapt to my feet. Thankfully, nothing gave way. I was facing Reilly now, and I could see his dark outline skipping nimbly across the rocks toward me. A light gleamed in his eyes. I stood my ground and tightened my fists. I would not go down without a fight.

And then, suddenly, he wasn't there anymore.

He yelled, and I heard water splashing and a man grunting with a combination of shock, pain, and exertion. I fumbled for my phone with shaking hands and pulled it out. I flicked the flashlight app on and shone it around the beach.

Reilly sat on the ground as water swirled around his hips. One leg was bent behind him, and the other disappeared beneath him. He tried to stand up, but he couldn't. He swore and kept on swearing as he flailed about, tugging at his leg. "Help me," he said. "It's stuck."

His right leg was trapped in a crevasse between two rocks. Waves crashed over him as the tide moved relentlessly in.

I edged around him, careful to keep myself out of range of his hands, keeping my eyes fixed on his face, hoping he wasn't playing a trick on me. But the frightened look in his eyes, the twist of pain in his lips, the angle of his leg told me this was no trick.

"I'll go for help," I said.

"I'm stuck. You have to get me out of here. The tide's coming in."

"I'll get help," I repeated.

"There isn't time." He began pushing at the rocks trapping him, but they were large and slick with wet seaweed and didn't move. The water climbed higher, washing over my lower legs. It was almost up to my calves now.

Between Reilly's shouts I could hear voices calling. A strong light swept the stretch of beach at the bottom of the stairs.

"Help, help!" I leapt up and down, waving my arms. "We're over here."

The light moved toward me. Another joined it.

I abandoned Reilly and ran toward the stairs. The beam of a powerful Maglite hit me full in the face, blinding me. I stumbled, yelped in pain, and covered my eyes with my hands. The light was lowered.

"What's happening there?"

When I could see again, I recognized Officer LeBlanc in front of me. Behind him Officer Bland jumped off the bottom step onto the ground.

I pointed down the beach. "It's Reilly Miller. He killed Tommy Greene. He tried to kill me. His leg's stuck in a rock pool."

A wave rushed between two boulders to wash against the legs of the police officers and threw white-topped spray onto the staircase.

The wave receded. High tide had been reached.

Chapter 23

I scrambled up as fast as I could go, my feet slipping on the slick, wet stairs. Hands reached for me, and I was pulled onto solid, dry land. I bent over, my hands on my knees, gasping for breath. A strong hand rubbed my back.

When I straightened up, a circle of faces was watching me. Bernie launched herself at me and wrapped her arms around me. She hugged me so hard, I was uncomfortably reminded of Reilly's strong fingers gripping my arm, but I let my friend hold me. Finally, she let go and stood back. "Looks like you'll live."

"You'd best get some clean clothes on, love," Rose said. "You'll catch your death." She tried to keep that English stiff upper lip in place, but her lip quivered, and her voice threatened to break.

"Good idea," I said.

Police officers passed me, heading down the stairs. Chuck Williams said in a surprisingly kind voice, "You do what your grandmother says, Lily. I'll have to take a statement from you, but first, I need to find out exactly what's going on here."

"Bernie, you take Lily to get into some dry clothes, and

Matt and I'll put the kettle on," Simon said, and I realized he'd been the one rubbing my back while I struggled to get control of myself.

"I can do that." Matt gave me a bright, encouraging smile.

"Off you go, love," Rose said.

Bernie put her arm around my shoulders and began to lead me away.

The onlookers stepped back, Claudia and Scarlet among them. Josh stood alone at the railing, watching the activity on the beach. He turned to face me. "Reilly?"

"I'm afraid so," I said.

"Tommy?"

"Yes. I'm sorry."

His face twisted, and he looked away.

Police radios burst with static as someone shouted for medics and added, "We need a crowbar down here." Reilly must be well and truly stuck.

At home, while I calmed a frantic Éclair, fussed over her, and offered her a doggie treat, Bernie ran the shower. When it was steaming, she practically shoved me under it. I stood beneath the hot water for a long time, letting the warmth seep into every pore. Finally, I got out, toweled myself off thoroughly, and dressed in ugly but warm track pants, heavy wool socks, and a thick sweater.

"What brings you here tonight, anyway?" I asked Bernie. "Not to mention Matt and Simon. How was your date? I hope Simon didn't go with you?"

"He did not, and it was very nice. Matt invited me back to his place for a . . . nightcap . . ." She gave me a broad wink. "We arrived to see every light in Victoria-on-Sea on, and people running around the veranda and the front lawn like a pack of chickens with their heads cut off. While we were debating whether or not we should see if we could be of assistance, police cars came screeching down the driveway behind us, and we had to move outta the way mighty quick. Matt called Simon, to let him know something was happening. If you'd rather not talk to Williams or anyone else tonight, I'll tell them you fell asleep."

"No. I'm fine." I shivered despite the warmth around me. "I want to get it all out."

"Reilly Miller. I always suspected it was him."

"You did not."

We found Detective Williams, several police officers, Scarlet and Claudia, and a substantial number of B & B guests gathered in the dining room, along with Rose. Most of the guests were dressed in some assortment of night-wear, with slippers on their feet. Scarlet's nightgown was a frothy pale green affair with a deep neckline trimmed with lace, the hem sweeping her feet. Claudia wore paisley pajamas that were about two sizes too large for her. With no makeup and hair ready for bed, neither one of them would be taken for TV stars.

Matt and Simon served coffee and tea and some of my baking they'd found in the freezer and quickly defrosted.

"Goodness," I said from the doorway. "A proper tea party."

Rose, also in her nightgown, indicated the chair next to her. I took it. Robert the Bruce eyed me as I sat down.

"First," I said, "how's Reilly?"

"He's been freed," Detective Williams said. "His leg's broken, and he's on his way to the hospital under escort. He's been charged with attempted murder of you. Other charges should be forthcoming."

"Josh went with him," Claudia said. "The poor man. I can't imagine what he must be going through."

"Reilly killed Tommy, then?" Scarlet said.

Williams spoke up. "Okay, ladies and gentlemen. It's late. Anyone who isn't directly involved in this matter can return to their beds. Thank you for your attention."

One by one the guests got to their feet, muttering some sort of good night. They appeared to be in no hurry to leave, but eventually, a uniformed officer shut the door behind them.

"Did Reilly specifically tell you he'd killed Tommy?" Chuck Williams asked me.

I tried to remember exactly what had been said between us. "He said he could tell I'd figured it out. Although he didn't actually say what I'd apparently figured out. Does that matter? I have absolutely no doubt he intended to kill me. He was going to shove me over the cliff and then run down the stairs to finish me off if the fall didn't do it."

I shuddered. Simon had come to stand behind me. He put his hands on my shoulders, and Rose took one of my hands in hers. I gripped it tightly. Bernie placed a cup of tea on the table next to me. I breathed in the rich, heady scent. "He would have done it, too, if someone hadn't shouted out an upstairs window."

"That was me," Scarlet said. "You and your grand-mother have a nice place here, but I've been too jumpy to enjoy it. Unable to sleep, thinking about what happened with Tommy, about problems with Josh, with the show. I heard a woman scream and stuck my head out to see what was going on."

"Giving me enough time to make a break for it," I said. "Thank you." I sipped my tea. Far too sweet, but I was grateful for the sweetness tonight.

"It was totally obvious Reilly was trying to take over the show," Scarlet said. "Using the disruption around Tommy's death to do what he'd been wanting to do for a long time and shove Josh out. I thought . . . I thought for a while Josh had killed Tommy because he thought Tommy was going over to Reilly's side. But Tommy wasn't, was he? He was finished with us and our ridiculous show."

"You suspected Josh was responsible," Williams said, "but you didn't tell us what you were thinking. Why not?"

She dipped her head. "I'm not as brave as Lily. I wanted all the trouble to just go away. I'm sorry."

Claudia stood up. She cleared her throat and faced Detective Williams. "I have a confession to make, Detective, and I regret not speaking up earlier. Your partner asked me if I was in the garden on Tuesday night. I said no. That was a lie. She asked me if I'd seen Tommy after I'd returned from dinner that evening. I told her no, and that was also a lie."

"You can be charged for that."

"I know, and I am truly sorry. In my defense, I'm not sure it would have helped with your investigation."

"It would have helped an innocent woman not be suspected of murder," I said, suddenly angry. These people and their secrets. I'd almost been killed. Cheryl had faced arrest and imprisonment. Scarlet hadn't wanted to get involved in the murder of a man she worked with, and Claudia had her own secrets to keep. "You asked Tommy for money before he died."

"Yes. I did," Claudia said. "My room faces the ocean, and I saw Tommy talking to you that night. You left, and he stood at the edge of the cliff for a long time, leaning on the fence, looking over the water. Obviously deep in thought. When he walked away, I expected that he'd be coming in, so I went downstairs to intercept him. I found him outside, walking in the rose garden. I joined him there. I . . . I asked him for a loan. He turned me down flat."

"You were wearing that puffy pink shell over your pajamas, right?" I asked.

"Yes. How did you know that?"

"Lily knows things," Bernie said. "She's smart that way."

"I . . . I've run into some financial difficulties," Claudia said. "Nothing serious, mind, and I'll be back on my feet in no time."

Rose snorted, and Robbie made a similar sound. "You keep telling yourself that, dear. With that attitude, I'm not surprised Tommy wasn't going to lend you money. He wasn't foolish enough to throw good money after bad."

I squeezed my grandmother's hand. "Claudia doesn't need a lecture right now."

Claudia swallowed heavily. Tears filled her eyes. "Maybe I do. Tommy told me he was finished with the show, and he intended to tell the network the next day. I . . . I should have told you, Detective. But I honestly didn't realize that was why he'd been killed."

"You didn't want to know," Rose said.

"I didn't want to have to tell anyone why I'd been talking with Tommy in the rose garden at that time of night. That I'd had to ask him . . . beg him . . . for money."

"You let Robyn Sullivan tell the police Cheryl had been in the garden, when it had been you," I said.

"I didn't know about that," Claudia said. "No one had any reason to tell me she'd identified someone else. If I'd known . . . I hope I would have come forward."

"We can talk about all this again tomorrow." Detective Williams put down his coffee mug and stood up. "I have a long night ahead of me." He hesitated, and then he crossed the room to stand in front of me. He held out his hand. I stared at it in surprise.

"Good work, Ms. Roberts," he said.

I stood up. I took his hand in mine, and we shook. His grip was surprisingly limp. No sign of a dominance display.

Chapter 24

Wednesday was a normal working day for us. Cheryl was cheerful, and so she should be, as the murder charge hanging over her head like a noxious cloud had been lifted. Marybeth was quiet and thoughtful. At one point in the busy afternoon, as she was arranging sandwiches on a platter for a light tea for four, she said, more to herself than me, "Makes you realize, doesn't it, what's important in life? I don't know how I'd be able to go on if my mom . . . had to go away."

I laid my hand lightly on her arm, but I said nothing. Words seemed inadequate.

She wiped at her eyes. "You and your grandma are really close. What about your mom?"

"My mom," I said. "Maybe I'll give her a call later."

And we went back to work.

Bernie texted me at three o'clock: **Drop everything at six and follow Cheryl.**

Me: **Why?**

Bernie: **Never mind.**

I wasn't prepared to drop everything at six, but I did go with Marybeth and Cheryl into the main dining room.

The last of the day's guests had departed a while ago, the linens had been scooped up prior to being washed, chairs were upside down on the tables to allow the floor to be vacuumed, and new place settings had not yet been laid.

Except for the big table in the center of the main room. The white tablecloth was freshly ironed, as were the green napkins. Seven places were set with our second-best china. A huge cut-glass bowl overflowing with peach roses sat in the center of the table, and a fluted champagne glass graced each place.

"What's going on?" I asked.

"Sit," Cheryl said.

"Why?"

"Because Bernie told me to make you sit."

I did as ordered as I heard the tapping of Rose's cane. Simon's arm was linked through hers, and they were followed by none other than Amy Redmond.

"What's going on?" I asked again.

"I assumed you'd want to know what's been happening today," Redmond said, "so I called your grandmother to arrange a time to tell you. She, in conjunction with Bernie, decided to make a grand affair of it."

"Fine." I started to rise. "But the airpots have been turned off, the coffee dumped, the baking put away, and the dishes are all done."

"Sit," Simon ordered.

I sat.

"It's all taken care of." He helped Rose into a chair. "Marybeth and Cheryl, you sit also. I'll give them a hand."

"Give who a hand?" I asked.

The expression on Rose's face was the same as the one on Robbie's when he'd licked up the entire contents of the cream jug before I noticed what he'd been up to. Marybeth and Cheryl looked as confused as I felt.

Bernie and Matt came in, laden with bakery boxes. Simon carried a tote bag clanging cheerfully as bottles clinked together. Bernie was in a vintage dress she'd worn to tea before: layers of ivory and gray silk reaching to a couple of inches above her ankles, gray lace trimming the neckline and bodice, and elbow-length sleeves. She'd matched the dress with short white gloves, a waist-length string of pearls, and a white fascinator decorated with gray beads.

She put the boxes on a nearby table and said, "Afternoon tea. Delivered straight to your door. As we don't want anyone jumping up and down making tea, we decided to do without it, and we brought champagne instead. The good stuff, courtesy of Matt and Simon." Simon bowed, Matt began taking bottles out of the bag, and Bernie opened the bakery boxes. She laid out a chocolate cake covered in a thick layer of shiny ganache, piles of brightly decorated donuts, and large oatmeal cookies.

"Those look like the sort of things made at North Augusta Bakery," I said.

"They were. I can't have you catering your own tea party. I paid a call on Allegra earlier. I thought I'd do the old 'let bygones be bygones' thing. She didn't throw me out of her place. I guess that's an improvement, but she's not ready to make nice."

"I never did anything to her."

"Irrelevant, as she sees it." Bernie laid the treats in the center of the table, and Matt and Simon passed around glasses of sparkling wine.

When everyone had been served, Simon lifted his glass. "Cheers."

"Cheers," we chorused. I took a sip, and bubbles danced in my mouth. It was the good stuff.

When everyone had helped themselves to the best of Allegra's baking, Amy Redmond tapped the side of her glass with her fork. "This might be the most pleasant debriefing

I've ever given, but the charm of the surroundings can't hide the seriousness of this business. Before I tell you what's been happening, Lily, I shouldn't have to remind you, but I will, that you should have told me or Detective Williams your concerns."

"You were busy."

"Yes, I was. I would have made one phone call to ensure you were protected and then gone back to what I was doing. I'm sorry to have missed the climax. Chuck phoned me in Boston to tell me what had happened. I was able to organize a neighbor to look in on my grandmother, and I came straight back here. I got to the station as Reilly Miller was finishing his breakfast and his lawyer was arriving. We've had an interesting and informative chat."

"Has Reilly confessed?" I asked.

"No. He and his lawyer are claiming that you grossly misrepresented the situation last night."

I almost choked on my champagne.

"Stuff and nonsense," Rose declared.

"Exactly," Redmond said. "He claims he tried to talk to you about the show, but you thought he was coming on to you and you ran away. Concerned about your welfare, he followed you down to the beach and fell into that hole."

I sputtered.

"We'll have no trouble dismissing that claim. Scarlet McIntosh's prepared to testify that when she looked out her window, she saw you struggling to free yourself from Reilly."

"What about the murder of Tommy Greene?" Cheryl asked.

"And the attack on me?" Simon said. "I'm assuming that was Reilly, too."

"He's denying both of those incidents but also trying to explain how he would have done it, if he had. He's nowhere near as clever as he thinks he is, and his lawyer's not having much success in getting him to shut up. Reilly admits he wanted his father to step aside and hand control of the show over to him. He spent some considerable time lurking around here in the dark, keeping an eye on things, he said, before his lawyer finally told him to stop talking. Why he needed to keep an eye on things in the middle of the night, he did not explain."

"Spying on them," Rose said. "Josh, Scarlet, Claudia. And Tommy."

"Yes. A couple of the people who work with him tell us they thought he seemed exceptionally tired this week. Pressure of the shoot, they thought at the time. I believe he was up most of the night watching Victoria-on-Sea."

"What a dreadful thought," Rose said.

"He was looking to cause trouble," Simon said.

"And he did," Redmond said. "I told him Claudia had been outside after dark on Tuesday, talking to Tommy. I implied she'd seen him, Reilly, there. He admitted he'd seen Claudia and Tommy talking, arguing, and he watched as Claudia went back inside, clearly angry. Tommy then walked through the garden, heading here. For the tearoom. Reilly says he approached Tommy and asked if something was bothering him. Tommy said he'd decided to leave the show. He, Reilly, told him to give it some more thought, and Tommy said he would."

"I don't buy that," I said. "My impression of Tommy was that he was a decisive man. He'd made up his mind."

"Regardless of what was said between them, Tommy let himself into the tearoom through the unlocked kitchen door."

"And there," Cheryl said, "all my troubles began. Why would he come in here?"

"He told me he missed cooking," I said. "He missed being on the ground in his own restaurant. He was in a pensive mood that night, debating his life choices, on the verge of making a major decision. He went to the nearest thing to a restaurant he could find—Tea by the Sea—to soak up the atmosphere and remind himself what he loved about them. He probably tried the door and was surprised when it opened."

"Reilly says when he left, Tommy was alive and alone. We'll break that defense down easily enough. As I said, he's eager to justify himself. He slipped up and stated that Tommy was admiring your marble rolling pin, Lily. Which, if he didn't come in with Tommy, he wouldn't have seen, now would he?"

"Why me?" Cheryl asked. "Why try to frame me?"

"I don't believe that was his initial intention," Redmond said. "This chocolate cake's good. You should put something like it on the menu, Lily."

"I'll get right on that." The cake was good. Exceptionally good. I'd never admit it.

"Reilly killed Tommy on impulse, without stopping to consider how he could get away with it. He must have been torn. If he packed up the filming and left North Augusta, he would have been out of our reach. But continuing with the program was the entire reason he'd killed Tommy in the first place. He had to keep *America Bakes!* going in order to be able to show the bosses he was in control and could make a success of it even without Tommy. Once you were in the frame, Cheryl, he hit on the idea of strengthening the case against you."

"No," I said, "he had more initiative than that. Now I remember it was Reilly who first pointed out that Cheryl had been angry at Tommy. When you were interviewing everyone in the B and B Wednesday morning, Reilly told you what happened between Tommy and Marybeth, and that Cheryl had been furious at Tommy. Reilly deliberately tried to implicate Cheryl."

Amy Redmond's eyes narrowed as I spoke, and I could

see a question forming behind them. I almost bit my tongue off. I'd overheard that snippet of conversation from my hiding place in the secret room. If Amy realized I hadn't been in the drawing room at the time . . . Reilly Miller wasn't the only one who didn't know when to stop talking.

"He must have seen you lose your earring, Cheryl," I said quickly, "and he scooped it up when no one was watching, probably with the intention of planting it somewhere. That night, as he was creeping around, he saw Simon, and . . . we know what happened."

Simon rubbed the back of his head. "Yeah, mate, I do."

"What happens now?" Bernie asked.

"Reilly's been charged with one count of murder, one count of attempted murder, and one count of assault," Redmond said. "For starters." She was no longer looking at me, and I hoped the moment had passed. "He's not going anywhere. We'll get him on all three charges. I have no doubt about that."

"Fine," Bernie said, "but I meant about the show. Is Josh going to continue with it?"

"No. Everyone's packing up and leaving. I can't see it ever resuming, not with a murder charge hanging over it. Josh Henshaw's been at the station all day. He's the one who arranged for the lawyer for Reilly."

"They checked out this morning," Rose said. "Claudia and Scarlet couldn't get out the door fast enough. Scarlet called a cab to take her to the airport, and Claudia begged to be allowed to share it. Scarlet looked like she was going to say no, but then she relented, and they left together. Josh asked me to recommend a cheaper place for him to go to as, he told me, the *America Bakes!* budget won't be covering it."

"If one good thing comes of this"—Marybeth smiled at

her mother—"maybe Josh and Reilly can build a solid father-son relationship."

"Allegra Griffin," Redmond said, "is fit to be tied. This morning a couple of our officers stopped at the bakery for a coffee before coming on shift, and they said the screaming from the back was pretty intense. That was probably around the time Allegra realized the film crew wasn't coming back."

I fixed my stare on my grandmother. "If you ever, ever, get a call about another TV program, you will slam down the phone immediately. Do you get it?"

"I'm thinking it would be nice if someone made a movie version of my book," Bernie said. "They could use Victoria-on-Sea for the mansion in which Rose, my Rose, grew up."

"No!" I shouted.

Redmond chuckled. She wiped her fingers on her napkin and said, "Thanks for this. I'd better get back. We have another round of questions for Reilly. One thing I've been wondering, Lily. Was there anything in particular that made you realize it was Reilly who killed Tommy?"

I nodded. "He was in the breakfast room yesterday morning, pushing his weight around, giving orders not only to Scarlet and Claudia but to Josh, as well. Scarlet said, 'Who died and made him god?' A common enough saying, but at that moment, I realized that someone had died, and Reilly was acting like he was indeed the god of *America Bakes!*"

Amy Redmond dipped her head toward me and left Tea by the Sea.

The party ended shortly after that. Marybeth had to pick up her kids, and she'd driven to work with Cheryl. Matt asked Bernie if she'd like to see the progress he was making on his kitchen. She accepted, and he politely asked

Rose to join them. The edges of my grandmother's mouth turned up as she demurely declined, saying she was tired. Matt tried not to look too pleased at that.

Eventually, only Simon and I were left at Tea by the Sea. He got up and checked the remaining bottle of champagne. "Another?"

I handed him my glass. "I think I will."

He poured for us both and sat down. We smiled at each other across the table.

"All's well that ends well," I said.

"For everyone except Reilly. And Josh, I suppose. How's your reservations book looking for tomorrow?"

"Jammed full. I hope it doesn't rain, as we need to be able to squeeze them into the garden."

"I've nothing on tonight, if you need some help in the kitchen."

I leaned back in my chair and saluted him with my champagne glass. "I've got enough to get a start tomorrow. Right now, I'm perfectly happy sitting here."

He grinned at me. "As am I. I'm going to have another piece of that cake. Would you like one?"

"Only if you promise never to tell anyone I liked it."

"My lips," he said as his eyes danced with amusement, "are sealed."

Recipes

Herbed Cucumber Sandwiches

A modern take on a traditional teatime classic, Lily serves these with her sandwich course.

Makes 24 teatime-sized sandwiches

Ingredients:
52 thin slices of cucumber
½ cup mayonnaise
2 Tbsp minced fresh chives
2 Tbsp minced fresh dill
2 Tbsp minced fresh parsley
1 tsp fresh lemon juice
½ tsp finely grated lemon zest
½ tsp salt
½ tsp ground black pepper
12 slices white sandwich bread, crusts trimmed off

Directions:
Place the cucumber slices on a plate lined with paper towels to absorb the excess moisture and set aside.

In a small bowl stir together the mayonnaise, chives, dill, parsley, lemon juice and zest, salt, and pepper until well combined.

Spread a layer of the herbed mayonnaise on each slice of bread. Arrange 9 cucumber slices on each of 6 bread slices, making sure that the cucumber slices do not overlap. Top each of the cucumber-laden bread slices with the reserved bread slices, mayonnaise side down, to form 6 sandwiches.

Next, cut each sandwich into four triangles and arrange the triangles on a platter or individual plates. Serve at once.

Coconut Lime Cake

Lily serves this cake often in her tearoom. It's quick and easy when made with a lime drizzle rather than a layer of icing for a lighter touch.

Ingredients:
1 cup unsweetened flaked coconut
½ cup unsalted butter, softened
1¼ cups granulated sugar
1 Tbsp finely grated lime zest
2 large eggs
1¾ cups all-purpose flour
2¾ tsp baking powder
½ tsp salt
¾ cup whole milk
2 Tbsp fresh lime juice, plus 2 Tbsp for lime drizzle
1 cup icing sugar

Directions:
Preheat the oven to 350°F. Butter a 9- by 2-inch round cake pan and line the bottom with a round of parchment paper.

Toast the coconut in a small baking pan in the oven, stirring once or twice, until golden, 8 to 12 minutes. Set aside to cool. Leave the oven on.

Beat together the butter, sugar, and lime zest with an electric mixer until fluffy. Beat in the eggs one at a time. In a medium bowl stir together the flour, baking powder, salt, and ½ cup of the reserved toasted coconut. In a small bowl combine the milk and 2 tablespoons of the lime juice and stir. At a low speed, add the flour mixture to the butter-sugar mixture in 3 batches alternately with the milk mixture, beginning and ending with the flour mixture.

Spoon the batter into the prepared cake pan. Bake for 40 to 45 minutes, or until golden and a wooden pick inserted in the center comes out clean. Cool the cake, and then turn it out onto a plate and discard the parchment paper.

Whisk together the icing sugar and the remaining 2 tablespoons lime juice, and pour over the cake. Sprinkle the cake with the remaining toasted coconut and serve. The cake may be stored in an airtight container in the refrigerator for up to 3 days.

Coffee Cake

Lily regularly makes this coffee cake to serve for breakfast at the B & B. It's a favorite of hers because it freezes
well and thus can be saved for emergencies. Of which they
seem to get a lot at Victoria-on-Sea.

Ingredients:
3 Tbsp granulated sugar
4½ tsp instant coffee granules
4½ tsp unsweetened Dutch-process cocoa powder
2 cups all-purpose flour
1 tsp baking powder
1 tsp baking soda
1 tsp salt
½ cup unsalted butter, at room temperature
1 cup sugar
2 large eggs, at room temperature
1 cup sour cream, at room temperature
1 tsp pure vanilla extract

Directions:
Preheat the oven to 350°F. Butter and flour a 10-
inch Bundt pan.
In a small bowl stir together the sugar, coffee, and
cocoa powder and set aside.
In a medium bowl whisk together the flour, baking
powder, baking soda, and salt until well combined
and set aside.
Place the butter and sugar in the bowl of an electric
mixer and mix on medium-high speed until pale and
fluffy, 3 to 4 minutes. Reduce the speed to medium,
add the eggs one at a time, and mix until incorpo-
rated. At a low speed, mix in the reserved flour mix-

ture in 3 batches alternately with the sour cream. Next, add the vanilla and mix the batter for 1 minute.

Spread one-third of the batter into the prepared Bundt pan. Carefully spread half of the reserved coffee-cocoa mixture on top. Layer another third of the batter on top, followed by the remaining coffee-cocoa mixture. Spread the remaining batter over the top. Run a thin knife through the batter to lightly combine the layers.

Bake for 35 to 38 minutes, or until a cake tester inserted in the center of the cake comes out clean. Let the cake cool in the pan for 30 minutes and then invert it onto a cake plate.

The cake may be stored in an airtight container in the refrigerator for up to 4 days. If freezing the cake, wrap it tightly in aluminum foil and store it in the freezer for up to 1 month.

Read on for a special preview of the next Tea by the Sea
mystery . . .

STEEPED IN MALICE

**At her Cape Cod tearoom, Tea by the Sea, Lily Roberts is
feeling the strain, thanks to the Great Teacup Shortage—
and a family fracas turned deadly . . .**

Afternoon tea isn't just about flavorful brews and delicious
treats. It's also about presentation—fine china teacups
(never mugs!), with carefully coordinated saucers and plates.
With her fragile stock running low, Lily has an excuse to
indulge in one of her favorite hobbies: visiting an antiques
fair for replacements.

Among other finds, Lily snaps up a charming Peter Rabbit-
themed tea set in a wicker basket, perfect for children's
events. But a few days later, a woman named Kimberly
marches into the tearoom, rudely demanding to buy it
back—then later returns and removes an envelope hidden
in the basket's lining.

An acquaintance of Lily's named Rachel is on the trail of the
tea set too. Apparently, she and Kimberly are half-sisters,
searching for their mother's final will. To her annoyance,
Lily is dunked into the middle of this mess—especially when
her ex-boyfriend turns out to be involved. But it's more than
a storm in a teacup when one of the sisters is found dead on
the grounds of the B&B owned by Lily's grandmother, Rose.

Is this a simple case of greed boiling over, or are there other
suspects in the blend? It'll take some savvy sleuthing from
Lily, Rose, and their allies to find the answers before a killer
shatters more lives . . .

Available in August 2023 from Kensington Publishing Corp.

Chapter 1

At Tea by the Sea we take tea seriously. It is, after all, the entire reason for the business. As far as I'm concerned, mugs are for coffee, and cups with saucers are for drinking tea, and I do not—shudder—serve tea in mugs. Presentation is a vitally important part of the image of a traditional afternoon tea.

The reason I mention this, is that at the moment I was going through the Great Teacup Shortage. Every restaurant has a substantial turnover in crockery. Things get damaged: dropped by staff, chipped in the sink or dishwasher, sometimes even stolen or deliberately broken by customers. Only yesterday a gentlemen picked up his entire tea service—teapot, cup, saucer, side plate—and hurled it against the wall. Point made, anger abated, he paid handsomely for the damage before storming out and leaving his embarrassed family behind to enjoy their own tea selection as well as the (fortunately) untouched arrangements of scones, sandwiches and sweets.

"You can't use mugs from the B and B?" Cheryl asked.

"I'm not serving Oolong or Darjeeling in coffee mugs!" I replied.

"You might have to," Marybeth said.

"Not gonna happen," I said firmly. Then I added, less firmly, "I hope."

As well as the aforementioned gentleman with a temper, it had been a bad week damage-wise. This is a tearoom, and we set every place with fine china, including when serving from the children's menu. Slightly damaged cups are often relocated to the ancient oak in the center of the garden patio, where they hang from colorful ribbons and make a cheerful display as well as a pleasant sound on a windy day.

"We'll have to wash faster," I said to my assistants. The supply of fine china had been getting low over the past couple of busy weeks. I'd put off noticing until now, when I couldn't not notice any longer. Marybeth had run up to Victoria-on-Sea, the B&B owned by my grandmother, Rose Campbell, to get extra cups and plates. She'd returned with not only teacups but coffee mugs. Mugs I refused to use on principle.

I folded and patted scone dough and glanced at the clock on the oven. Four o'clock. Unless we had a rush of customers without reservations, we'd make it to the end of the day.

Marybeth finished arranging food on a three-tiered tray in the traditional arrangement of scones in the middle, sandwiches on the bottom, desserts on top, and carried it into the dining room, while Cheryl scooped tea leaves out of cannisters, added them to teapots, poured in hot water from the airpots, and set the individual timers. Different teas require different water temperatures and steeping times, and we adhere closely to their requirements. My English grandmother taught me not to bother making a cup of tea if you aren't going to prepare it as it deserves.

The kitchen smelled of heaven itself—fresh tea, sugared pastries, warm baking.

"Once these scones are in the oven," I said, "I'll take over washing-up duty. I'll do the cups and saucers that can go into the dishwasher by hand rather than wait for it to finish its cycle. We'll be okay until closing, and I have a plan."

"A plan." Cheryl clapped her hands. "What plan?" I detected a note of sarcasm, but decided to ignore it.

"Tomorrow's Wednesday. Usually, the quietest day of the week in here. If I stay late tonight and call in reinforcements, I can get enough baking done so I can take the morning off. By fortuitous coincidence a big antique show's starting tomorrow in town. What do you find at antique shows?"

"Teacups?"

"Bingo," I said.

I have to confess that I wasn't making any sort of great sacrifice by going to the North Augusta Antique Fair in search of vintage tea sets. There isn't much I love more in life than fine china, and browsing antique shows is my happy place.

Working alone in my kitchen after everyone has gone, making fragrant, delicious things, is also my happy place, and I didn't mind working long into the night, preparing sandwich ingredients and baking cookies, pastries, and scones to have ready to serve tomorrow. I decided not to call in reinforcements, meaning the B&B gardener Simon McCracken, who knows his way around a kitchen, and my friend Bernadette Murphy, who does not. Better, I thought, to save the calling-for-help part for a genuine emergency.

It was coming up to midnight when at last I took off my apron and hairnet, shook out my hair, gave my shoulders and neck a good stretch, checked the stoves were off, turned out the lights, and locked the door of Tea by the Sea, highly satisfied with my night's work.

The antique fair opened at ten o'clock, which suited me perfectly because although I was taking the morning off from the tearoom, I still had my other job to go to.

I was in the B&B kitchen at six, putting the coffee on and getting the breakfasts underway. Luck was on my side this week: we had no overly demanding guests and everyone came down for breakfast in good time. I was finished by nine and left Edna, the breakfast waitress and kitchen assistant, to clean up. I had enough time to take a mug (not a cup!) of coffee and a slice of coffee cake with me to enjoy an all-too-brief period of relaxation before plunging into the next round of the day's activities.

I live in a small cottage on Victoria-on-Sea property. My front porch overlooks the sparkling waters of Cape Cod Bay. It was a beautiful summer day, full of the promise of heat to come, and I made myself comfortable on the porch, sipping my coffee, munching on my own baking, and watching the activity on the bay, while my Labradoodle, Éclair, explored the patch of yard she'd explored a thousand times before. At twenty to ten, I drained my coffee mug, licked my index finger to scoop up the last of the cake crumbs, pushed myself to my feet, and called Éclair to come inside.

Last night, I'd phoned Bernie and asked her if she wanted to join me today. She was waiting on the veranda when I rounded the big old Victorian house the B&B's named after. My grandmother was with her. I hadn't invited Rose to accompany us, as she's anything but an early riser, but I should have known. I'm Rose's granddaughter, but she and Bernie are as thick as the currants in my scones. I might physically take after Rose, fine-boned with blue eyes, pale blond hair, and a complexion that's sometimes called "English rose," but our personalities are totally opposite. She and Bernie, however—hotheaded and impulsive are the words that spring to mind. Whereas Rose doesn't look the part, being tiny and demure, Bernie, at near six feet tall with wild red curls and flashing green eyes, does. We've been friends since grade school, and I've always called her the Warrior Princess.

"Are you joining us this morning, Rose?" I asked.

She tapped her way down the veranda steps, needing only a minor amount of help from her pink cane. "I thought a day of antiquing might be pleasant."

"Hope it's okay that I invited her," Bernie said.

I smiled at them both. "Of course it's okay. Now remember, the purpose of going is to buy china for the tearoom. If you see me getting out of control, it's your job to stop me."

"As if," Rose muttered. She was dressed for the outing in wide-legged purple pants, a bright yellow T-shirt, and a huge red hat topped with an orange flower. My grandmother is a woman who likes color. Her lips and cheeks were a slash of red and her eyes rimmed by thick black liner.

I went to the garage for Rose's Ford Focus, Bernie helped Rose into the passenger seat, and then she jumped in the back and we set off. Tea by the Sea sits at the top of the B&B driveway, and as we passed I could see Marybeth raising the sun umbrellas prior to setting the patio tables. She turned at the sound of the car engine and gave us a cheerful wave.

"How's the book coming along?" I asked Bernie as I turned onto the main road. Bernie was working on a historical mystery novel. Her progress was, shall we say, sporadic.

"Don't ask," she said.

"That well, eh?"

"That well. Which is why I agreed to come with you today. A change of scenery will do me good. Get the creative juices reenergized and flowing."

"You must be in serious trouble if you think the North Augusta Community Center is a change of scenery."

"I'm thinking more of antiques. Grandfather clocks going *tick-tick*, silver tea services, wooden children's toys, dolls with creepy faces. The sort of things my characters would have had around them in their daily lives."

As I'd planned, we arrived as the doors to the community center were opening. I was a woman on a mission, and I wanted to be one of the first to get my choice of what good china was available.

The cavernous room was crammed full of vendors and their wares. People chatted and laughed, called greetings to acquaintances. The air was full of the scent of wood and silver polish and dust rising from old fabric, and the bright overhead lights sparkled on glassware, candlesticks, and Tiffany lamps. For the next hour I wandered happily up and down the aisles, trailed by Rose and Bernie, exploring the booths, checking everything out before deciding what I wanted to buy. I was delighted to see a wide range of china, ranging from what would have once been everyday stuff in a middle-class home, to some truly lovely pieces. Once I saw what was on offer, I plunged eagerly in. More than tea sets caught my eye, and it took all of my self-control, plus Bernie's strong arm and Rose's disapproving stare, to drag me away from the purchase of a rocking chair, a porcelain chamber pot, a set of silver salt and pepper cellars in a mouse-chewed, velvet-lined box, an antique log-cabin pattern quilt, and two china dolls with painted faces and hand-sewn clothes.

Many of the vendors had tea service items among their wares, but one in particular specialized in fine china and that's where I spent most of my money. The sign over the booth said *D. McIntosh, Fine Antiques, Chatham, MA.* While I checked prices and quality and struggled to decide which pieces to get (I wanted them all), Bernie asked the vendor where she found her stock.

"Estate sales and the like mostly. I drive all over New England in the spring seeking out garage sales. Not many people want this stuff anymore. Used to be when Grandma kicked the bucket," she peeked at Rose out of the corner of her eyes, realizing that comment was a mite indiscreet, "I mean, when the older generations passed on to their eternal reward, their silver and china would be cherished by their descendants. People these days want modern stuff." She herself was probably in her mid-thirties, same as Bernie and me. "Unlike your friend," she added, meaning me.

"I own a tearoom in North Augusta." I dug in my purse for my business card and handed it to her. "We serve traditional afternoon tea, and I'm always needing china. Fine china, as you know, is fragile."

She accepted the card and read it. "Tea by the Sea. Nice name. I might pop in while I'm here." She slipped it into her apron pocket.

"How long's this show going to last?" Bernie asked.

"Through the weekend. We break down on Sunday afternoon."

I continued selecting china and putting aside the pieces I liked. There were few full sets, meaning matching teapot, cups, and side plates, but I didn't worry overly much about that. I like to mix and match china to present an interesting and varied tablescape. *When did I start using words like tablescape?* I selected a good variety of things, adding some modern, brightly colored or black-and-white geometrical patterns to the traditional flower design and pastel colors.

"This is charming." My attention had been drawn to a brown wicker box, cracked and worn with age. The lid was open displaying a lining of faded blue cloth and a children's tea set. Six teacups with matching saucers and side plates, teapot, milk jug and sugar bowl. The china was half regular size, white with a thin gold rim, each piece illustrated with a scene from the Peter Rabbit books by Beatrix Potter. I examined it all carefully and found no chips or cracks.

Bernie and Rose came to stand beside me. "Reminds me of my youth," Rose said. "A similar set was in the nursery at Thornecroft Castle." She was referring to the English stately home where she'd been a kitchen maid before (literally) running into my grandfather, Eric Campbell, outside a Halifax tea shop, marrying him and moving to America. "It also had illustrations from Beatrix Potter, although a different image."

I read the price tag. Two hundred dollars for the set, including the box. "It's a bit on the expensive side for the tearoom."

"Moving right along," Bernie called cheerfully. "Now that you're finished, pay the lady and I'll help you take this lot to the car."

I ignored her. "I do like it, though. Children will love it. American children don't often get to use lovely things designed especially for them."

"Sure they do," Bernie said. "My sister's twins have their own dishes. Nice bright cartoon illustrations."

"Your sister's twins are barely weaned and are still throwing their food at each other. Their dishes are plastic, not fine china."

"Lady Frockmorton," Rose said, "was justifiably proud of her afternoon tea service. She had several sets of china. I wonder what happened to them all."

I balanced one of the teacups in my hand. It was truly

lovely, but it was expensive, and impractical for children, for whom fine china has a high casualty rate.

"My job here today," Bernie reminded me, "is to supervise your spending, Lily. That's a lot for six teacups."

I reluctantly put the cup down. Sensing she was about to lose the sale, the vendor swooped in. "Because you're buying so much, and because I hope we can do business again: twenty percent off."

"Sold!" I said.

Rose chuckled and Bernie sighed.

My wallet was light but my car was heavy as we bounced down the road heading back to Tea by the Sea.

Visit our website at
KensingtonBooks.com
to sign up for our newsletters, read
more from your favorite authors, see
books by series, view reading group
guides, and more!

Become a Part of Our
Between the Chapters Book Club
Community and Join the Conversation

Submit your book review for a chance to win exclusive
Between the Chapters swag you can't get anywhere else!
https://www.kensingtonbooks.com/pages/review/